Lucky in the Corner

Also by Carol Anshaw

AQUAMARINE

SEVEN MOVES

LUCKY
in the
CORNER

....

Carol
Anshaw

HOUGHTON MIFFLIN COMPANY
BOSTON · NEW YORK
2002

For information about permission to reproduce selections
from this book, write to Permissions, Houghton Mifflin Company,
215 Park Avenue South, New York, New York 10003.

Visit our Web site: www.houghtonmifflinbooks.com.

Library of Congress Cataloging-in-Publication Data

Anshaw, Carol.

Lucky in the corner / Carol Anshaw.

p. cm.

ISBN 0-395-94040-0

1. Mothers and daughters—Fiction. 2. Lesbian
mothers—Fiction. I. Title.

PS3551.N7147 L83 2002

813'.54—dc21   2001051891

Printed in the United States of America

Book design by Robert Overholtzer

QUM 10 9 8 7 6 5 4 3 2 1

This book is for Jessie.

Lucky in the Corner

crash

NORA IS BANKED and blanketed in sleep. At first, the mayhem outside is absorbed and accommodated by a dream she is having about the Good Humor truck that used to troll past her family's house in the summers. She and her brother are running after it the way they used to in real life, jostled from afternoon naps, still in their underpants, fists full of change, yet in the time-pleat of the dream they are their adult selves, running in their underwear nonetheless. And then the nostalgic tenor of the dream shifts abruptly as the ice cream truck explodes.

Nora's eyelids flip open. Her partner, Jeanne, is already out of their bed, stumbling across the room to the window, which overlooks the street. "Something bad is happening," she says. Then, when she is at the window and has rubbed away the frost with the heel of her hand, she says, "What is this? No, this is very terrible."

Nora pulls the comforter around her and listens to what is now absolute silence reflecting off the ice-white night outside.

And then it begins again — a lowercase armageddon, judgment rendered automotively. A car careens around the corner and hurtles down their block. Nora understands that this is its second pass; the first was what awakened her. Then there is the gunning of an engine in neutral, the high whine of reverse, rubber tread crunching frantically through snow. The slam of steel on steel. A sucker punch of fender into door. The pull of metal snagged, then stretched, groaning. Slam and creak overlaid with shatter of glass. Then, a peeling-off into the wider night, leaving behind the tripped horn of a wounded car. Which, when Nora makes her way, reluctantly, to the window, she sees is her Jetta.

It has been struck with such impact that it has left its parking space and now rests on the front lawn of the house across from theirs — home to a jumbled assortment of family with two burly father possibilities, both with furry hairdos and high trucks. A wife who stands on the porch through all but the harshest weather with cigarette and cordless phone. Several giant, sullen teenagers. These familiar strangers are now barely awake, bleary but curious, pulling on parkas, gathering up their forces as they lumber across the front yard, their way illuminated by blinking holiday lights.

The storm door downstairs slams as Nora's daughter, Fern, shouts behind her, "Hey! Come on!"

More neighbors add themselves to the scene. A small group forms, bringing to bear on the situation the weight of flesh and blood, and speculation.

Nora turns to see Jeanne pull on pants and a sweater from a pile on the chair in the corner. She comes back to the window and puts a hand on Nora's shoulder, a gesture to release her from whatever glitch is keeping her still when she should be leaping into action. Jeanne, of course, can't know that within Nora is actually quite busy, gathering up all the false notes she is soon going to need to pretend she is surprised by what has just happened.

nap

FERN AND TRACY stretch out on the wide, lumpy futon where they used to laugh, shaking like bowls of jelly through stoned sleepover nights as if there were no tomorrow, tomorrow being adulthood. They lie on their sides, facing each other, languid and silent, listening to the soft sweep of a sprinkler fanning Tracy's mother's garden, green aroma drifting up in the afternoon heat in the same lazy way a Cubs game from an unseen radio fades in and out on the soft waves of breeze.

On the floor beside the bed, Lucky also lies on his side, legs stretched out straight. Fern had him clipped at the beginning of the summer, and now his fur has grown back some. He looks like a rusty lamb. At the moment, he appears to be pondering something, staring off into the middle distance dogs keep an eye on. Fern drops a hand, gives him a good scratch behind one ear. She ran over here with him an hour or so ago, although going on a run with Lucky, who's deep into his golden years, means loping together for maybe thirty seconds, then sprinting on ahead for half a block, then doubling back and jogging in place while he finishes a two-minute sniff of an especially fascinating blade of grass.

The girls are quiet because Tracy's baby, Vaughn, is asleep between them, pacifier fallen from his mouth into a small puddle of drool on the flannel bunched next to his face. Vaughn is four months old. Tracy puts the lightest pressure of a fingertip on the edge of his ear, which causes him to raise his arms and squiggle into a horizontal dance move, toes clenched.

"He's in a dream club," Fern says, noticing that Tracy's swollen breasts are leaking milk through her old Smashing Pumpkins T-shirt. The Pumpkins are part of their past life when they were stuck in an edgy, static place. Now everything has changed. Vaughn is a sign, a sign that anything is possible.

Tracy and Fern have been best friends since seventh grade, but Tracy won't tell anyone — not even Fern — who Vaughn's father is. "He was a bad idea I had for about one minute. Totally irrelevant" was what she said when she first told Fern she was pregnant, and since then she hasn't added anything to that small piece of non-information. Fern interpreted the statement to mean Tracy wasn't all that sure herself who Vaughn's father is. She was moving pretty fast at that point.

Tracy's boyfriends have all been bad news. For a while in high school, she was involved with a gang guy, Luis. He weighed about three hundred pounds but wasn't fat, that kind of guy. For a whole summer, Tracy wore vinyl shorts and drove around with him in his low-rider while he dealt crystal meth, checked out graffiti in alleys, and planned fights. Over the course of that summer, she herself became moody and chemically overanimated. She traded make-up tips with huge-hair girls. Her own hair got huge, her lips got lined. Fern was sure she'd lost her, and then suddenly, in the fall, Luis was history and Tracy was back, her old self shakily reassembled.

The next year, when they were juniors, Tracy disappeared for three weeks with someone named Don who ran the Tilt-A-Whirl in a traveling carnival that had set up in the parking lot of St. Ben's. She lived in a trailer with him and his little dog through all the carnival's stops in Indiana. Her parents freaked; Tracy was calling them from along the way, but not telling them where she was. The guy was forty-three.

Tracy's emotional life has been harrowing and exhausting for years. For a time, Fern envied it. She kept an eye on Tracy's euphoria, Tracy's sufferings, while she herself was only able to stand on the other side of heavy glass, reaching toward the smoking beakers of passion and derangement, her hands encased in heavy protective gloves, shielded from the chemical burn. Then Fern met Cooper and got some experience of her own. This has put them on more equal footing; now they both have stuff they don't want to talk about.

Vaughn is starting to come out of sleep. His lashes flutter, his fat hands ball up into fists. Everything about him is so new — perfection awaiting the wear and tear of the life he's about to live.

She tells Tracy, "If you want to get out — you know, get a break — I could take him tomorrow." Fern enjoys hanging out with Vaughn, especially when it's just the two of them, plus Lucky. A small, nonverbal community.

"Thanks, but I'm on at the store." Tracy works part-time at a stupid store up on Clark called Aroma One's Own. They sell scented candles and soaps, crystal jewelry, audiotapes of waves and dolphins, and what Tracy calls "spiritual clothing" — fanciful dresses and capes patterned with celestial motifs. "Thalia lets me bring the papoose to work. To show what a feminist and nurturing person she is. But the truth is he's good for business. He's a charmball, puts customers in a warm and fuzzy mood. Which can turn into a candle-purchasing mood."

"Then what about coming over? Next week sometime? Friday. I'll fix dinner for everybody. Mom and Jeanne. My uncle. They're all nuts for Vaughn. They'll goo-goo, give you a break. Plus it'll give me a chance to do my Stepford Daughter impersonation. Like — if I'm standing there cooking, I must be okay. They don't have to start worrying about what's really going on with me. It saves us all a lot of trouble."

"We can invite your dad and Louise, too," Tracy says. This is a joke. Fern hates Louise.

"She has a new gym," Fern tells Tracy. "Some gonzo fitness place where they pinch you with calipers to check your percentage of body fat. She's moved on to the stationary bike thing. Spinning. She's a spinner."

"What happened to the StairMaster?" Tracy says. "I thought Louise was Queen of the StairMaster."

"They had to talk with her because she was hogging too many time periods. If you read history books, all the things Louise does were once ways they used to punish prisoners. Next she'll find a place where they put her in the hold of a ship and lash her to an oar." Suddenly Fern is tired of trashing Louise; she flips back to her dinner plan. "I'll make my peasant spaghetti."

Tracy sits and picks up Vaughn, who has started to fuss. She gives him a breast — her left, which in the old, pre-Vaughn days had a small gold ring through the nipple.

Fern stretches half off the futon and reaches for a stack of CDs, flips through them to find a Lucinda Williams disk, then plucks it from its case and sets it into Tracy's boom box. Fern has only recently tuned in to Lucinda Williams. She has developed an ear for songs of murky obsession. They wait until the music starts.

"Lucinda sings the way I feel," Fern says. "Like she's learned so much from experiences with guys, but she's also ready to do something stupid again in about ten minutes."

"Yeah, Lucinda's cool," Tracy says. She reaches down with her free hand and touches the side of Fern's neck. "This, too," she says, meaning Fern's tattoo. "Way, way cool." Fern herself already has serious doubts about the tattoo, which is a small black ankh. When she got it done a few months back, it seemed so ancient and mystical, so Egyptian and all. There was also the bonus that her mother would hate it, but there's only so much she can get off on that. Lately Fern has been thinking there are probably too many people with tattoos, that they're becoming cheesy personal statements along the lines of bumper stickers. She's grateful for Tracy's reassurance, though. This is one way in which Tracy is always a good friend. She can figure out exactly the thing Fern is having doubts about and boost her up.

"Does it seem to you that things are moving pretty fast?" she asks Tracy.

"It seems to me like they've stopped entirely."

"But in terms of change around us. Vaughn, big change. My dad marrying Louise after all those years alone. Louise and her Bible-beating family and that hideous wedding with the minister telling them that Dad was the farmer and she was the mule pulling his plow or something like that. And — bam! — now these religious nuts are part of my family. Same with Jeanne. Before she came to live with us, she was just this Frenchy person my mother was sleeping with. But then all of a sudden she was, like, my assistant mother."

"I envy you," Tracy says. "I still have my same nightmare parents. Worse, they still like each other; they'll never get divorced. But you, you got a nice big divorce. Lots of drama."

"Please."

"Well, it's true, and as it turned out, it's cool. It got you Jeanne, who is way cooler than your father."

"Yeah. Right," Fern says. Tracy flat-out likes Jeanne and she's probably right. Still, Fern likes to appear to be keeping her suspicions up, on principle, the principle being not to let her mother push all the pieces around on her and totally get away with it.

Actually, when it's just the two of them together, Fern likes Jeanne fine. It's only when she has to witness Jeanne's devotion to Nora that Fern's sentiments starts wavering between contempt for Jeanne for being such a fool and pity for Jeanne for being such a fool. Sooner or later, Fern knows Nora will betray

Jeanne, the way she betrayed Fern and her father. She will become distracted and walk away toward whatever is distracting her, forgetting even to look back over her shoulder. Sometimes when she is with her mother and Jeanne, Fern gets a mild chill, as though a draft is passing through the room. Jeanne can't feel this cold air, is incapable of imagining Nora's treachery. That's all right. Fern imagines for her.

"And Louise," Tracy is on a roll. "Even Louise might not be all that bad. I mean, she gave you that check for your birthday."

"It *wasn't* a check. It was a dorky savings bond. I have to wait until I'm retired or something to cash it in. When I'm ninety, I can stand all stooped over in line at the post office and get fifty dollars for it." She stops herself. "Oh man, do I sound like a total whiner, or what?"

Vaughn lets go of his mother's breast, appears totally satisfied for a split second, then bunches up his face in distress.

"Burp alert." Tracy hoists him over her shoulder and starts patting his back in time to the music.

What's actually bugging Fern is her own dead standstill in this great flutter of rearrangement. It seems she should be able to come up with some large, surprising event of her own. Instead, in place of actually being able to create a dramatic future for herself, she has become adept at making up one to suit the occasion or questioner. On the spot she can spin out to whomever — her mother or father or the head of the Anthro Department at school, or Turner, the therapist her parents had her seeing for a while — some detailed plan for the next few crucial years. She likes school but has no idea what she will do with all this education. She bluffs by putting together a full-color package featuring grants and fellowships and grad school programs and field study semesters on this island or in that remote mountain village.

Her line lately is that she wants to study the Nenets, an Arctic tribe in Siberia, some of whom are reindeer herders adhering to a lifestyle so primitive they wear clothes made of reindeer skins and live in reindeer skin teepees, make nearly everything they need, and spurn all modern conveniences except ceramic teacups. They have the narrowest worldview imaginable. A Nenets proverb, for instance, is: "If you don't eat warm blood and fresh meat, you are doomed to die on the tundra." The Nenets play into Fern's fantasies of being in a much simpler situation, a place of limited expectations.

She stretches off the mattress onto the floor to uncover the clock from beneath a pile of Tracy's clothes, then gives Lucky a little massage on his chest. "Can you keep Lucky for the rest of the afternoon? I have to go to work. I'm on from four to eight tonight. Rush hour. Right after they run the infomercial."

Vaughn curls up as though squeezing the sleep out of his body, pulling his legs and arms in, then pushing them out again. He smiles and explodes with something that sounds like *"pow!"* and becomes once again center of all the attention in the room. Even Lucky rallies. He gets up on his feet to stand quietly watching the baby for his next surprise.

It occurs to Fern that Vaughn's needs will be rapidly changing and expanding. Soon he'll be tottering around, rummaging through danger-packed cabinets. Then he'll have to be placed in preschool and go to summer oboe camp and get expensive braces on his teeth, and then in spite of all the attention and concern of the adults around him, he'll do something brainless like inhale air freshener on a dare, or steal a car. Or flunk out of a decent college and have to finish up at someplace nobody ever heard of in Ohio. But then he'll get it all together and find some niche in the universe. His own pattern of connect-the-dots. It's hard to imagine; all of this seems remote as another galaxy on this still summer day that smells like lawn and tomatoes and seems as though it could hold itself in place forever.

"What do you think he's smiling about?" Tracy says, giving up her index finger to Vaughn's grip. "What can a baby's dreams be? What can he know yet?"

"He knows he's a miracle," Fern says, putting her face close to his head, which smells like powder and sweat and is covered in thick dark brown hair like a cheap toupee. Everyone says he'll lose this, but so far he hasn't. "He's thinking, So far, so good. He's resting on his laurels."

complaint

"DID HE TOUCH YOU?" Nora asks. She has to shout a little to make herself heard over the huge, shuddering air conditioner stuck in the window behind her. "Any of these times in the lab?"

"Sometimes, sort of," the student, Ellen Schroeder, says. She dabs her nose with a Kleenex that has nearly gone back to pulp. Her nostrils are brilliantly red.

Nora will write up this complaint and put it into the channels the college provides, but she needs to hear it all herself first. Mercifully, she doesn't get many of these in her program, which has been snappily renamed Access College, but is really just the old Continuing Ed extension of the real college. (And Continuing Ed was only a euphemism for the original night school.) She has to acknowledge that some of the courses the program offers — cooking classes, language intensives for travelers, current events discussion groups — are lightweight and have a social component, and so attractions do occur, but these are consensual and between adults, matters of the heart that are none of her business. In Mediterranean Cuisines last spring, a romance that had formed in the class led to some nuzzling around the chopping block, and she had to call the offenders into her office for an embarrassing chat about toning it down, but that sort of thing has been the worst of it. She doesn't think there's a need for her to be the morals police in classes that involve tabooli preparation or tango lessons.

Ellen Schroeder's complaint, though, is of another order, dead serious. She is taking two psychology classes, both for credit, in an attempt to boost her grade point enough to be admitted to the regular bachelor's program in the fall. Her complaint concerns Claude Frolich, a tenured full professor in the Psych Department and Ellen's instructor in Behaivioral Research. Nora flips him up in her mental Rolodex: pear-shaped, sententious, mid-fifties. She vaguely remembers something about him in the mid-distant past. The Psych Department calling him on the carpet. She'll have to phone someone over there.

All she can do now is listen to what has been happening down in the psych lab. Claude Frolich cozying up to Ellen around the cages of the mice they inject with whatever, or deprive of whatever else. She sees Claude insinuating his meaty thigh against Ellen's bony one while telling her he thinks she has the makings of a first-rate research psychologist. Sliding into an offer of mentorship, accompanied by an arm around her shoulders.

"It was kind of subtle," Ellen says. Nora flashes up a little picture of Claude at the college's Christmas party with his wife (Irene?), a tiny woman with enormous glasses, the two of them looking as though they'd been married a thousand years.

Nora hates these complaints, hates that they exist at all. She thinks everyone should be able to keep his hands to himself and his penis in his pants while in the workplace. Girls shouldn't have to come in here, nervous and weepy and worried for their grade, but more nervous that if they don't come here the rubbing or double entendres will go on. All Ellen wants is to get into the degree program without having anything to do with Claude Frolich's thigh or having to act as though she finds him attractive even though he's an old guy with pasted-down hair and pipe breath.

She catches herself. Although she likes Ellen Schroeder and believes her, she can't condemn Claude just yet. There is the remote possibility that Ellen Schroeder is a crank, that her complaint is vindictive, payback for a lousy grade or something. These aberrations occur, and make her grateful for the school's mechanisms of judicious mediation. She won't have to draw and quarter Claude Frolich herself, tar and feather him, run him out on a rail. Then wonder if she's done the right thing.

"Don't worry about this" is all she has to say, all she *can* say to Ellen at the moment. "I'll start things in motion, send a report over to the ombudsman's office." She pulls a bag of Pecan Sandies out of a desk drawer. When she opens it, a gust of cookie scent escapes into the air over her desk. She extends the bag toward Ellen. To show her, without having to say as much, that she is on her side.

After Ellen, she has an appointment with a guy named Edward Carlson, who called a couple of weeks back wanting to teach a course titled "Tapping Your Inner Potential." The Access poohbahs are big on inner potential, on tapping it.

As it turns out, Edward Carlson arrives lugging a briefcase bulging with legal pads, the pages of which, she can see, are filled from top to bottom, no margins, with a quivery handwriting. He would like to help students release their internal energy fields with the help of magnets. She talks to him as though he is absolutely sane, at the same time keeping an eye on the wall clock over his shoulder. She and her secretary, Mrs. Rathko, have an agreement that if a visitor to Nora's office appears to be a nut, Mrs. Rathko will pop in at the twenty-minute mark to inform Nora that it is time for her "meeting with the vice president." This time, though, she doesn't poke her head in until almost half an hour has gone by. A small nasty trick from the bag Mrs. Rathko keeps at the ready.

The afternoon rumbles on in this way: waves of too much to do peppered with sharp longings for a smoke. It has been five weeks since Nora quit with the help of a hypnotherapist recommended by her friend Stevie. Nora was skeptical, but she has managed to stay off for thirty-seven days. She's also wearing a nicotine patch and going to yoga classes, which she hates — slow, silent torture, all that finding her way into a pretzel position, teetering forever on one foot, staring down an arbitrary point on the wall, pretending she is part of some deep, philosophical Eastern belief system. Someone in a loincloth on a mountain, instead of in a loft on Lincoln above a tattoo parlor and a German delicatessen that specializes in disturbing lunch meats.

She casts about for a good enough reason — a minor crisis, a fit of nerves — that would permit her to go down the hall and bum a weed off Geri in Admissions, but she can't come up with anything. By design, her life is resistant to casual crises, like those Incan walls that absorb subterranean tremors by rippling, then settling gently back into place.

"This memo you wrote on add/drop procedures. I suppose if people read between the lines, they'll eventually see what you're getting at," Mrs. Rathko says, standing in the doorway, imperious even in a dress patterned with tiny polka dots, holding the offending document between two fingers, as though it is dripping with its own incompetence.

Mrs. Rathko has had Nora on the run for years. She has figured out precisely the right sequence of buttons to push to shift Nora onto the defensive. Nora feels like a Russian chess champion pitted against a supercomputer. Her own moves will be absurdly inadequate to the task of outmaneuvering Mrs. Rathko. The charms with which Nora is able to woo most people just bead up and roll off Mrs. Rathko, who has never given any indication that she finds Nora amusing or intelligent or interesting in any way. Her unspoken stance is that Nora is a nitwit who has, by some inexplicable twist of circumstance, been placed in a position over her. There is a parallel assumption that Nora also understands the absurdity of their situation. Nora does her best to brush all this nonsense away, but is still left with the gloomy fear that those who hold a good opinion of her are simply less discerning than her secretary.

"I'll look it over," Nora says in the monotone that is one of her pathetic tactics against Mrs. Rathko.

"How's the smoking?"

"Fine," Nora says. These interactions have made her a master of the nonresponse.

Jeanne calls. It's Thursday; she teaches a night class at Berlitz until nine-thirty. (She used to teach here at the college, in Modern Languages, but the pay was too crummy.) She is calling not because she has anything to say, but so this won't be a day when the two of them don't speak between getting up and going to bed. She is a compendium of these sorts of small kindnesses and considerations. If Nora had to account for why she loves Jeanne, she would have to parse her explanation into a thousand slivers as tiny as this.

Jeanne wants to talk about her lunch with her friend Bernice, another teacher at Berlitz. "She had calamari."

Nora doesn't say anything; there doesn't seem to be a response, really.

"It is like rubber bands. Why would anyone want to eat rubber?"

"Oh, I don't know," Nora says. "I kind of like it myself. Sometimes, nights when you're not home, I fry up an old bathing cap." This is an old kind of joke she makes up especially for Jeanne, who enjoys pure silliness and has too little of it in her teaching days, during which she wears a businessy suit and assumes a strict, pedagogic posture, rapping her ruler on the classroom desks where corporate executives sit, failing to rumble out their r's properly.

"Fern left a note in the kitchen," Jeanne tells her. "She wants to fix us dinner next week. Friday. Tracy and the baby are coming."

"Great." She flips to the next page in her datebook. "It'll mean skipping yoga, but I'm always happy for an excuse. I don't think it's working anyway. Last time, when we did that resting part at the end? Where it's dark and we're lying on the mats, freeing ourselves of worldly concerns? I thought, what a nice time it would be to have a little smoke."

"Oh, but I think it *is* helping. You have more calmness. You could go another night instead? Thursday perhaps." Jeanne's mechanisms of control come cloaked in good-natured politeness.

"No. Thursday I have an orientation reception for the fall semester. I hate Continuing Ed." This attitude comes over her frequently since she quit smoking. "Why can't people just get educated once and for all and give it a rest? Instead of coming in here at night with their big life changes and ridiculous identity crises. They've been accountants for thirty years and now all of a sudden they think they might have a knack for Web site design, or day trading."

"Or belly dancing," Jeanne says, unnecessarily.

"You know Leila conned me on that one. Her course title was Desert Rhythms. As soon as I got wind of what was going on, it got dropped from the schedule." Nora hates the little catch of defensiveness she can hear in her voice, but she's up on her high horse and can't get off. "Look, I know Access is not a totally serious enterprise. But it's still this huge machine to operate. It still pumps out a giant toxic cloud of meetings and memos and complaints." She stops, remembering that Jeanne is not the enemy, or the unconverted. "Where are you, anyway?" She hears traffic in the background.

"Down the street from Willie's." Jeanne has been living in America for twenty years, but at heart, she is still French, culturally averse to exercise. Wilhelmina is her masseuse. Jeanne goes once a week, lies on a padded table, is rubbed and stretched and pounded, and given something called "electric stim." She refers to these sessions as "conditioning."

"I'll probably get home before you. Let's do something nice. I'll make cappuccino. I never see you anymore. Are you still short?"

"You are crazy busy," Jeanne says.

"I know. I feel like Lucy. Lucy *and* Ethel when they were working on the assembly line at the chocolate factory and the chocolates were coming so fast they started ramming them into their mouths." She waits a minute, then realizes Jeanne doesn't have Lucy in her cultural data bank, that she was still in France when Lucy was working in the candy factory, and being pushed out of the kitchen by her over-yeasted bread, and riding the suds from her over-soaped laundry load. "It's nice about Fern's dinner, though. I wonder what inspired her to such a grand gesture?"

"We can play with Tracy's baby," Jeanne says. Childless herself, she adores babies, the way non-Catholics adore nuns.

"Man, I hope Fern doesn't get pregnant anytime soon," Nora says.

"Oh, but I cannot even imagine her having sex. I think she is too alienated from the human race, too *nihiliste* to make herself naked with someone else."

"I think she was doing something. With somebody. You know. That time."

"Perhaps."

"All those late nights out and sleepovers at Tracy's. It was fishy as hell." She can't win on this. She doesn't want Fern to be twenty-one and have had no sexual experience. On the other hand, she doesn't want to think of her going through this evolution furtively, without guidance.

She flushes with a terrible memory of Fern at twelve and way out of synch with the Lolitas who attended her school. Next to them, Fern seemed stuck, swaddled in orthodontia and shyness, miles taller than everyone in her class except for a set of beanpole twin brothers. Her manner back then was composed of explosions of goofy humor alternating with gloomy silences. Nora tried to help; she ordered a boxed set of pamphlets and videos, "Gal Gab: Mothers and Daughters Talk about Sex." On the box was a photo of a mother and daughter, snuggled side by side on an overstuffed couch, the daughter fascinated as the mother smiled and pointed to a diagram of ovaries and fallopian tubes. This was Nora's hope for her and Fern, exactly what was pictured on the corny box.

They never got to the couch. Fern looked at the box, and said, "Please," in a tone that was panicky, not sarcastic (which would have been marginally better), "don't make me do this."

Fern slipped into adolescence silently, as though it were quicksand. Even, all these years later, now that she has surfaced into early adulthood, Fern is still unfindable behind her superficial presence. She is always available to talk, to be positively chatty while revealing nothing of her true self, whoever that might be. She is someone, apparently, who thought it was a good idea to get a tattoo on the side of her neck. Nora will never mention the tattoo to Fern. The tattoo is a nonsubject.

"When I think of Fern and our future together," she says to Jeanne, although she can tell Jeanne is only being patient until she can get off the line, "we're not together. She's moved to Seattle. Or Sweden. She tells her friends there she *had* to get away. She lives with some guy who collects exotic goldfish, spends nights in the basement synthesizing sounds on his computer. They have a kid. Fern's an advocate for soy baby formula or home schooling . . ."

While Nora is on this roll, time-traveling through the near future, the call with Jeanne gets cut off with several beeps and the sound of coins being swallowed by the pay phone. Nora hangs up and waits for her to find some change and call back, but the phone sits silent on her desk. Perhaps Jeanne felt the conversation was effectively over, even though they hadn't said goodbye.

canasta

FERN LETS HERSELF IN with a key her uncle has made for her. She understands that in giving her this, Harold was also giving up a piece of his privacy. He was deferring to Fern's need of a slipknot, a release from the house she lives in with her mother and Jeanne. Where things have become purely claustrophobic.

Last weekend, Saturday morning, she woke with a terrifying sensation of suffocation, then realized it was the subconscious drift from the thick fragrances of domestic ritual seeping under her bedroom door — the buttery aroma of Jeanne's croissants baking, the charred air kicked up by her mother's vacuuming, the suspended pollen of lemon Pledge.

Jeanne is not the problem; she's only guilty by association with Nora. Nora is the problem. Anyone else's mother would be easier. Tracy's, for instance — huge phony, bad nose job, thinks she can win you over by reading your tarot cards. But it is precisely these limitations that make her bearable. Tracy's mother always occupies the same, predictable amount of space. As opposed to Nora, who spills over all her edges, then over Fern's.

The problem starts with the way she looks. Those compellingly irregular features, the haunted eyes — what Tracy once labeled "your mother's fuck-you looks." Tracy has a whole riff on this, like why hasn't Nora given in to fate — moved to New York and signed some huge modeling contract and started sleeping with rock stars and getting herself a tricky little addiction, maybe an eating disorder?

But Nora is not interested in anything involving cameras or stages. She's in a lifelong flight from her family's fascination with show business and doesn't really want this sort of attention and blah-blah-blah, and Fern more or less believes her, but not really. Something about the way she blows off looking so dramatic and movie-starrish — all the baseball caps and sunglasses — only sets her more apart, pressurizes and intensifies her little magnetic field. Which she then, of course, uses to her advantage.

Meanwhile Fern, with her gawky height and bland features, will always suffer by comparison. This is the result of Fern's mother having married Fern's father, who, although he is in advertising and dresses in a moderately hip way, nonetheless looks totally like a dentist, and has left his stamp on Fern. So in their family configuration, Nora will always remain the gorgeous one, while Fern will have to make the best of an appearance that is not so much unattractive or attractive, but rather that of someone you'd feel comfortable coming to with a toothache.

She has been working against this blandness, what she thinks of as her dentality. She worries that this was, in some part, what Cooper slipped away from. And so she has been trying to carve out some angles with the tattoo, the diet she doesn't mention to anyone, a major hair change. Early in the summer she went down the street to Big Hair, which specializes in chaotic cuts, and now she has hair that's short all over, disorganized on top and three colors — her own dishwater blond, a Coca-Cola brown, and a synthetic red. For a week of mornings after, she surprised herself in the mirror.

Her mother has said nothing about the tattoo, has yet to notice the diet, and looked at the haircut as if she was about to come forward with an opinion, then thought better of it. It's never that Nora doesn't *have* an opinion — the best you can hope for is that she will restrain herself from expressing it. This is the most incredibly annoying thing about her, her relentless certainty. She is so smug about her career choice (college administration!) and sexual orientation and her relationship with Jeanne and having left Fern's father in the dust, but now they're good friends so no real harm's been done (in Nora's view at any rate). How, Fern wonders, can anyone be so certain of what's right and wrong, the proper axis of the planet, the order of the universe, her position in it?

A worse part of this confidence is that it includes an exact idea of who Fern should be. Nora just *knows*. Of course, she won't reveal in any direct way what this idea is. Instead she lets Fern know that she is constantly falling short, or to the side of this ideal, and is by now miles off the mark. Nora is a mistress of disappointment, and of meaningful silence, her gaze tactfully shifting to the floor. Fern hates The Shifting Gaze. She can feel it coming even before her mother's eyes have begun to move.

She can't go and live with her dad, can't even spend weekends with him as she did through the years after her parents split up, because now there's Louise, and now Fern meets her father once a week for dinner, without Louise. Mercifully, the only substantial time she and Louise spend together is the week Fern spends every summer at her father's summer cottage in Michigan, around the lake. This is a long-standing tradition he insists on keeping up. He thinks Fern is short on traditions.

An apartment of her own is what Fern needs, a place for just her and Lucky. Instead, she is still sleeping in the back sun porch off the kitchen. She claimed this room as hers when they moved here. They have lived in this house for eight years, and Fern has repainted her room five times. Wedgwood blue, sunshine yellow, Day-Glo orange, purple. This last time, she came up with a color she initially thought of as neutral, and only later realized was a maximum-security gray.

She was all ready to get out last year. She and Tracy were going to rent a place together in Bucktown. They had a plan and a budget, a sofa bed from a friend. And then Tracy got pregnant with Vaughn and that was that. Fern can't swing it alone, which means she is probably going to stay put for another year, until she finishes college. Because she goes to the same college where her mother works, they get a tuition break. At first, she thought they'd be running into each other all the time, and it would be weird, but this hasn't happened. She sees Nora surprisingly little on campus.

Home is another story. Her strategy for living there is to stay away as much as possible, lie low when she is there, and try not to feel like someone arrested in her development, lost amid her stuffed animal collection. She has cultivated what she thinks of as a breezy air when everyone's around, as though she doesn't exactly live there, but rather has stopped by to be amusing for the length of this conversation, that pancake breakfast. Her spaghetti dinner next week. She sees her interactions with her mother as scenes in a little play in which nothing anybody says holds any real meaning. The audience would have to consult a key, as with *Ulysses*, something with psychological and historical footnotes, to decipher what's actually going on.

Here at her uncle's apartment, the atmosphere is much less tricky. It is Thursday afternoon; Harold will be hostessing his canasta club. Fern opens the door of the apartment and hears the soft flipping action of the giant, vintage card shuffler, backed by Della Reese on the stereo, over-enunciating some heartbroken delusion — "Someday," Della belts, "you'll want me to want you."

As Fern comes through the short hallway into the living room, she nods to the group — Vera, Gwen, Iris, and her uncle, who on Thursday afternoons crosses over into Dolores. The four of them are vamps from another era. They shave close, pad their brassieres, powder their noses, and cross their legs provocatively in dresses with back-slit skirts. Slouchy hats on top of lustrous pageboy wigs, silk gardenias tucked behind their ears. Their nylons have seams. Kid gloves lie like fallen birds at the corners of the card table among the ashtrays and cocktail glasses, fluttering lightly in the breeze of an ancient electric fan set on the windowsill.

Their drag has a cut-rate quality. Although vampiness hangs in the air like musk, it's not as though they're impersonating Lauren Bacall or Barbara Stanwyck, but rather some second rung of actresses in the movies Harold loves (and loves Fern to watch with him) — the bad girls who get shot in the last reel, or dumped by the detective hero, or casually turned over to the cops. Audrey Totter. Lizabeth Scott. On Thursday afternoons, the room is filled with their ghosts. Everywhere, hair falls in heavy waves over eyes, lips are darkened to reddish black. Dolores and her friends look like women who are playing canasta, but would also like someone to help them murder their husbands.

Playing cards, here in this apartment, is their only group activity. Their drag is not quite ready for the wider world. Gwen's stubble pokes through her face powder. Vera's wig is a bad fit. Iris and Gwen are large men with muscular calves; both are telephone linemen when they're not at the card table.

They seem content to cut themselves a lot of slack. It's as though they learned through some correspondence school instead of from observing actual women. Of course, how could they, really? Women like them haven't existed for fifty years.

They are all straight apparently, all married except Harold. Fern saw Vera once in the Loop, selling luggage at Field's. It was shocking to encounter him as a man. As though *that* were the impersonation.

"Would you like a gimlet, dear? Our cocktail *du jour*," her uncle says, lifting a stemmed glass. Fern understands the offer is a formality.

"Thanks, but I just need to use the phone for a while," she says, slipping into the bedroom. She is shy around Harold's friends, a shyness she extends on their behalf. They aren't ready for inspection by someone female from birth, especially someone as careless with femininity as Fern, tossing around what they are trying so hard to get right.

She closes the door behind herself, takes the receiver from her phone, and settles on the bedroom floor, propping her back against the bed — a hulking, lumpy double with a dark wood frame out of an Edward Hopper hotel room.

She phones into the Star Scanners central number, punches in her employee code, then hangs up to wait for callbacks. As she waits, she hunkers down into a parallel universe of livelier possibilities.

For the past few months, Fern has been working as a 900-number psychic. She works here, pays for the additional line, and Harold provides her with the solitude of his bedroom. Working from home is not an option. Nora and Jeanne think the job is ridiculous. They make goofy faces whenever she says she's off to work; rippling swami salutes cascade from their foreheads. Harold doesn't think it's so funny. He looks at the upside of the business. He says she gives people a little hope.

In her more optimistic moments, Fern thinks maybe he's right, yet she also thinks she tells more clients than she probably should that they're going to find new loves, or get old ones back. And she tells *way* too many that they're going to be taking a long journey, by sea. This flight of fancy seems to get them mystified and happy at the same time. The bad thing is that Fern is spinning her clients along and sailing them off at about four dollars a minute.

In the training session she had when she started this job — half an hour on the phone with a supervisor named Mindy — she was told that the important thing was to keep the caller on the line as long as possible. Psychics with the longest calls get more future calls fielded their way. To keep clients on the line, you try to intuit their needs. Fern was told that except for the elderly — who are concerned with their health or are lonely — most callers are looking for news of money or love.

Money is easy; it is always on its way, coming soon. Stacks of bills as thick as bricks. Coins tumbling out from a slot machine. "Work up a lively picture," Mindy told her. "Then pass it along to the client." Mindy consistently referred to the callers as "clients." She told Fern to expect that eighty percent of them would be women and the guys who called would mostly be gay. "Basically, just assume they are."

"Love is harder. You have to listen to what the client is looking for. Are they at the start of something and don't know if it's a good idea?" For this situation, she gave Fern a spiel to fall back on. She's supposed to say, "You're in a dilemma about your love life. There are two paths in front of you. Your head tells you to take one. Your heart tells you to take the other."

Other times — much more often, actually — she picks up that the caller is suffering from a broken heart. In these cases she's supposed to say, "You don't trust people right away. Now you have and you feel betrayed, sadder but wiser." Often they want to know if this person is coming back. Mindy told her that at Star Scanners, you *always* hold out hope. "Hope is what keeps our clients on the line, keeps them calling back again."

And so Fern tries to imply that those who've left are on their way back, but more and more she slumps into sadness, imagining a world composed of two populations: one stationary, sitting in dusk-filled rooms with the radio on, waiting for the other half, a roving band out late, laughing, dancing, clinking glasses and making toasts to their new lives with no backward glances. She has come to hate telling clients that these lost loves will return when she has little belief that they will. Which is odd because, although she finds most of her callers' cases hopeless, she can nonetheless put her own broken heart into a different category. She is still able to imagine any given day as the one in which Cooper will reappear in her life.

The phone rings.

"This is Adriana," Fern says, pushing her voice into a deeper, more sophisticated register, burnishing it lightly with an accent she thinks of as "European." "I'm picking up some very strong vibrations from you."

"That looks fabulous on you," Fern says when Harold comes in, about an hour later, when the girls have left. He sits in the fatigued, fuzzy armchair in the corner, crosses his legs at the knees; his feet are snug in huge, cartoonish navy and white spectator pumps. He's wearing a dark blue dress with a short jacket that has a fake leopard collar. The thing of it is, even though his make-up isn't quite right, his outfit a little overdramatic, Harold, who is a pretty handsome guy, also makes a pretty attractive woman.

"It's new," he says, referring to the outfit, brushing invisible lint off a knee. "Well, new for me, but old, of course."

Fortunately for Fern, drag doesn't make him look like Fern's mother. *That* would be a little too weird. As a guy, he is very much Nora's brother, but as a woman he is quite specifically Dolores, a creature of her own design. She has her own personality — a slightly more lurid, more purple shade of Harold. She is more cynical, but this is only a cover for her sentimental belief in romance and glamour. Fern tries to treat Harold and Dolores as separate people, which has turned out to be not all that complicated.

Dolores dangles one shoe from her toes, then lets it drop to the floor and massages a foot encased in seamed nylon. "Oh, these poor dogs of mine. They are *barking.*" She nods toward the phone. "Business slow?"

"The funny thing," Fern says, "is that there are definite patterns. Events are arranged in some sort of order, but the order's invisible to me. Like, in a four-hour shift, I usually get, I don't know, maybe fifteen calls. But then there are days like today when I only get one or two. Everyone's all right, hanging out in the here and now. They don't need to prowl around in the future.

"And then there are the days that come up dark and *agitato*. Gloomy. Electric. I wake up and I can already feel the calls lining up to come in one after the other. I'll barely have time to hang up between one and the next. There will be terrible despair in all of them. Mostly about love gone wrong. Sometimes, though, they're longing for someone they haven't found yet, but they know this person is out there. Basically, it seems like there's this huge, low moan echoing through the universe."

"I'll bet you're wonderful at this," Dolores says, "working out of your fabulous intuition. And — if you don't mind my bringing it up — your own personal experience along these lines." Dolores is referring to Cooper. Fern doesn't particularly want to talk about him, but Dolores presses. "How's that all going?"

"Same," Fern says. "I'm totally nuts. My greatest accomplishment in life is my impersonation of sane."

The length of her obsession with Cooper is embarrassing. The actual relationship lasted only a few months. But it was definitely a time with a higher degree of density, a calendar made of blotter paper, each day saturated with cryptic messages in invisible ink.

She met him at a rave, with Tracy. The rave was also the first and last time she did ecstasy. She found herself at three A.M. out at the far edge of the warehouse parking lot in St. Charles or Dolton, someplace like that, in the back seat of Cooper's Camaro. It wasn't the way she would have imagined anything important happening, and he wasn't the sort of person with whom she would have imagined anything important happening

— hot in a grungy way, but studied, she could see that even at first, even through the haze of drugs and lust. Like his goatee, so neatly clipped.

He is Vietnamese-American, but never talked about his family or his ethnic background. He seemed like a backgroundless person, as though he had just arrived on the planet full-grown, and Asian-American was the model he came in, a stylish fusion blend. He was, like most people, shorter than Fern, which didn't seem to bother him at all. When they were together, she was grateful for this. Now she suspects she was a kind of style accessory — tall girlfriend.

He was vague about what he did for a living, but there was always money around, pockets and dresser drawers filled with rubber-banded rolls of bills. Part of what he did was scalp tickets, but there was other stuff. As he described it, his was a business of obtaining the difficult, whatever that meant to the client. His life was filled with client relationships, and lots of phone calls to keep these relationships lubricated. The cell phone was like a third person in their relationship. It was always there, holding the threat of interruption. Once he answered it while they were having sex and he didn't stop either the phone conversation or what Fern was doing to him, didn't let one affect the other. It was scary.

And when he eventually left her, it was like those bloodless professional murders from the movies, where the hit man is so skilled he simply presses the curare dart into the exact perfect spot on the neck and the victim drops silently, still unaware that anything bad has happened.

Since his departure over a year ago, he has taken the concept of "gone" seriously and Fern's nightlife has shifted location to her bedroom, where she fantasizes about him so fiercely, it's like being in a centrifuge. In this centrifuge she has found that she is able — through the application of obsession and juju thinking — to maintain something like a relationship with him.

"It's not like I have imaginary conversations with him," she tells Dolores, who, aside from Tracy, is the only person in her life who knows about Cooper. "Nothing really colorful like that. More like an outline. Like, I scan for his car when I'm driving around." She can spot green Camaros from a ways off, can separate older and newer models from his, but sighting *any* green Camaro is a good omen. Sighting two or three in a day is extremely significant, although she couldn't articulate what this significance might be. Or the even higher significance of seeing his actual car, parked somewhere.

Once he was in his car, driving, when she spotted it. He was turning left in front of her at the corner of Belmont and Sheffield, but she couldn't bring herself to look straight at him, to see if he was looking at her. She couldn't bear that much exposure. It's better when she takes him at a couple of removes. Through music, for instance.

"I listen for songs we liked." These still sometimes come up on the radio and raise her hopes, particularly if they come in the same day, or one after the other on the playlist. And now there's a new musical category — current songs she knows she and Cooper would share, if they were still together, groups she has discovered since him. Wilco. Wilco would definitely be one of their favorites.

"We keep in touch in a way. I assume all hang-ups are him, and I call him back, late at night, when I'm sure he'll be out. I get his tape, then hang up before it's finished." So she won't leave a click on his machine, a sound footprint.

Sometimes she can persuade herself — it takes only a little fiddling with facts — that he is not permanently gone from her, or even moving away. Rather that he is taking an extremely circuitous route back. She doesn't tell anyone this part, not even Dolores.

Dolores pulls a smashed pack of Pall Malls out of a jacket pocket, lights one with a Zippo that gives off a metallic aroma as flint meets wheel and a blue flame floods the wick. She inhales deeply, exhales, then picks a speck of tobacco off her magenta-coated lower lip as she emerges from some deep place of reflection.

"Sometimes missing someone is the best relationship you can have with them. You still have most of the perks — those delicious little rushes of adrenaline, the fantasy highlight reel — but without having to deal with those nasty imperfections, like their ambivalence and petty cruelty, that made life so nerve-wracking when they were still around."

Fern recognizes this as tortured logic, but is grateful anyway. She is also momentarily distracted as it occurs to her that Harold doesn't smoke.

"And don't worry about being a nut," Dolores adds, "about only being able to impersonate sanity. That's really the best anyone can hope for." She clenches the smoldering cigarette between her lips, and hauls herself out of the chair while dangling her shoes from two fingers. "I'm going to get out of this girdle and soak in a tub. Those girls are *murderous* at the card table. I feel like I've put in a shift in the mines."

The phone rings as though it has been politely holding off.

"Take your time," Dolores says, waving goodbye with a wiggle of fingers behind her as she heads for her bath.

road trip

NORA AND HAROLD were sharing the back seat, but not happily. She licked a finger and drew an invisible line down the middle of the white leather upholstery of the Pontiac Bonneville.

"Cross this and I'll be forced to kill you," she told him. He was seven and bored in the car and whined to persuade their mother, Lynette, to stop at the Giant Glass Beehive or the Mystery Mansion, or whined to get Nora to play License Plate Bingo. Through Pennsylvania and Maryland, before Lynette brought the milk bottle aboard, he had whined to stop at gas station rest rooms about every half hour. Now he peed in the bottle, then gave it to Lynette, who held it straight-armed out the window as she zoomed down the interstate and various shortcut, two-lane highways, letting loose a golden stream that made Nora slide below window level in embarrassment.

Plus, not all of Harold's pee made it into the bottle; his aim was wobbly and a squirt often dribbled onto the floor or seat, or worse, onto Nora, which was one of the reasons she had drawn her line.

It was midafternoon in the middle of February deep into Georgia, the state where they had finally left the winter behind. The car was a rolling oven. They had all the windows open; air rushed in with a deafening roar but no cooling properties. This was the second day of their trip south from New York to Dania,

Florida. Their mother had pulled them out of school for her three-week gig singing and dancing with Ray Bolger in a high-season dinner theater production of *Anything Goes.*

"Bolger's a genius. His feet are little geniuses in shoes. He came out of retirement to do this show. It's a real break for me," she had told them as she packed their small suitcases. "Something that could lead to something bigger."

She let Nora and Harold in on all her career plans and worries. She was thirty-eight, getting old for musicals, plus she now had the two of them to think about, and with their father on the road so much of the time, he couldn't be as much of a help as he might be. Opportunity wasn't knocking as often as it used to, and when it did, she sometimes couldn't even get to the door. She was determined not to let this particular knock go unanswered.

Nora wished she wasn't stuck in the back with Harold. She longed to be up front next to her mother, who drove in a speedy, freewheeling way. In the passenger seat, Nora could pretend she herself was doing the driving.

Lynette paid little attention to them and their back-seat squabbling. She kept the radio turned up; one speaker was on its way out and quavered under the strain of Dionne Warwick singing "Do You Know the Way to San Jose?" from the dashboard. Lynette picked stations that didn't play rock and roll, which she eyed with suspicion. She was in a trance, locked into this song, plugged into the current that Dionne was sending through the airwaves. Lynette was syncopated with the road — wheel in one hand, cigarette in the other, a covered cup of coffee jiggling on the dash, both the mottled tan filter and the coffee lid greased coral with her lip-print. She had the radio and the road and her mission, to get them to Dania and the Sand Bar Motor Hotel and Dinner Theater by tomorrow afternoon.

"Palm tree!" Harold shouted. "We're there!" But it was a suppressed shout. He understood that everyone was enormously tired of him at the moment. He had been announcing their arrival since they hit Maryland.

"No," Lynette said, holding a map over the top of the back seat. "See. We still have almost the whole length of Florida to go."

"Oh," he said, then grew deeply silent, his narrow chest rising and falling under the skimpy plastic lei he had been wearing since their stop yesterday at the Aloha Juice Stand, a Hawaiian outpost in North Carolina.

"We'll stop soon," she promised. "Start looking for a motel. Start looking for VACANCY. A little vacancy is what we need."

Art — Lynette's husband, Nora and Harold's father — was in Las Vegas, managing Vicki Ashford, "The Purring Kitten," a singer with long blond hair that fell over one eye and a husky voice ("Stop by Some Night, Late" was her current big hit, number twenty-seven on the *Billboard* charts). Vicki was like a kitten onstage, but behind her back Art referred to her as "The Shrieking Jackal." Art had managed Vicki for two years, and her career was beginning to skyrocket, but the more famous she got, the more demands she came up with, and the more she drank. And the more she drank, the more she demanded. Demands for her dressing room (champagne on ice, Hershey's Kisses in a crystal bowl) and wardrobe and special lighting and photo approval and musical arrangements, and of course, always for more money. Keeping Vicki happy was hard, highly acidic work; Art stashed a bottle of chalky white liquid antacid in the pocket of his suit coat, and often had a white mustache from swigging it through a long day of Vicki.

That night, at the motel where they'd found some vacancy, on the beige phone on the nightstand between the beds, Lynette talked with Art about Vicki. They tried to save money on long distance by making lists of what they needed to say and most of Art's list was about Vicki. Lynette listened, then calmed him down in a low voice. Before Vicki, Art had had a client list consisting of Lynette; the Balkan Tumblers; a ventriloquist act, Dan and Herkimer; and Joey Zee, a comedian who told jokes so filthy he could be booked only into bachelor parties or late-night shows.

"There's no going back to those days," she told him.

On her next call, this one to California, to Fern Lawler, her friend from their Rockette days, she made the same point. "Vicki is this family's meal ticket. Art is going to have to keep her happy, no matter how many ulcers it gives him."

"Can we go out to the pool?" Nora pantomimed to her mother, pointing to the door, then to herself and Harold in their bathing suits even though it was already purple outside, the sky saturated with dusk. *Laugh-In* was on the TV on the dresser, but with the sound off. Nora watched while she waited for her mother to answer. Jo Anne Worley was screaming. Even with the sound off, Nora knew she was saying, "Is that another *chicken* joke?!"

Lynette nodded as she tilted a green bottle of Canada Dry over a glass of ice cubes and continued talking to Fern Lawler.

The pool — billed as OLYMPIC SIZE — seemed too big and glamorous for the Ho-Hum Motor Lodge with its sign featuring a yawning man in a nightgown and tasseled cap. There were a few other kids in the illuminated water — tired holdovers from an afternoon shift, who were getting in their last splashes. Their squeals and shouts echoed through the motel's courtyard. Nora put down the towels she had brought from the bathroom and strapped Harold into his orange life jacket. He always wanted to swim, then got nervous once actually immersed in water, his head tilted back as he treaded furiously. This didn't seem like any fun at all, but he always wanted to go in again.

"Stay where you can touch bottom," she told him, then kept an eye on him while she lined up for the diving board. When her turn came, she cannonballed into the water, resurfaced, lined up again. She loved cannonballing.

There was another girl making the same circuit. Pretty in a sunburned, chlorine-blond way, smaller than Nora, about her age probably, but it was hard to tell. She had breasts, or at least had a bathing suit with cups inside that made it seem as though she had breasts. Nora was twelve and fried-egg flat, although this didn't bother her. Still, girls with breasts seemed in another league and so she was made shy by this one. She turned out not to be at all conceited, though. Her name was Cheryl and she opened up the conversation.

"You do a really good cannonball."

"I'm training for the Olympics in diving, that's why I don't have to be in school. I'm only fooling around tonight. That's why we're staying at this place. The Olympics people only let me stay at places with Olympic-size pools. It's kind of a regulation."

"Oh," Cheryl said, and left it at that. She was either an extremely trusting sort of person, or didn't care if Nora was lying. The wind went out of Nora's sails, which had been billowing with lies the whole trip. She abandoned the stories she was about to tell about her childhood spent traveling alone across Europe by train, the thyroid operation during which she almost died.

"My father's an astronaut," she said, but there was no steam in it.

"Do you have a radio with you?" Cheryl said.

Nora shook her head.

"It's okay. I do," Cheryl said, and hoisted herself out of the pool to get it.

Nora paddled over to Harold, who was standing in water deep enough to push his life jacket up around his ears. Under water, Nora could see his swim trunks ballooning around his hips.

"We're going to have a dance party," she told him. "I'll let you come."

Cheryl brought out a sea-green plastic portable that came to life with a huge chaotic burst of static. With a safecracker's fingers rolling the dial, she tuned in to a new Aretha Franklin song, "Chain of Fools."

The other kids had disappeared by now, had drifted off to showers and pajamas. It was still warm out; the air and water were a perfect match in temperature. The girls pulled T-shirts on over their suits. Harold kept his life vest on. The three of them danced, mostly shuffling side to side, sometimes taking each other's hand and doing a shambling jitterbug. The girls occasionally gave Harold a yank and a twirl, or grabbed him and bent him backward into a giggly dip.

Lynette wandered out and sat on the foot of a webbed chaise and watched them for a while.

"I'm going to put you two in the show when we get there," she said. This was a frequent, but idle threat. With their looks they should be on the stage or in front of the cameras. She said this all the time. Nora wasn't interested.

She and Harold shared the same combination of Lynette's thick black hair and Art's wide-set pale green eyes. Something about them startled people. Neighbor ladies clucked over them. Teachers gave them the benefit of the doubt, rounding their scores off to the higher grade. More recently, Nora noticed boys watching her in a way that indicated they didn't want her to know they were watching. This gave her the creeps. The whole attention thing made her feel as if she were being followed around by a little spotlight.

The light actually shone down on her whole family; they hadn't successfully blended into any of their neighborhoods, especially not their latest one in White Plains. There, against the background of pampered lawns and pastel living rooms, her mother's bright clothes looked like costumes rather than outfits. She spoke too loudly, had too many racy backstage anecdotes. It was as though she were an immigrant from a backward culture, trailing her strange, vaguely embarrassing customs behind her into coffee klatches and PTA meetings.

Nora's father was no better. He wasn't like any of the other fathers on their block; his job had nothing to do with industry or the stock market. And Nora could tell he had no interest in belonging to their club. She could tell from the quick, stiff conversations he had with these neighbors that he was bewildered by their interest in sports, their vengeance on crabgrass.

"Time to get out of those wet suits," Lynette said, stubbing her cigarette in a sand-filled urn by the side of the pool. The water shimmered with subsurface lighting.

Cheryl looked at Nora quickly. Something passed with a flicker between them. As Nora met the glance, then looked down quickly at the cement of the pool deck, she knew they were setting up a small conspiracy, an alliance invisible to anyone else. They were entering a private space beyond the sunlit spot children were supposed to occupy.

"Help me put my radio back in my room," Cheryl said, as though the radio were cumbersome as a steamer trunk, as though her room were up a tricky, twisting staircase. Nora told her mother she'd be back in a little while. Harold frowned, broody with rejection, but went off with his mother because he was too small and young to assert any power in this situation.

Cheryl had her own room next to her parents', but there was no door connecting them. The parents were out to dinner anyway. Cheryl made a point of mentioning this. She didn't turn on a light; there was only the muddy orange neon drift from outside. The air was dense with the smells of carpet shampoo and bleached sheets and Comet.

Cheryl set her radio on the dresser and turned it on. The Stone Poneys were singing "Different Drum." It was a song that could be danced to either way — slow or fast, and Cheryl decided on slow, putting her hands shyly on Nora's shoulders, as though waiting to see if Nora would shrug them off. When she didn't, Cheryl put together the dance they were going to do, rocking Nora a little side to side, moving her around with small pushing steps. The soles of Nora's feet were iced by the cold terrazzo floor. Although their faces weren't quite touching, she could feel Cheryl's breath passing over the line of her jaw.

At this point, events — which seemed to have been speeding along — suddenly froze. Nothing further, she knew, would happen unless she made it happen. Cheryl had brought them this far and now it was Nora's turn.

She pulled back a little and, with her eyes closed (she couldn't look), she covered Cheryl's mouth with her own. From there, everything was a brief tumble of imagined colors and temperatures. Their lips were blue, the insides of their mouths red. The room held steady at orange, and something inside Nora clicked. A photograph was already starting to develop inside her.

orientation

MRS. RATHKO HAS ORDERED her standard festive platter from the Jewel: crushed, colored foil topped with bologna roll-ups; triangles of an oily, brilliantly orange cheddar; canned olives; toothpicks with cellophane tassels. She has thumped onto the table two boxes of wine — Country Red and Summer White. Cans of store-brand pop sit in ice in the fake crystal bowl she drags out for these occasions. At Christmas, she dusts off empty gift-wrapped boxes to set under the artificial tree. For Thanksgiving, she folds out an accordion-pleated crepe paper turkey. Mrs. Rathko knows how to cut celebration down to size, portion-control it.

In spite of the heat wave — which is into its third day over a hundred degrees — there are maybe fifty students at this reception in the ballroom of the Student Union, about a quarter of those enrolled for the fall semester at Access. Even this year, with her nicotine-hungry nerves and apathy toward her job, Nora is still a little fluttery and hopeful about launching the new school year. Although Access has its share of goof-off courses, it also provides a little academic trampoline. Marginal students can build their confidence and grade points here, then move into the degree program. And now there's a strong English as a Second Language Department, serving a population recently arrived here, impelled by unfortunate circumstances. These foreign students seldom show up at any of the school's social events. Nora extrapolates from their serious manner, imagines them working long hours in hard jobs, places thick with steam or fumes and too few windows. They have no time for any sort of frivolity or social break. Maybe for a wedding, a birth, a religious festival, but not for a school reception.

These sorts of gatherings mostly attract the other segment of the student population — those looking to the program for distraction or redirection. They are unhappy in their jobs or marriages, or are unpartnered and don't understand why. People in a rut or at a crossroads, or hoping a crossroad will turn up along the way of their rut. Most of the students who have come tonight look as though they fit one or another of these profiles. They look dulled, worn out, as though they've come here to revive themselves, are waiting for plasma or megavitamin shots rather than merely for culture or hot dates.

One of them, though, is not dull. According to the block letters on her paper nametag, she is P A M . She's very tan. There's a slight list to her stance, a confident, relaxed quality in her expression. She is, Nora suspects, someone conversant in the language of seduction. She has the look of someone who has run a long gauntlet of women but come out unscathed, instead has left the gauntlet battered and bruised. She's postbutch — narrow black pants, black sneakers, a black rayon camp shirt. Where the collar opens at her throat, a silver chain is visible, a semiserious chain that rides the line between jewelry and statement. There's a small hickey under the chain. Actually, it's a neck that's hard to imagine without a hickey.

She has a crewcut.

Nora tries to picture this woman in a job. Deep-tissue massage therapy. Dog training maybe.

To the ordinary eye, she wouldn't appear to be doing anything provocative at the moment, only standing in the middle of this reception, holding a plastic glass of Country Red, nametag stuck to her shirt. It's only to Nora that she is alarming, the alarm an echo from the past. It was precisely women like this who brought Nora out. Neo-vamps adept at using mischief and mayhem to draw not-so-very-straight women like Nora out of worn grooves of marriage and fidelity. There was a time when she desperately needed these women, needed their sullen smoldering, needed the chaos they provided, needed them to call and then not call, to drive her crazy and use up all her available nerve endings on their superficial and transient interest in her. Assembled, they provided a swaying rope bridge out of some jungle movie, unraveling beneath her as she went, creating so much drama and suspense around her transit that arrival on the other side, the initial point of the journey, turned out to be rather anticlimactic.

Eventually she ran through these women, and arrived at Jeanne. At first Jeanne was attractive simply for who she was not. Not a morning dope smoker, or an all-night cokehead. Not someone who flipped out in the middle of making love, and left. Or someone who, if Nora talked to another woman at a party, was suddenly standing there, like a Sicilian husband, holding Nora's coat.

When Nora approached her, Jeanne stood still, waiting both to hold Nora and to steady her. And all these years since, she has maintained this unswerving posture. What she offered, continues to offer, is a connection in which love is given the opportunity to flourish. She is never capricious with Nora's heart.

They each came into the relationship looking for something big and permanent. They were in their midthirties then, old enough to be dragging around tattered histories of grim dating, awkward near misses, hopeless affairs, less-than-successful long-term connections. In Paris, Jeanne had lived with a woman for a few years, an orthopedic surgeon she met by way of a fall on slippery steps. Nora, of course, had her marriage behind her, a terrible mistake, with Nora bearing the entire weight of its failure. Both she and Jeanne came in with complicated reasons for wanting to make good this time.

One of Nora's reasons was her daughter. She wanted to link up with someone who would help her create a new home for Fern, and from the start, without hesitation, Jeanne understood that a life with Nora would also include Fern. And somehow, with her charm and good nature, she moved into a position that wasn't presumptuously parental or even stepparental, but rather provided Nora and Fern with a buffering presence between them. Nora knows Fern's adolescence would have been even rougher-going if Jeanne hadn't been there to simmer things down, smooth them out. For this alone, Nora is hugely indebted to her. No one else could ever occupy Jeanne's place, which has been achieved through so much shared history.

Not that their relationship is a monolith; it still, even after all this time, sorts out into its good and bad days. There is still a lot of push and pull — a subtle handing over and taking back of power, control, confession, intimacy that sometimes seems so terribly interesting. In other moments, this seems a more fatiguing way of doing things than might be necessary.

The fundamental tone of their partnership, though, set by Jeanne in the very beginning, is one of kindness. This simple measure has made Nora a more considerate person. She used to be thoughtless in small ways — late without calling, forgetful about plans made. Now when there's something important to be done for Jeanne, Nora writes it on her palm, then checks her hand at the end of the day. She has a sign taped to her desk that says, CHECK HAND.

Sometimes they arrive at larger differences, but weather these with a tacit understanding that there are borders on disagreement, that no argument will explode into something truly threatening. At the center of the love Nora holds for Jeanne is a sense of safety — from terrible craziness rising between them, and from the rough side of life. Also from women like this one, here at the reception, from her attraction to these women. Which has already come into play — warm liquid flooding her joints, an intransitive sense of urgency. (Something must be done, but about *what?*) Nora sees that this collection of old, familiar symptoms is probably what has inspired her interior pause to mark the merits of her relationship with Jeanne.

She has to be on guard against herself because even after all the years away from women like this, Nora can still hear their soft, deliberate footfalls as they pace the perimeter of her desire. She can still, given about two seconds, come up with a fairly detailed scenario — something fast and wordless in a gas station rest room along some deserted highway. Or something in a motel room backing onto railroad tracks. Sheets still wafting up sex recently transacted as well as the promise of more to come soon. The scene also includes drinking Cokes from small, icicle-cold bottles from a red 1950s cooler outside the door. Drinking Cokes and smoking Camels.

She gathers herself up, readies her handshake, and tries to get down to the business of greeting students. Her radar is still on, though, and so there is no surprise at all, not so much as an instant of wondering whose fingers have dropped lightly on her forearm.

She turns around.

"Someone . . ." the woman, Pam, says, "I hate to bug you, but someone told me you were the person to talk to about getting a parking permit for the semester."

"Oh. Right." Nora loses her sure footing for a moment. Pam waits patiently while Nora pulls a couple of sentences together. "Come by my office before your first class. My assistant handles the passes." She immediately regrets having used the words "handles" and "passes."

Pam nods, shyly. This shyness throws Nora off-balance; she was expecting swashbuckling. Shy is trickier.

"Actually," Nora says, "come by if you have any questions or problems at all. That's what we're there for." She feels good about having come up with this bureaucratic plural. As though her office is hopping with peppy, uniformed staffers, ready to give efficient, impersonal service.

"Oh, I'm not expecting a problem," Pam says. "I'm only taking pottery." She looks down at the floor again.

Nora feels an old power flood through her like a narcotic. She has had so much training in this part, is so adept at its extremely small moves. Simply continuing to stand here looking at this woman who can't look back, not letting her gaze fall or drift is, in itself, a move. The trick is to keep whatever is said or done hovering over the blurry line between something and nothing. These are skills she learned during the women before Jeanne. Surprisingly, they don't feel at all creaky or withered from lack of use. Rather, they seem greased up and at the ready, as though she has been working out in some secret gym, at night.

"With all your responsibilities," Pam is saying, "I suppose you need to introduce yourself to some of the others, the other . . ."

"Students," Nora says. "Yes, I suppose I should."

While Pam heads off toward the refreshment table, Nora searches for a familiar face, any colleague will do. Instead she finds herself being nodded at by Mrs. Rathko, who was apparently on her way over anyway to say "Disappointing turnout. If only you'd gotten those flyers to me a little earlier." She goes on in this rueful vein for a while (what a pity they've been sabotaged by the weather, and she's already gotten so many withdrawals for the semester ahead). When Nora finally manages to disengage and is free to scan the thinning crowd, Pam is gone.

She herself stays until the ice melts around the cans of pop, and the buffet runs out of everything but a scattering of carrot sticks, and the students have diminished to a self-sustaining group of perhaps a dozen, chatting in small clumps. Still, even though three-quarters of an hour has elapsed, she is not really surprised when she comes out the front door of the Student Union, to find Pam sitting on the ledge to the side of the stairs. Her shirt is soaked through in places, stuck to her skin at the collar-bone, deeply stained at her armpits.

"First," she says, "let's not say anything about the heat."

"Okay," Nora says, idling in neutral. "What's second?"

"Oh man, I didn't have a second thing." Pam runs a hand over her damp, bristly hair.

Nora feels a drop land on her cheek. She loses track of what Pam is saying. It's not important. The hair is what's important, its dampness. Nora pushes an internal PAUSE button, freezing the little scene that pops up when she puts a picture of Pam to-gether with the concept "damp": they're in the bathroom of the railroad motel and Nora is pulling a shower curtain aside, hand-ing Pam a towel, then playfully reneging.

In the real world, on the steps of the Union, hoping she has missed only half a beat of real time, Nora tries to find a conversa-tional analogue of throat-clearing, tie-straightening, cuff-tug-ging. "Well, then. I hope you enjoy your class. Have some fun."

"I'll make you an ashtray," Pam says, not joining in the straightening up. She's still in the motel room, lazy between the sheets.

"I quit smoking," Nora says.

"You might start again, though."

Night is falling. Nora pulls her car out of the lot behind the Ad-ministration Building. She hears on the radio that large patches of the North Side have had their power knocked out — payback for having sucked up all the available electricity with a few mil-lion air conditioners running on high. Everything looks normal and regular for a few blocks, then lapses into darkness. It's a little scary, also fascinating, to sail along a daily route made eerily un-familiar by minor catastrophe. Nothing is quite itself. Block after unlit block, here and there a candle or flashlight visible in a win-dow, on the street a sweep of headlights. Amateur anarchists splash in the water gushing from uncapped fire hydrants. Ancient beaters ghost by, heading toward the lake with their windows rolled down and mattresses strapped to their roofs. On the radio, she hears that the parks and beaches are filling up with a temporarily transient population looking for a cool spot to spend the night.

Sailing through all this, it occurs to Nora that if anything were to happen between her and this woman, they would already have this little piece of history in place, something to refer back to, a meteorological marker of their beginning.

turbo cooler

FERN LIES ACROSS HER BED waiting for her next call. The heat wave has forced her to work from home. Harold's power is still out. She called and found him in a rare downcast mood. He had to cancel the canasta club and had two trays of Crab Rangoon appetizers spoiling in a dead refrigerator.

"I'll just hang over here, then," Fern told him. With any luck, her mother and Jeanne will be late getting home. Even though she has all the windows on the sun porch open, and has stripped down to gym shorts and a tank top, the heat presses on her with dead weight. For Lucky, she has been running a tea towel under cold water, wringing it out, then draping it over his back. He moves *very* carefully, to keep his tea towel in place; he understands that the towel is crucial.

They don't have air-conditioning. All three of them hate its artificial feel and the sealed-in quality, and, really, on all but a few days of summer, they're perfectly fine with the ceiling fans. When an unbearable stretch comes along, they usually cave in and call Sears, only to find they're sold out. And then the heat breaks and they completely forget about air-conditioning for another year.

And so now, Fern tries to lie absolutely still waiting for the phone. When it rings, she husbands her limited psychic energies, cuts to the chase by almost immediately telling the caller she sees a reunion with a loved one. "Someone who has gone away. There's a long journey involved. By sea."

"Where do you see me?" the caller asks. "What sea?"

Fern thinks he might be an exception to the rule, a straight guy, older. He has an affected accent. She imagines him wearing an ascot, his hair in a comb-over.

"I can't tell exactly," she says, treading until she sees what direction this call will take. "Someplace you've always wanted to go."

"Greece?"

"Yes." Without even trying, she can feel the Greek sun beating down on ancient temples. No, too hot. She moves toward the cool water. "I see small islands with white houses. Silvery fish pulled from the sea in heavy nets." Fern tries to fill in the blanks with whatever she can remember from Jeanne's travel magazines and the few times she has eaten down in Greek Town. She decides against bringing flaming cheese into the picture.

"And this is going to be soon?"

"Within the year, yes," Fern says, her voice vibrant with confidence. It is this tone, she is sure, that makes her so successful, brings so many repeat callers to ask the Star Scanners operator for Adriana.

"Are you Greek yourself?" the caller asks. She's not crazy about dealing with a straight guy. Women and gay men are truly interested in the future. With straight guys, sometimes their interest slides off the future, onto Adriana. Fern listens carefully to his breathing, tries to determine if this one is whacking off. Sometimes there's confusion along these lines. They think "900 number" and "woman" and put them together in a faulty way. She suspects this caller falls between the rows, neither interested in his Greek odyssey nor in something sexual with her. He is probably just lonely.

"Actually, I am," she says. "Greek. I was born in Athens." She adds, "In the shadow of the Acropolis," her mind racing through high school geography, hoping the Acropolis wasn't in Sparta, hoping his next question isn't about her pantyhose.

"I'm calling Sears!" Nora says as she comes in through the back door.

"I already tried," Fern says from the bed, where she is being very still, waiting for her next call. "They're out of everything except one that's mainly for factory use. A million BTUs or something. We'd have to get special wiring."

"Man, it's weird out there. Lights off everywhere. Hydrants popped all the way up Damen. At least we haven't lost *our* electricity. Oh." Nora stops as she sticks her head in Fern's room. "Are you . . . *working?*" She puts a tiny spin on the word.

"I can't go to Harold's. His power has been down for hours. He's in a foul mood. His canapés are melting. So I need to do this here, if that's going to be okay."

"Why ask me?" Nora says, but just because she has to be a little bitchy about Fern's job. Something — the heat probably — has knocked the usual fight out of her. She seems dreamy and preoccupied. She disappears for the next couple of calls, but then, while Fern is in the midst of consoling a client who has been dumped — dumped terribly, from the details — Nora drifts past the doorway, miming "boo-hoo-hoo," fingertips tracing imaginary tears down her cheeks. She's having her little bit of fun. Fern calls the Star Scanners number and logs out early.

"I didn't mean for you to stop," Nora says.

"I can't do this in an environment of sarcasm. You totally don't take my work seriously."

"Well, there *is* a serious side to it. My sympathies do genuinely go out to your customers in their real moment of sorrow, when they open their Visa statements and see how much they've blown on these calls."

"You have a point," Fern says. This is one of the stock phrases she uses to sidestep arguments with her mother. The best thing to do with her mother, she has found from hard experience, is not hand her anything she might later use as a club. And that could be anything — an interest in something new, a person Fern might find attractive, a book or movie she might have enjoyed. So the trick is not to give up anything of herself to her mother, ever.

This is especially easy today; she can hardly come up with conversation, let alone confrontation. The heat makes even the gathering of thoughts difficult. It is all she can do just to lie in a torpor, the chenille of the bedspread blotting up her sweat.

Then the house, which has been silent except for Lucky panting in a mildly alarming way on the floor next to her, is suddenly alive with action. Nora is dragging an old metal box fan across the floor of Fern's room, into the tiny bathroom at its far end. She then turns the shower on full-blast, puts the fan up on a wooden chair she drags in from the kitchen, then stands looking with pride at her handiwork, which she presents to Fern as the "Turbo Cooler."

Fern can see that her mother is trying to make amends for clipping her about her job. Instead of apologizing, though, or not clipping Fern in the first place, she's trying to make it up with charm. In moments like this, Fern can see her mother as Harold's sister, products of the same improvisational childhood that makes them subtly different from everybody else. And this is the very stuff she loves best about Harold. If *he'd* rigged up this contraption, she would have sworn it worked even if it hadn't. In fact, though, the Turbo Cooler works fabulously. The sea breeze she imagined on her Greek island is suddenly, deliciously wafting over her.

"So . . . ?" Nora says.

"Whatever," Fern says. She knows this is her mother's most hated response.

"Then we shouldn't waste the water; I'll just turn it off."

"No," Fern says. "Leave it on. It's better than nothing." Then she wonders if she might have come across as too enthusiastic.

gadget

THE HEAT WAVE BREAKS in the night between Thursday and Friday, with a terrific storm that whips against the house and down the street. Nora leaps up to close windows, then decides against it.

"It just feels so great," she says to Jeanne as she presses her palms to the screen. "So things get a little wet. So what?"

Fern's dinner on Friday feels like a celebration, a thanksgiving to the gods of rain and coolness. Nora brings home a kitchen gadget, a present for the cook. She doesn't want the already touchy relationship she has with Fern to degenerate into snappish little scenes like the one they had last night. She's hoping she can change the tone.

"Somebody's going to make a million bucks on this gizmo — the Miracle Garlic Peeler." Nora demonstrates. It's a soft rubber tube. "Put in a clove," she says, lifting her voice into a pumped, infomercial tone. "Roll it back and forth on the counter, and it's done!" She shakes out the clove, neatly shed of its skin.

"Cool," Fern says, as though she means it. Nora watches her daughter looming over the kitchen island, her height giving her a cheflike majesty. She has a style all her own, although Nora suspects she isn't very aware of it. She pulls from the grab bag of visual rhetoric available to girls her age and makes it look completely like her own idea. Her confetti hair, the ironic way she

wears lipstick only with the most non-lipstick-compatible outfits, like today — a dark red that's comic in combination with a
T-shirt, a pair of plaid Bermudas, and a multipocketed fishing
vest.

This nose-thumbing approach to fashion is part of a complex
joke Fern seems to be assembling about the universe she inhabits. She sees the humor in what everyone else finds merely annoying. She has a repertoire of urban imitations, like a pitch-
perfect rendition of the six-sound car alarms that drive all of
them nuts in the middle of the night. She also thinks Vahle's Bird
Store on Damen ought to have a striped ticking cover pulled
over it at night. She inhabits a hilarious city in which she is always scouting out new landmarks like the Decent Convenient
Store and the Little Bit Cleaner, both catering to customers with
low expectations; or the Stationary Store on Leland, which customers can rest assured will still be there when they pick up their
business cards. Fern links this to the Toujours Spa on Clark,
whose promise seems to be that it will resolutely remain a spa, as
opposed to changing willy-nilly into a tapas bar or optometrist's
office. Nora suspects that, as with the way she dresses, Fern is not
entirely aware of how delightful she is, which only makes her
more delightful.

At the moment, though, Fern is not being very delightful at
all. She takes the garlic peeler, looks at it as though it has historical significance, like the cotton gin. Then she puts it aside on the
countertop and gets a knife from the drawer and peels a few
cloves in the old, labor-intensive way, whacking them first with
the side of the blade.

From a shelf full of books on the difficult adolescent, Nora
understands that Fern needs to blow off the garlic peeler, do
things her own way, form her own style of peeling, form her own
personal relationship to garlic. Nora understands this, and still,
in these moments, her hope and goodwill evaporate and all she

can see is the two of them on the floor, flat on their stomachs, positioned to arm wrestle, and — it being *her* fantasy — Fern has a weak grip and it's an easy piece of work to force her hand to the ground.

Harold is sitting across the kitchen table from her, crunching Lucky's ears, bending to lift a velvety flap and whisper a sweet nothing. Nora tries halfheartedly to catch his eye, then gives up. Why bother? She will never make him see how skillfully Fern operates. He can never ascribe any malice to Fern; he has her in a little grotto, surrounded by small vases of cut flowers, flickering votive candles. Then, of course, she feels awful for wanting to tint his opinion. Why does she need an ally against her own child?

Until he appeared half an hour ago at the kitchen door, Nora wasn't aware that her brother was going to be part of this dinner. He arrived bearing a bowl wrapped like a mummy in foil, giving off frosty steam in the mild air of the early evening.

"I found an old ice cream freezer at one of my junk shops on Belmont. I made Pistachio Rocky Road, from scratch. The thirty-second flavor."

It's Friday night. Nora wonders why he's not working.

In spite of never having had a discernible career, Harold nonetheless appears to be on a gently downward slide in terms of employment. At first, the waitering jobs were a way to subsidize his acting. And for a while after he followed Nora to Chicago, he was a lively presence in local theater — in roles requiring a dash of the sophisticate, an edge of the sinister.

He also, for a few years in the earlier portion of his thirties, worked for an escort service, and swears that in his case, it never went any further than escorting. He took single businesswomen to social functions, widows to weddings, none of them to bed. Topics were the problem — the constant search for conversation openers and continuers, the avoidance of awkward silences.

Over time, he has gotten less and less stage work. Nora suspects that, along his way, he acquired a reputation for being difficult, a superstar-type perfectionist but without star clout, without, actually, any clout at all. There has been a parallel slippage in his waitering. He started out working in high-style places with zinc bars and pale wood tables, in the early era of chic food. Serving entrées flecked with sun-dried tomatoes, salads dressed with raspberry vinaigrette. But three or six months into a job, there were always troubles, peculiar disagreements and subterranean feuds with this cook, that hostess, brooding skirmishes difficult for him to articulate when Nora probed. For the past three years, though, he has been working way up on Lincoln, at Der Schnitzel Haus, which has a beer hall in the back famous in tourist guidebooks as the "Home of the Singing Bartenders." Nothing about the place is trendy. He wears a cummerbund, serves huge platters of roast duck, sauerkraut, spaetzle, giant wedges of Black Forest torte. And he has, it seems, no troubles. The hostess and co-owner is Gretel. She runs a tight ship. No feuds or flaring tempers under her command.

"She doesn't wear braids wrapped around her head, but you feel like she does," he has told Nora. "When I'm away from the restaurant, I could swear she has braids."

He has a crush on Gretel, Nora can tell. She can imagine the two of them pretty graphically, scenes in which one or maybe both of them is wearing a girdle.

Harold's life is a detailed demonstration of getting by. He operates out of a cheese-paring frugality. He rents an apartment in a pocket of nowhere up on Ashland, dirt-cheap but with the understanding that the landlord does next to nothing in the way of repairs. He roots around in secondhand shops for clothes. He gets his books and videos from the library, goes to free concerts, takes wood shop through the Park District. He has an unkillable car, a fifteen-year-old Chevy he loads up at a giant club store in

Skokie or Morton Grove. Everywhere you look in his apartment, every hiding place — under the bed or on the high back shelves of the closet, or behind the sofa in the living room — is stuffed with a hundred cans or rolls or boxes of something.

Within a disposable Western culture, Harold inhabits a miniaturized Third World. He discards almost nothing. His kitchen drawers are filled with wiped, then neatly folded sheets of aluminum foil; a trove of rubber bands; restaurant matchbooks; dust rags cut from worn-out underwear. He gets his broken appliances fixed, or fixes them himself. He has his shoes resoled, knows a tailor who still practices "invisible reweaving."

He wears a lot of black and is devoted to dyeing, which, to avoid detection, he does nocturnally in the back row of the laundromat. The T-shirt he's wearing today, she can tell, is a product of midnight craft — stretched at the collar, but crisp in color. Because of the worn thinness of its material, the outline of a brassiere beneath is visible.

Nora doesn't think this fascination with drag signals anything troublesome. What is it, after all, but a hobby, a set of model trains in his basement? One time she and Jeanne had a little party for people they worked with — from the college, from Berlitz. Harold turned up in a sport jacket, but also wearing eye liner and mascara. This unsettled Nora for about two minutes, and then she let it go. It was subtly applied and if anybody noticed, so fucking what?

"My mother sent along . . . you know . . . some stuff," Tracy says. She is awkwardly negotiating the back door with Vaughn, cozy against her breasts in his baby sling. She has her hands full with offerings — a loaf of bread and a Tupperware container — its translucence almost certainly camouflaging a clot of her mother's turgid homemade cheese. "Plus I have a couple of discontinued candles." She takes them out to read a label. "Bayberry maple."

Vaughn gets a big round of welcomes and, as soon as Tracy has him out of his sling, he receives the fanfare with fists balled up in glee. He seems to already grasp the principle of visiting.

"He just had his nap," Tracy says. "I hope someone's up to entertaining him for a while. He's discovered he has hands. Just to warn you."

Harold tugs at Vaughn's toes, telling him, "Ooky, pooky, dooky. How's my little snooky?" One of the best things about Harold is that he has absolutely no fear of appearing foolish.

Lucky shambles over and licks the baby's dangling foot. It takes the dog some time to get across a room now.

Nora takes the baby from Tracy, over to the old sofa against the far wall of this big room made out of the house's original kitchen and dining room. She settles in, making a lap for him to sit on. His smell — the sweet and sour of baby powder and spit-up milk — and his body so jam-packed with babyness combine to tumble her back into her own early days of motherhood, when holding Fern could so overwhelm her with love that she worried she might be deranged.

She makes monkey faces for Vaughn, who has a rather funny face himself — a long nose for a baby, and eyes that droop a little at the edges, brows that sweep upward, giving him an aspect of curiosity. Then there is his thick, stand-up hair, like a fright wig. She shoots him into midair, tickling him as he goes, holding him high and dangling, but secure in her clutches. He bunches up his odd features, then smiles hugely while shouting "yayaya," the prototype of a laugh.

Fern glances up and across the room from stirring the pot of boiling spaghetti, and tells Nora, "He doesn't enjoy that sort of thing."

"Yes, he's miserable," Nora says. "You can see."

"Yeah, well, he laughs, but then he throws up," Fern says, nibbling a broken-off piece of Parmesan.

Nora retreats into silence. She flips back to the beginnings of her long, unwinnable war with Fern.

When she came out to herself, Nora went from fierce nerves and brooding to pure exhilaration. Up until then, everything had seemed so in its place, with Russell still a copywriter at the agency and she still working in the ombudsman's office at the college. Of course, they didn't know the "still" part, didn't think of this as being merely the first part of their adulthood. The future appeared deceptively plain in front of them, looking much like their present only maybe painted a slightly different color, maybe with a room added on. Fern was just starting school, coming home with peculiar drawings, odd stories about aliens from outer space visiting her class, or coming home with nothing at all to say about an entire day. And all of this was so fiercely interesting, so preoccupying, so ongoing, each day opening directly into another. And yet, in the middle of this, for Nora to be right, to be who she really was, who she had already become, all of this would have to be overturned.

And it was in this overturning, Nora fears, that Fern — already a mysterious child, tricky to find in the best of moments — became profoundly lost to her. A vacuum was set up between them and has persisted through the years, Fern signaling her indifference in the face of all that Nora offers, keeps offering nonetheless, in hope and in penance.

"My turn," Harold says, and takes Vaughn from Nora. He lies down on the wood floor of the kitchen, sets the baby onto his stomach, and gives him big thumbs to hold.

Tracy joins Fern in fixing the dinner; the two of them politely help each other at the chopping block. They are no longer the giggling, silly friends they used to be. Nora suspects this is not a loss of innocence, rather simply that they are no longer smoking dope out in Tracy's car as a prelude to encounters with adults, gliding into the house like deer emerging from the dark forest, their pupils huge. Now they are practicing at being adults. Now Tracy has a baby and Fern is studying anthropology. Nora supposes they are repositioning themselves *vis-à-vis* each other, accommodating the fact that their circumstances have set them on divergent paths. Nora still has trouble adjusting to the notion of Tracy as a mother; she has grown so used to thinking of her as the ur–bad girl with her terrible boyfriends and school suspensions. Motherhood makes her seem vulnerable for the first time, a tentative young woman with a circus-animal plastic diaper bag and a blood-dripping dagger tattooed on her ankle, doing something quite difficult in an eerily solitary way.

"This kid has so much personality," Harold says in a voice squeezed from having his nose clenched in Vaughn's fierce grasp.

Fern overlaps this, shouting "Almost done!" to all concerned, tossing the spaghetti with the garlic and olive oil, the red pepper flakes and flat-leaf parsley. Nora goes upstairs to fetch her girlfriend from her study.

Although the evening is mild, Jeanne is wearing a light cardigan. This over a retro rayon dress. She will be more dressed up for this dinner than anyone else. Even if she wore jeans, they would be jeans into which she had ironed a crease. Part of this formality is because she is French, part because she is Jeanne.

"I have a small chill, it seems," she says.

Nora puts one hand to her lover's forehead, the other to her own for comparison. "You *are* a little warm."

"*Un peu enrhumée*, perhaps. I always get a cold in the summer, when everyone else is well, then never in the winter when my classroom is full of sneezes."

She looks tired, an older version of her usual self. Jeanne's small maladies — colds, tickly throats, occasionally a stomach-ache she ascribes to her liver — Nora has come to understand, are tugs on her awareness. Jeanne is not hypochondriacal, but she doesn't like to ask for things directly, and Nora has noticed that these minor ailments tend to come on when their time together has been pinched by the rest of life. They are, she thinks, Jeanne's unconscious way of asking for a slight increase in Nora's attention. Sometimes this seems sweet; other times Nora wishes Jeanne could just spit it out. Grab Nora by the hair and yell at her, or drag her into bed, or whatever all this politeness is a cloak for.

"It has been a long week," Jeanne says. "Too many students. And they grow stubborn or discouraged, and my job becomes even so much harder."

"How's it going? Your article." Nora nods toward the screen of Jeanne's computer, the flush of three-by-five cards across the surface of her worktable. Jeanne is far past her deadline with this piece, for a feminist journal. The article is to be a reappraisal. She hopes to show that while Colette undeniably slept with women, she wasn't really a lesbian. That there is a distinct difference between doing something and defining oneself by it. Jeanne's argument is that it is wrong-headed to attempt to plug historical figures into a contemporary set of assumptions, that although loving someone of one's own sex has always existed, gay identity is a modern construction. Colette is the centerpiece of the article, but along the way, Jeanne has tacked on Emily Dickinson and Eleanor Roosevelt. When she started talking about including Melissa Etheridge, Nora understood that the piece was slipping out of control.

Jeanne holds up a copy of a letter from Colette to her lover, Missy. "All of this is a problem of translation, but not of language. Here, it is that the French — specifically in the time of Colette's youth, *la belle époque* — experienced life in such a different way than we do now, here. And also, Colette was something of a foreigner in her own place, an anachronism in her own time, which adds to my difficulties."

Jeanne doesn't want to be teaching grammar and syntax; she wants to be teaching French literature or cultural studies. But her Ph.D. dissertation languishes in a box somewhere while she fritters her time away on articles like this one. There is no talking to her about any of this. Nora has tried. Discussion only brings out her defenses, and does nothing to get her off the dime. They have been together eight years, long enough that many of their topics and issues have gone into reruns; some have been taken off the air altogether. The two of them are long past the dazzling, opening stretch of relationship where each of them thought they were going to be a huge agent of change for the other.

"Is it time for Fern's dinner?" Jeanne asks.

"Yes. She's being very awful," Nora says. "Come down and protect me." In the hallway, she adds, "I don't deserve this. All the literature says you replicate your own parents' limitations. But I haven't. My mother was so all over me all the time. I was determined to give Fern room to grow, some private space to hold her secrets. Which I continue to do. I've never, for instance, if you've noticed, so much as alluded, not once, to the fucking tattoo."

On the stairs, Jeanne tugs at the back of Nora's tank top, makes her stop and turn around, kisses the side of her mouth.

"I think Fern is in a place now that is a little dark. You know, patting her hand around on the wall to find the switch to turn on the light. And I think soon she will find it, but also that she needs to be alone in her darkness until she does. I think this is what she is saying to you, what you perceive as anger or indifference."

"I know, but —" Nora starts, but Jeanne pats her butt to get her going down the steps, and says:

"Patience."

They move out to the backyard for the dinner; they eat at two long folding tables pushed together to make a square. These tables are layered with an assortment of Nora's vintage tablecloths

— pink and blue, a green and yellow map of the States, a holly-patterned Christmas cloth — set with brightly colored Mexican plates. The rains have revived the garden, loosened the deepest fragrances from the flowers, the earth itself, the basil and the tomatoes — especially the tomatoes. Fern's boom box sits on the sill of her bedroom, facing out. Otis Redding's greatest hits slip through the window screen.

The big bowl of pasta rests in the center of the table, next to it a platter of Caprese salad with fat slices of tomatoes and fresh mozzarella and a confetti of chopped basil leaves. Tracy's mother's many-grain bread sits, sliced, on a board. The homemade cheese, which they all know too well from long acquaintance, remains in the kitchen, on the counter next to the sink, safely confined to its plastic tub. The bayberry maple candles have made it onto the table, but no one has made a move to light them.

It's a mystery where Fern comes by her talent for cooking; she was raised on spaghetti sauce from jars, rotisserie chickens from the supermarket. And then, when she was early into her teens, she started bringing home cookbooks. Like a child from some backwoods shack without so much as a radio, coming upon a grand piano and teaching herself to play.

"We are so lucky to have you," Jeanne tells her, as plates are being passed around, and Fern smiles and lowers her head and closes her eyes, made both happy and shy by the compliment.

Nora wonders why she herself couldn't have come up with this little bit of praise and elicited this particularly sweet smile from Fern. But of course, if Nora had been offering the compliment, it wouldn't have been received in this easy way. Fern would have been searching for some hidden jab, or pretending to take it as though it had been delivered sarcastically, bravely trying not to appear wounded.

"I'm going to have to switch to working lunch at the Haus," Harold tells them all once they've begun eating. "I have a part. A new theater company, up on Clark. They're doing some *very* interesting things."

"Is it big?" Fern says. "The part?"

"Well, it's ridiculous in a way. You could say it's a large part because I am onstage through the entire play. But I don't have any lines because the fact is, I am deceased. The whole thing is set at a wake and I'm laid out in the casket. I was a very complicated person when I was alive and all the other characters have to sort out their feelings about me."

At first, no one finds anything to say to Harold's remarks, except Harold.

"No matter how fascinating you were when you were alive," he says, "once you're embalmed, you're pretty much reduced to one aspect. Which is to say, dead."

"Man, though," Fern says. "I mean, no blinking."

"What if you sneeze?" Tracy says, lifting her shirt to nurse Vaughn, who has begun to fuss on her lap.

"Yes," Harold says, "well, you can see that even though it's hugely boring, it is nonetheless going to require all this control." He closes his eyes and tilts his head back, holding the position while they all watch. There is not the slightest flutter of lashes.

"Could be very powerful," Fern says, and Nora forgives her everything.

When they've finished dinner and had coffee and Harold's ice cream (a big success) and everyone has requested that Fern play the Otis Redding disk again, she does, then comes back out and claims Vaughn as her dance partner, swooping him around dramatically to "I've Been Loving You Too Long." The baby adores Fern, goes into a sort of rapture, Nora has noticed, whenever she picks him up, as though he knows he is totally loved by this particular human. Which he is. Nora sees Fern's love for Vaughn as something other than maternal or auntlike or whatever she might understandably be feeling for him coming out of her closeness to Tracy. Rather it seems to Nora that what Fern and Vaughn have is some profound version of friendship, an affinity.

It's almost ten by the time the kitchen gets cleaned up with a little effort from everyone but Fern, who gets a cook's dispensation. Soon after this, Tracy leaves with Vaughn, who has long since nodded off. Harold says his goodbyes after looking at his watch and muttering something about having to meet someone. He chests his social life like a good hand of cards. Whatever he has on tap for tonight must be very good to risk the wrath of Gretel for blowing off work.

Nora and Jeanne, tired and sleepy with wine, offer a final round of praise for Fern's dinner, then pull themselves upstairs. Nora picks a copy of *The Death of the Heart* off the pillow along with her glasses, and sets them on the dresser. She was hoping to get a little reading in tonight, but it's too late now. She and Jeanne fall into bed, crash-landing without taking off underpants or watches, only brushing each other's lips by way of good night.

They sleep like synchronized swimmers, freestyling parallel through the night, flipping over to catch, then release, each other into the universe of the subconscious. Nora has come to know Jeanne in sleep as much as through daylight observation. Let loose in a room of a hundred women, she could find Jeanne by the shape of her shoulder, the scent under her arm, the taste of the inside of her ear. In the morning, they often lie limb over limb, shuffling through their dreams.

Nora's are tricky skirmishes in an ongoing war with dark forces. Hitchhikers unsheathing knives in the back seat as she drives along desert highways, the sound of metal brushing against leather before the blade is pressed sharp to her throat. Other, more hulking figures, springing from beneath the steps in the shadowy stairwell. Or large, writhing rats racing over her in some dimly lit, too small space, their tight fur bristling across her palms as she tries to push them away. If sex enters the frame, it is something sordid with someone inappropriate — Harold, or her mother. Once with Mrs. Rathko, in a train berth.

Jeanne, meanwhile, reports dreams of flying low over their neighborhood, using her arms to take off and land gently. Even what she considers nightmares seem merely whimsical or slightly odd. She has little hands for ears. She gives birth to a chipmunk. Last night, Queen Elizabeth startled her by opening her handbag to show off her trained mice in little outfits — polka dot dresses, checkered suits.

"I think you should bring *my* dreams in to your therapist," Nora says. "They're so much meatier."

"I ran into her yesterday. Christine. At the Dominick's. She was buying artichokes with her girlfriend." Nora knows it's idiotic, her jealousy of Jeanne's therapist, her worry that this person she has never met probably knows more about Jeanne than Nora does, or at least more of the interesting stuff. She also hates that Jeanne refers to her therapist by her first name. Instead of calling her Dr. Jungundfreud or whatever. But of course, she *isn't* a doctor; she's a lesbian therapist — though not the worst of the lot. She doesn't barter her services for French lessons. She doesn't work out of her house, or have her dogs prowling through her sessions with clients. She hasn't tried to date Jeanne. The worst indictment Nora has been able to come up with for all her probing is that her office is filled with deadly, cliché therapist art (gallery posters from the Southwest). That, and Nora doesn't like her voice when she's on the machine changing an appointment. She sounds way too *understanding*. There's also this big mystique around her, some veiled tragedy in her recent past. All in all, she's a little too romantic a figure to suit Nora. What happened to all the pudgy bald guys everyone used to go to?

"What was she like, the girlfriend?"

"Tall, dark. Handsome in a Katharine Hepburn way. It was

like in school, when you couldn't imagine the teacher had a life outside the classroom. I am afraid I appeared very silly. I know I was falling over my words. Rouging."

"Blushing."

"Yes."

It's Saturday and soon they will have to get up. Jeanne will bake croissants (usually just frozen ones, but occasionally she tackles the project from scratch) and then they'll set about cleaning their house, one of Nora's favorite parts of the week, a few hours to bustle and putter, flounce sheets like energetic chambermaids in something from *Masterpiece Theatre*. Today Nora's plan is to attack the furry tile grout around the bathtub; she has set aside an old toothbrush especially for the job.

Jeanne turns from her back onto her side, to face Nora. She is such a small person, so light in her movements. This rearrangement under the sheet makes Nora think of a small flock of birds fluttering inside a soft sack.

"What about your reception at school the other night? I didn't get to hear. It was a success?"

"Oh, I think so," Nora says. "Not so many students as I'd hoped. There never are. But some of them seemed to connect with each other. Mrs. Rathko was terrible to me, what else is new?"

This nattering is successful. By the end of it, Jeanne is brushing Nora's hair back, kissing her forehead, popping out of bed in search of coffee, on her way into the day. The moment has passed when Nora could have, by the by, brought up the woman at the reception, so she and Jeanne could have shared her, allied themselves lightly against an innocuous moment of flirtation. This happens more and more often — Nora sees exactly how some small next piece of her life should be happening and, instead, like the bus driver weary of his route, alone on the night shift, veers off a little, down some unscheduled side street.

park

WHEN HE GOT HOME FROM WORK, Fern's father would take her and their new dog, Lucky, to the park. Even in February, lots of dogs came out with their owners around this time and mostly they got along and had fun without too many scraps because the park was no one's territory, there was no protecting or guarding to be done. These were some of Fern's happiest times, out there not only with Lucky, but with all the dogs — Ben and Kiko, Maggie, Bridget Olive, and the wild blond dog, she didn't know his name. Sometimes there were as many as a dozen or even twenty dogs out at once and she would stand with her hands out so she could peel off her mittens and pet them as they milled around her in the gathering darkness, exhaling clouds of frosty breath, smelling one another and looking for balls to fetch and allowing themselves the casual love of humans.

Lucky was a year old. They picked him out at Anti-Cruelty in the spring, a present for Fern's seventh birthday. He had already had two previous owners, had been brought back twice for bad behavior. He was the fastest dog in the park. When the chasing and running around started up, he was always at the head of the pack — red fur flying behind him as he went, tongue dangling out the side of his mouth.

"He's a great dog," Fern said.

"If only he didn't have a screw loose," her father said, standing beside her. He meant Lucky's problem with anyone, as he put it, of the "postal persuasion." The first week they had him, he'd gotten out the front door and gone after their mailman, Raymond, who shouted from the sidewalk up to Fern and her mother, standing on the porch, "I'm going to have to mace him."

And Fern's mother said, "Go ahead," because if he didn't, Lucky would tear into Raymond. So Lucky got sprayed and it was terrible to see him wobbling around the lawn blearily, pooping everywhere, but there was nothing else they could have done.

The problem was bigger than simply their own mailman. If Lucky was in the car with them and spotted some stray mail person, he would begin growling in the back seat. Even if he saw just a mail cart by itself on the sidewalk. So they always had to keep an eye out for mail carriers, plus people wearing shirts or jackets with emblems on them. In these cases, Lucky had to decide if what they were wearing counted as a uniform, or not.

These small trips to the park made Fern feel that everything was in its place, holding together. She had a dog and a father and they went to the park together. Like a page in a storybook.

This was the best thing about her father — that he was always where she expected him to be. Not only here in the park, but also in the living room at home watching sports on TV, which he loved. Out in the backyard grilling, even in winter. During the day he was in his office at the ad agency; at night he was home. She never felt she had lost him or was about to lose him, the way she did with her mother.

This happened once in the Jewel when Fern was six. She was in the cereal aisle, looking for Cocoa Puffs, couldn't find them, then couldn't find her mother. It turned out she was only around a couple of corners, picking up a package of chicken drumsticks, but in the short, heart-pounding burst of time it took before Fern found her, she imagined the whole rest of her life as a child alone in the world, walking down a highway with her backpack.

What happened in the Jewel stayed with her a long time, and

made her fear that every time her mother went out the door, she would never come back. But in fact, in this real-life way, she always came back. The leaving that frightened Fern was something else, odd moments when she could tell that her mother had retreated — not by walking away, or getting into the car and pulling out of the space in front of the house. The retreat was into herself, pulling back from Fern and her father and shutting a tight door, like on a refrigerator, a door with a seal. You didn't know if, inside her, the light was on or off. It was from this place that Fern feared her mother would never return.

skateboard

SATURDAY. They're hanging out in Tracy's backyard, by the side of a huge baby pool from Tracy's own childhood, resurrected from the back of the garage for Vaughn, who sits near it, in the shade of the yard's huge maple. He is content in his bouncer, alternately holding and throwing to the ground a multicolored rattle Fern brought him. Fern can mark off the summers of her adolescence — like rings in the wood of a tree — by memories of the conversations she and Tracy have had hanging out in this yard.

Behind them, Lucky lies panting, even in the shade. She picks him up and sets him gently in the pool. Under his fur, he feels stiff in her arms, with his brittle bones and arthritic joints. Although he has never been much of a swimmer, he always becomes elated in water, standing up to his knees in it, then looking over his shoulder at Fern, as though he has accomplished something pretty significant. She plunks herself down in the pool next to him, scoops a little water over his neck to cool him down. When he leaves her to step carefully to the other side of the pool, then stands stock-still, waiting, she gets up, lifts him over the side, and sets him back on the grass. He shakes his fur free of water, then settles onto the lawn with an accordion sigh.

Tracy pushes her shades down her nose and gives Fern a look over the top of the frames.

"He's doing great," Fern says. She doesn't want anyone saying he isn't, or thinking it, or even just giving that look. He's slowed down, sure, but he still enjoys life in most of his old ways. Going for walks. Flustering any birds who might be idling a little too complacently on the ground. Hating the mailman. The whole Lucky thing is too complicated. Fern can't think about it. He has been her dog since forever; his presence beside her spans the whole distance from her childhood to this very minute. When he goes, there will be a terrible space next to her, a shadow with nothing casting it.

After a lightly rainy morning, the afternoon is warm and sunny, but there are signs that summer is thinning out beneath them. The leaves on the neighborhood trees are still green, but dusty and beginning to dry. They scratch against one another, making a high, pale din, like sheets of waxed paper. In a couple of weeks, Fern's fall semester will begin. She lies back and closes her eyes for a moment to enjoy the future. She has signed up for Observational Models, and got advance placement in a graduate seminar, Peasants. She's taking a final semester of Spanish for her language requirement, and for an elective, Basic Zoology.

She loves college, can get down into a kind of Zen calm sitting at her bedroom desk, or in the library at school, highlighter poised over an open textbook, assigning importance to certain sentences, determining the most crucial pieces of knowledge. She loves that learning is a thing in itself, a closed circuit. She particularly loves the shutter that anthropology opens on the possible ways of living a life. Nothing is a given; the most peculiar sort of behavior in Chicago would be absolutely normal in some remote mountain village, on some island somewhere. Celebrated even, with pageants or ceremonies.

She has been reading about the dream travelers of Borneo. They go nowhere physically, feel no need to. They stay where they are, elongating their earlobes several inches with weights.

They are tourists in their dreams, then return to report these dreams to one another. The dreams serve as both journey and as the raw material of story; in this way, they are always on the go, always engaged in both their real and their parallel lives. They would look at American girls obsessing over old boyfriends and longing for their own apartments as foolish creatures with pathetically small earlobes.

Tracy flattens the *Reader* open on the grass in front of her and points to the ad she placed in the "Missed Connections" section, then reads it out loud: "*Tower Records, Sunday night. You: interestingly wasted Rage Against the Machine lover. Me, blond, plugged into Beck. We crossed cords at the listening station. Was the eye contact all in my imagination? Tracy. Voicebox 698.*"

"*How* wasted?" Fern asks her.

"Doesn't matter," Tracy says. "He won't call. What are the chances he'll see this? The only people who read these are the fools who put them in. Too stupid to act when it might have possibly mattered. And say he even does call, what kind of social life can I possibly have with leaky tits and this little ball and chain?" She snaps Vaughn's bouncer, springing him upward a little sharply. He looks disturbed, but only for a moment. Then his startled expression regroups into laughter as he decides this is a game.

"You, though," Tracy says. "Looking good. How much have you lost?"

"Eleven pounds," Fern says. Tracy is the first person to notice.

This has been Fern's summer self-improvement project. She would most like to be shorter, but, that option not being available, she is trying to get thinner. She started running in the mornings and going to Weight Watchers meetings where she has learned how to break food into a system of points.

Tracy wants details.

"Well, the main thing is to boost you up about the whole project. And tips, there are tons of tips. Sometimes someone brings in a deranged recipe, like skinless, boneless, fatless chicken breasts, grilled with a molé sauce you make from sugar-free cocoa mix, nonfat mayonnaise, and, I don't know — garlic powder. Like that. Everything's free or low or substitute or skinless. Or lettuce. I'm hoping I don't run into anyone there who knows my mother. She can't find out about this. I have to make this seem like something that just *happened*. She'd be so supportive. I don't know which would be worse — being fat, or having to endure my mother being supportive about me getting thin."

"You weren't fat before."

"No, right. Not fat. I was more like those sturdy peasant girls in old paintings, doing the haying. Wide in the loins, good for birthing. Kind of a birthing and hay-heaving look. As opposed to a runway model look."

"As opposed to my loins, which were *not* built for birthing," Tracy says, putting a hand on each hip. Fern was her birth partner. They went to classes together for a couple of months before Vaughn was born, Tracy doing breathing exercises, Fern learning how to comfort her through the process. And then, when push came to shove, Tracy lasted about ten minutes before calling the doctor a fuckhead and the nurses cunts and demanding an epidural immediately.

"I'm supposed to be on a garden walk with my mother," Fern says. "A bonding opportunity she cooked up."

"You waste too much energy hating her," Tracy says.

"I don't hate her. Hating her would be so much easier. What I am is confused by her. She is a confusing person. Do you remember in middle school? When we went to the exhibit of holograms?"

"No, I had impetigo, don't you remember? Everybody got to go but me. I had to stay home. I looked leprous."

"I remember. Your sister was charging her friends fifty cents to look at you."

"I forgot that part. The little jerk."

"Well, I don't want you to be bitter after all this time, but the holograms were totally cool. Like a person. You could walk around them. One was Thomas Jefferson. There was Amelia Earhart. And they were three-dimensional, but also transparent. They were only made up of laser beams or something. That's my mother. There, yes. But not really. *Never* really."

Nobody says anything for a little while, then Tracy lifts Vaughn out of his bouncer and brings him into the pool with her. He loves the water, has no fear at all.

"I haven't told him about drowning yet. That's why he's so cocky," she says, holding him out in front of her as he slaps the water and throws his head back, cackling like a mad thing.

Tracy's mother comes out the back door with a large pan and a roll of gauze that looks like bandaging for a wounded army.

"Cheese alert," Fern says in a low voice. Every weekend for as long as Fern has known Tracy, Tracy's mother makes cheese, the same cheese she brought to Fern's dinner, to all of Fern's dinners — pale curdy grout that hangs from a line in mesh sacks over the pan, draining through all the Saturday afternoons of their growing up. Tracy's parents were hippies and still make the cheese to stay in touch with their good old days. There's the cheese and the home-baked bread, plus they still wear Birkenstocks. When Tracy first figured out she was pregnant — peeing on the blotter stick from the home kit while Fern sat on the edge of the bathtub — Fern thought, well, at least Brad and Tina (they want you to call them by their first names) would be understanding. They themselves met in a drug- and sex-filled commune in the seventies and had Tracy before they were married. So it was surprising when they turned out to be upset, although Fern sees that their anger is not based on any moral system but on Tracy blithely tossing away her future, turning overnight into someone not terribly interested in leaving the house.

As far as Fern is concerned, it is Brad and Tina who are the big disappointments. They have turned out to be only superficially alternative; their attitude did a one-eighty when they started making big money, almost accidentally, in herbal supplements. The business started out as a basement operation but now has its own plant in some far-flung suburb.

Tracy has a sister, Wind. (Until she was twelve and took matters into her own hands, Tracy herself was Skye.) Wind is a trader. Even when she's visiting at home, she sits in the breakfast nook with hundreds of small pink slips and a cell phone and makes and takes calls on only two stocks. She asks, "What's it selling for?" Or "What's it at now?" Tight little questions for whoever is on the other end of the line. She buys, she sells. All day. This seems to Fern the most soulless occupation imaginable, but because Wind drives an Infiniti and has a condo overlooking Lincoln Park, Brad and Tina consider her a big success Tracy should imitate.

"Hey, Tina," Fern says. Tina's response today is muted — a slight nod and the hanging of a few more sacks of cheese. She's not the cheery talker she used to be, not with Tracy, of course, but also not with Fern, who has apparently fallen into the accomplice category.

"You were going to look into daycare places," Fern says, turning back to Tracy.

"Daycare, I'm beginning to find out, is for women with careers, or at least real jobs. Or women with SUVs and manicure appointments. Basically I'm one step up from the women you see dragging their laundry to the 'mat in a wire cart, with all their kids trailing behind them. Okay, maybe I'm *two* steps up from there. I have Tina's old car, and we have a washing machine in the basement. I don't need a wire cart. Beyond the cart is as far as I've gotten."

"But what about going back to school so you could be a person with a real job? Your parents would help, you know they would. They'd be pissy for a while, then they'd help."

"Maybe," Tracy says. "Probably. But I'm too tired right now to come up with a coherent plan. Right now, my little job is almost more than I can handle."

"Then —" Fern gets only this far before Tracy puts a hand on her arm.

"Thanks, but I'm okay. *We're* okay." She rubs Vaughn's furry head as though he's a good luck charm. "I'll figure something out. Just not now, okay?"

"I was only —"

"I know."

The sky grows overcast as heavy yellow-gray clouds muscle in. Tracy brings Vaughn out of the pool and bundles him in a big towel, then gets him into a fresh diaper and a T-shirt that says BIG BABY.

"Let's change out of our suits and go for a walk," Fern says. "We can put Vaughn in his stroller thing, what do you say?" It's an idle suggestion. Tracy isn't much for getting out and about these days. And so Fern is surprised when she says, "Okay."

Not far, over on Roscoe, then a ways down Damen, there's a nice little park. They sit on a bench enjoying the big breeze that's coming up with the clouds. They watch a trio of guys about their age — a little old for skateboarding, but very good at it. They look like old surfers, their hair bleached out at the tips, their tans oven-baked. They're doing tricks on the sloping asphalt paths winding among the park's trees. Taking long stretches easily on their back wheels. Hopping off their boards, turning in midair, reconnecting soles to fiberglass, flipping into an opposite direction. Showing off for one another and for anyone else who might care to watch.

"Oh man," Tracy says, and it takes Fern a beat or two to

see she's not referring to their tricks, but rather that she recognizes one of them, who nods in their direction. "Fuck," she says softly.

"A checker," Fern guesses, meaning from Tracy's checkered past.

Fern doesn't recognize him, but that's not surprising. For a long while, Tracy was a devotee of the one-night stand. She carried a baggie stuffed with condoms in her backpack, along with an address book of numbers and first names. Fern figures she probably doesn't know about most of Tracy's boyfriends. This one is tall and skinny in that flat way some guys have; when he turns to the side there's hardly anything between the back of him and the front. He has ropy muscles in his arms and legs. He's wearing long, baggy shorts and black, thick-soled shoes, a karate-style headband, wraparound shades.

Fern waits to see what will happen. More and more when the issue of guys comes up, Fern feels alienated from Tracy, or as though she has been left far behind. Tracy is already worn out, just from the amount of life she has lived so far — the time she put in being a creature of the night, out on Belmont or in Bucktown in black polyester pants and peculiar hats and thrift shop sweaters with politically incorrect fur collars and cuffs. Being politically incorrect is part of her tough act. Fern used to think that underneath all the toughness Tracy was really just a big softie, but lately what's underneath also seems tough, fibrous, as though she has taken a look at what's available out there and isn't terribly impressed. Her facial features, small and pointed, have now also hardened up. What used to be a dry-ice glare, used selectively, has become her default look, and it's hard to find her inside there. Too often lately, Fern gets embarrassed when her own enthusiasms run head-on into the abutment of Tracy. She has become guarded in revealing excitement, about certain things in particular, but also in her general sense that everything ahead is bursting with possibility. Possibility seems to be one of the things on which Tracy now casts a cold eye.

For a long while, Fern was Tracy's sidekick on their search for whatever. When she met Cooper, at the rave, she thought Tracy would be happy for her, happy to be a part of the discovery team. And she was, for about a minute. Then Cooper quickly became one of the things Tracy was bored by. While Fern was finding him so original and fascinating, Tracy acted as though she'd already come across a thousand Coopers and he was just one thousand and one.

"He's nothing," she told Fern. "He's vapor."

Fern didn't want to have to defend Cooper to Tracy. What she wanted was for Tracy to understand automatically why she was so totally vulnerable to him, why contact with him made her feel exfoliated, like she'd had about six layers of skin sanded off. Understanding this seemed like the kind of thing Tracy should be able to do, but she couldn't. So she turned out to be right about him, that's not the point. The point is that she couldn't come out of her own darkness to be happy in a particular moment for Fern.

The guy who is a problem for Tracy wheels over. He is in a state of extreme sweat, but in an interesting way. His chest is furry, the hairs glistening; the band around his head and the T-shirt he has knotted around his hips are soaked through. He tips gracefully off his board, and, as part of the same fluid motion, crouches down in front of Lucky, who is sitting at attention. The guy is close enough that Fern can smell salt. She can tell that Lucky is making his standard initial assessment of this guy — friend or foe? The guy lifts his hand and with long fingers starts scratching Lucky's chest. In reply, Lucky gives the guy's shoulder a long lick, as though it is delicious.

Tracy emerges from somewhere deep within to say, "Hey,

James." She's got her voice flattened out, but she's nervous, Fern can tell. She doesn't bother making introductions, just shifts her gaze down and starts pushing Vaughn back and forth a little in his stroller.

"Hey," James says in reply — to Tracy at first, but then he widens his focus to take in Fern and the baby.

"Fern," she says, introducing herself, lifting her hand in a wavelike gesture she immediately regrets. She suspects she looks as though she's wiggling a puppet.

He kind of notices her, kind of doesn't. She figures his distraction has something to do with him and Tracy, nothing to do with her, but she feels dismissed nonetheless. She is not very adept at being cool; she falls way short of negotiating the complex grid of attitude. So she retreats from the conversational volley; she leaves it to the two of them. They seem to be making a point of how little they have to say to each other.

How has Tracy been?

She's been fine.

He's been fine, too. He's working as a bike messenger between law firms down in the Loop. It's pretty good money, but he almost gets killed in traffic about five times a day. He has nightmares about getting "doored."

She's taking some time off from school.

Neither of them mentions Vaughn, although while he's talking, the guy brushes his hand casually through the baby's hatlike crop of hair, which prompts Tracy to start fussing, yanking Vaughn out of his stroller, onto her lap. James looks over at Fern with a kind of click in the back of his eyes. There's something about the look that makes her edgy in return, but not until he has waved in response to his friends, who are leaving, their boards under their arms, and made a quick set of goodbyes so he can catch up with them, and she has watched the way he moves in his long shorts the whole way out of the park, does she begin to figure out that this edginess has something to do with attraction.

"Anything you want to tell me?" she says to Tracy.

"An old acquaintance. Mr. Nice Guy. Not my type. Too broody."

It occurs to Fern all of a sudden that the awkwardness between him and Tracy might be that James is Vaughn's father. She's not sure where she has come up with this. Maybe their eyebrows; there's something similar about the way they wave up a little at the ends. But it's more than that. Before she became a psychic, she almost never had premonitions or suspicions or forebodings. Now she has them all the time. Occupational drift, but disconcerting nonetheless. She's not sure she wants to know so much, opening doors onto people's secrets.

Fern waits for Tracy to come forward with this piece of information about the guy, James, but she doesn't say anything, just plays a silent game of patty-cake with Vaughn.

After a longish while, Fern says, "I kind of liked him." She feels like she's throwing herself on a grenade.

But Tracy only looks at her and then back at the path down which James is disappearing, and says, "Yeah. You might."

almost there

NORA AND HAROLD go on a neighborhood garden walk. He found the tour advertised on a flyer tacked up somewhere, the same way he ferrets out church pancake breakfasts and VFW spaghetti dinners. For Harold, the city is a limitless universe of galaxies and he's a tourist in all of them. This makes him both delightful to know and exhausting to be around.

Nora asked Jeanne along (too busy with her article) and Fern (something else to do, that sad smile of regret, she's so adept at these, at making them look as false as possible). Later, Nora heard her on the phone with Tracy, discussing their lack of plans. Nora knew the garden walk wouldn't attract Fern's interest, but she thought maybe with Harold as a draw . . .

She gets this hazy idea from time to time, the three of them doing more together. But it seems that Fern and Harold already have their relationship in place. Very private, not based on social occasions, especially not on garden walks. She's jealous, of course.

The walk is in Andersonville, which has some huge old Prairie mansions Nora wouldn't mind snooping around. She can imagine herself gardening in some placid patch of her future. She watches Martha Stewart on TV — annihilating aphids, pruning rosebushes, training Boston ivy over pergolas — and can easily project herself into this cluster of patient pursuits even though, so far, in any given summer of her life, she has not found time to do more than stake a few tomato plants, or plug in a flat of impatiens alongside the garage. Even the basil was too much for her this year; she left it to Fern. Still, she's up for taking a look at what rich people are doing in their backyards — why not?

Saturday arrives bearing a light, misty rain, and she assumes Harold will have changed his mind, but when she calls, he's still up for it, and when she pulls up in front of his apartment, the rain has stopped and he's standing on the sidewalk, ready for an expedition, an umbrella tucked under his arm.

He has always been beautiful, but moving through his thirties, the throttle is out. Sometimes Nora doesn't see him for two or three weeks and in reappearing, he catches her off-guard. Much of his beauty, she thinks, is the incandescence of his goodness radiating from within. It's interesting that he dresses as both man and woman. Sometimes he pushes in both directions at once. Like today. In pleated black linen shorts and a pale green camp shirt, with his hair wet-combed back off his face, his gender is unspecifiable. He is the perfect androgyne.

Here is another way in which he and Fern are connected. Nora knows about Dolores, but only secondhand, through Fern. She is bothered by Harold's lack of trust in her, but at the same time knows she would do poorly if confronted face-to-face with Dolores. She could not, as she gathers Fern does, sit around having conversations, dishing the dirt or whatever it is you're supposed to do with Dolores. She herself would be able to go only as far as having a conversation with her brother in costume, whereas Fern apparently welcomes Dolores as another person, or at least a legitimate alternate version of Harold. How can she? Nora wonders, while at the same time understanding that this very thought disqualifies her, clicks the velvet rope across the entrance to the complete Harold.

He thinks Fern is coming with them today.

"She blew me off," Nora says, looking for sympathy. "She's not, basically, interested in spending time with me."

"I think she is an extremely private person," he says. "Like Garbo. Except without the Swedish part, or the movie star part. But still, it's like having Garbo around your house. I can see how that might be frustrating."

Harold is a mediator. When issues arise between Nora and their parents, or between Nora and Fern, he moves into position with a calming tone and a sympathetic demeanor, a kind of tilt down and forward with one shoulder, the one you can feel free to cry on. Sometimes he is a comfort, but other times, she wants to put a bucket over his head and start banging on it.

"I think she finds you kind of overwhelming," he offers.

"What? Is that what she tells you? I mean, how ridiculous is *that*? I can't even whelm her, much less *over*whelm her. I can't even get her to clean up the bathroom after herself. I don't really think you can be overwhelming to someone if you also have to pull that person's hair out of the drain catcher."

"You're right," he says. "I'm sorry. I forget you're perfect. How could she have any complaint against you?"

Nora doesn't bother to reply.

Harold gives it one more try. "Look. Fern is twenty-one. Do you remember twenty-one?"

"Sort of."

"You don't, really," he says. "The good news for you is pretty soon Fern will be forty and you two can get along then."

"Thanks so much for your insights."

It turns out this walk encompasses only the lower-rent streets of Andersonville, blocks of sensible middle-class brick two-flats.

"Maybe we should forget it," Nora says.

"Come on. It'll still be fun. And the rain's almost over," he says, pointing to a sunny sky pausing beyond a bank of clouds.

"What I'm really looking for," she says, "is a medicine-chest walk. A drawer-by-the-side-of-the-bed tour. I want to see the prescriptions and nipple clamps of strangers."

"Oh, darling, I *know*."

"Here's Number Fifteen," she says, half an hour later, pointing to a marker flag.

"This is a fucking *corner*," Harold says.

"Correcto mundo." Nora reads from the stapled program they were given for their six-dollar entry fee: "Number Fifteen — neighborhood corner planting." They look down at a skimpy bed of nasturtiums.

"I don't think they can count this," he says gloomily.

"Number Seventeen is a window box," Nora says, pretending to read further. It's hard to joke about a joke, though. Number 6 was somebody's muddy backyard with nothing but a crayoned sign propped on a lawn chair:

SORRY!

AZALEAS BOMBED THIS YEAR.

They pass other garden walkers along their way, recognizable as fellow travelers by their air of determination to get somewhere, but without much enthusiasm, and by the pamphlets rolled up in their hands.

Harold gets a broody look as they pass a house with six wind chimes tinkling and clanking and bonging in the slight breeze. He is thrown into despondence by what he considers stupid, worthless noise — mainly car alarms with their hair-trigger detonation, their pips of setting and unsetting that fill the air of the city. And, of course, wind chimes.

"I don't think wind needs enhancement," he says. "I mean, why can't it just be wind and we all leave it alone?"

"I think people get them as gifts," Nora tells him. She has told him this before. "They put them up, then forget they're even there."

"But I *don't* forget, that's the thing. I mean if it was the sound of some orphan's dialysis machine, you'd say, well, it's irritating, but you'd have to live with it. But this is only more worthless, knickknacky noise added to all the rest of the noise that's already there. Do you think they'll pass? That they're just a fad?"

Nora says in what she hopes sounds like a convincing, definite voice, "Oh, I think they're already on their way out." This is a total lie. She saw a huge display of them a couple of weeks ago in the snooty Smith & Hawken store down on Clybourn. If anything, they are only on their way in. From the look he gives her, though, she can see he believes her. Sometimes it's as though they are still twelve and seven.

Number 19 is mostly clumpy bushes and the odd begonia, but there's a flagstone patio with half a dozen extremely old people sitting attentively, or at least politely, while a sullen teenage girl in a pale blue sundress plays something lugubrious on a cello.

As they come back down the gangway, Harold whines in impersonation of the cellist, "I don't want to do it. It's about to rain again anyway and Brittany and Jessica are going to the mall."

Nora answers with a parental baritone. "Now, honey. Grandma and Grandpa are counting on you. Who knows how much longer they're going to be with us." There's a certain kind of fun Nora has only with her brother. It's about having a few million stupid jokes behind them.

Numbers 21 and 22 are nice gardens, both behind two-flats belonging to gay guys. At 21, there's a small black and white dog Harold takes a shine to. At 22, they're offered mimosas. Nora declines. Harold takes one and drains it in short order, like a cowpoke in a saloon.

"We've seen enough, don't you think?" he says, picking up on her weariness. On his own, she suspects he'd slog through to the bitter end, get his full six dollars' worth. "I'll take you to lunch, okay?" he says. "I need to go down to Chinatown anyway, to get some cookies."

They take the Drive along the lakefront, which, in spite of some threatening clouds in the distance, is so alive with people today it looks as though there's a Festival of All Humanity and everyone got an invitation.

"I was down at Filene's this week," she says, reaching around while she drives, pulling a package of T-shirts off the back seat and handing it over to him. "Couldn't resist these at the price." She tries to subsidize Harold's meager lifestyle when she can find small casual gestures that won't embarrass him.

She'll pick up the lunch check, too, even though, as it's Harold's choice, she knows the restaurant will be impossibly cheap. It turns out to be on a side street off Wentworth, tucked in among a row of jammed-together frame houses. There is no sign out front and inside there are only five Formica-topped tables and a wall menu in Chinese. Everyone besides the two of them is Chinese. No one is eating anything readily recognizable. Root vegetables, maybe. Marine life, both flora and fauna. Nora can only guess.

The owner is delighted to see Harold, who tells him, "The usual." What arrives is tofu and little bits of meat in black bean sauce and some thready noodles in a curry. Also greens on a separate plate, leaves mixed with oil and garlic and something that tastes like mushrooms but probably isn't.

"Good," Nora says, picking at this and that with her chopsticks.

"Nobody comes down to Chinatown anymore," Harold says. "Cantonese is totally unhip now. Or wasn't hip ever. But it's still great."

"Dad's not looking so good," he says a little later. He has just been down to Florida for a short visit with their parents. They pay his plane fare. He stays a couple of days, sleeps in their guest room. He helps Lynette with the big household jobs that are starting to overwhelm her. He cleans out the refrigerator, rents a carpet shampooer and does the whole apartment, wall to wall. He helps with the husbandly details in which Art has never had much interest. He takes their car in for maintenance and makes sure Art doesn't get ripped off. He soaks, then clips, their father's tusklike toenails. He is an excellent son.

"Gray," he says. "His color is gray with a little top coat of tan."

Nora nods, as though she is the specialist being brought in on Art's case, as though she knows anything about what's going on in her father's arteries, his liver.

"He must be seeing a doctor?" she says.

"The thing is, I don't remember him being this way before — maybe it's from hanging around with other old guys — but he's got this new bad-ass attitude. That it's going to the doctor that brings on the trouble, that you step into the office and that's where your troubles really begin."

"I'll get Mom on him."

"He has this serious paunch now. He sits on the sofa and has to lean back to get comfortable. He doesn't have a lap anymore. It's more of a slope, an embankment. And when he gets up, it's like he's made this huge effort. There's sweat on his forehead."

"Well, he better not go to the doctor, then. I have a feeling that doctor would only tell him he's not in great shape and that's where his troubles would really begin."

"I know," Harold says. A plate of tiny snails has arrived with little picker implements to pluck out the meat. He holds out the dish toward her.

"Not for me," she says, raising a hand. "I have trouble with them cringing in their shells."

"This is going to take me a while, then, all by myself." He starts in with his little pick. There look to be maybe a hundred snails on the plate.

Nora sits back and pours more Coke into her glass of ice. The cubes crack and sputter, rearrange themselves. "I'll call Mom. Get her to take him in to see someone. He won't fight Mom."

When Harold is done eating, he blots his lips with a flutter of thin paper napkins from the table dispenser. He exhales deeply and fills a small cup with tea that has steeped to nearly the color of coffee.

Nora looks to her brother for clues. He gives off an air of life fully lived, deeply enjoyed — all without seeming to have any of the sort of larger point to which one is supposed to aspire. He has an aura of success and accomplishment hovering around him, although he doesn't seem to have accomplished or succeeded at much of anything. Nora wants to understand this contentment. She would like a piece of it for herself.

She considers talking to him about the woman at the orientation reception. She would have nothing to fear; he is the most discreet person on the planet, and probably the second or third least judgmental. She could put a silly spin on the little episode. Make fun of her own vanity being tapped by the encounter. Then shake her head with relief that she hung up her jersey years ago and retired from this ridiculous sport.

She moves so close to this confession that she experiences the slight sensation in the jaw that precedes revelation. But then, instead, she says nothing, picks up the pale green slip that is the restaurant check, settles up, and moves quickly past the opportunity.

Around the corner from the restaurant, they find what he's looking for. A wholesale shop, profoundly dark and musty inside, its wares lurking in huge drooping banks of cloth sacks pushed against the walls, and in a freezer case where roiling frost obscures whatever lies inside. There doesn't seem to be a lively flow of buying and selling in the shop. Nora imagines a hole in the middle of the back room, leading directly to China, mysterious goods hefted out, then set to wait for some vague, nocturnal commerce.

"These will see me through a couple of months." Harold pats the giant bag of fortune cookies he has bought. He tears it open at the top, shakes it like a lottery maestro, and tips the bag toward her. "Go ahead."

She cracks open her cookie and reads:

YOU ARE ALMOST THERE.

"A great fortune," she says. She hands it to Harold.

"Yes," he says. "Excellent."

While he was buying the cookies, Nora found, on a shelf next to some bottles of hair tonic, a dusty, paper-wrapped bar of jasmine soap.

"For Jeanne," she tells him, setting it on the counter, feeling the guilt flow through her fingertips into this gift, tainting it. Even though she has nothing to be guilty about. Yet. The guilt comes from knowing there is a "yet" attached to the thought.

On their way home, he opens the bag and sniffs the soap, which sets him off on the subject of Jeanne. "You are so lucky," he says.

"Yes." She wants to head off the hymn of praise for Jeanne that is forthcoming. She won't be able to hear it right now, cannot have the conversation that is pressing its way forward. Instead she brings up his play.

"Previews start next weekend," he says brightly, meaning, Will she come?

"Saturday. On Friday, Fern and I have to go have a talk with Russell. She's supposed to be contributing to her own upkeep. She already gets half her tuition because of me working there. Russell makes up the shortfall on that, but there's still everything else, and most of what she makes from the psychic thing goes — well, she has her Body Shop habit, those Starbucks drinks. So anyway, we have to put on our rough-hewn garments, go into mendicant mode."

"He'll do it. Russell always comes through."

"Yes, but he'll make me suffer first. That's why we have to go over to have this humiliating talk. It's my penance. He can't just mail a check. And I have to bring Fern for moral support because I can't ever bring Jeanne. Louise says she can't accept our 'lifestyle.' She doesn't want to be confronted with it. What she actually said was she didn't want her nose rubbed in it."

"Someone should put a sock in her mouth. A smelly sock." Everyone hates Louise; Harold jumped right on that bandwagon, bless his heart.

"Oh, I think Russell is hiding behind her skirts. He can put everything off on Louise and her religion. She has a bumper sticker: GOD LISTENS. God must just be so bummed, don't you think, having to sit up there, listening to Louise?"

"That's Friday," Harold says.

"Yes, and so Saturday we'll come to your play. We're all looking forward to it."

They both taste the lie for a moment, then Harold says, "I'll drop off some comps."

"And I'll call Mom," she tells him as he gets out of the car in front of his place. "Get her on Dad's case."

"You won't be disappointed," he says, meaning the play. Unspoken between them is all the ghastly theater Nora has had to sit through over the years because Harold was a wife-poisoner in this, a spy in that. Once, he was Being in a theatrical interpretation of *Being and Nothingness*. They can never talk about that one.

meteorology

DON'T KNOW WHYYY . . . drifts out from Harold's living room as Fern lets herself and Lucky in the front door.

Dolores is home, propped against the cushions at the end of the sofa, in her version of leisurewear — a long kimono-style robe printed with fans. Her hair drapes her shoulders. She is soaking the fingertips of her left hand, to release the two-inch, vermilion press-on nails Harold won't be able to wear out this afternoon.

"Lena Horne doesn't have enough tragic range for 'Stormy Weather,'" she tells Fern. "I have the Judy Garland cover. With Judy, that sun's not merely hiding behind a couple of gray old clouds. The apocalypse has already happened. That sun has abandoned the sky, for good."

"Has it ever occurred to you . . ." Fern starts in, then gets cold feet, then warms them up enough for another try, which is, "I mean, have you ever noticed that your interests are sort of like the interests of, well . . . of a gay guy?"

"Oh," Dolores says, pulling her hand out of the soaking solution, plucking the nails off one by one, "wouldn't that just simplify *everything*?"

From the stereo, Lena acknowledges that she can't go on, that everything she has is gone, but her sorrows get muted by the bedroom door as Fern pulls it shut behind her. Lucky finds a corner, and, after several turnarounds, drops to the carpet for a nap. Fern is ready for work.

By conducting her business within earshot of Harold's stereo, its ancient turntable always stacked with sputtering seventy-eights from the forties and fifties, Fern is acquiring a slouchy outlook on love. Everything that has happened to her, or will happen, has clearly already happened to someone else. It was a cold hand on her heart, the realization that the people who first found meaning in these songs of wry despair are now her grandmother's age. In much the same way, all the vaporous futures predicted by all the fortunetellers before her are long since played out. But for her clients, who have their own contemporary anthems of sorrow, their troubles are still terribly alive, their futures lying around sharp corners, over steep rises ahead.

She positions herself diagonally on the bed; she has found she gets the best reception from this angle, that more information seems to come her way. This sort of thinking, which she would have found totally flaky a year ago, has become part of the new way she sees the universe.

It started with trying to be good at the job. At first she was punting with every call. Wildly scanning for clues — inflections in the client's voice, pauses that might be pregnant with meaning. Guessing general, using the formats Mindy provided, then going to specifics when the clients' interest seemed to perk up. Beating the bushes to flush out their pasts — hard childhoods, missed opportunities, estrangements.

Their present — a period of upheaval or searching.

Their future — growth and change ahead! Perhaps a new and significant person entering their life! Maybe money! (She tried to fill the future with capital letters and exclamation points.)

This is still her default method, but, more and more lately, she hears her callers' questions, then waits along with them for her own response. She is sometimes not sure what she's going to say until she says it. This is where the process gets interesting.

Star Scanners is happy with the increasing length of her calls, her rate of return callers. They want her to be plugged in from four to eight, three nights a week and Sunday afternoons, so her regulars will know when they can find her. In exchange for this firmer schedule, they have bumped her hourly rate up a couple of notches. Once she's back at school next week, she'll have to work the calls around her studies. Today, though, she can just stretch out and wait, passing the time thinking about all the potential in life as it lies ahead of her.

It's almost five; she's about to clock out when the phone rings.

"I know I'm late, but I just got in and I had to talk with you today."

This is Marsha, a nurse — nurses and beauticians are her most frequent callers. Marsha is a regular about whom Fern has not yet received so much as the vaguest psychic insight. All she can give her is common sense laced with a mystical flavor. Marsha has been involved for a couple of years with a married guy and has recently found out that he has also been seeing yet another woman — a girl really, a college friend of his daughter. Marsha is trying to bend the facts enough to keep thinking the guy — Phil — is an okay, simply confused person.

Fern wishes Marsha would stop calling. She is done with this client, has nothing more to offer her. Nada. She has told Marsha flat-out that she doesn't see this liaison occupying any good place in her future, that she sees her going on to someone who is neither married nor dating someone else (instead of both), that she sees the aura of distant travel, an adventure deep into a foreign culture. Not even this exotic note did much to pry Marsha off her Phil obsession. Although she pretends to take Fern's — which is to say Adriana's — advice to heart, and hangs up at the end of each of their sessions utterly resolved to get free of Phil, she has not yet made it a whole week before she's back on the phone to report a new glimmer of possibility.

"We had a very important talk today," Marsha says.

"Yes, I see it. I see you sitting very close to each other. Your expressions are very serious." She knows they were close since the only places Phil, nervous about discovery, will take Marsha is to a budget motel or out in his car where they park like teenagers.

"He's not serious about her," Marsha says.

"The new girlfriend?"

"No. His wife. Their parents were friends. It was practically an arranged marriage."

"But they've been married for years, right?"

"Eighteen, but it's been dead in the water for a long time."

"But what about the college girl?"

"If I can get him to dump the wife, the girl will be a piece of cake."

Fern doesn't like Marsha's attitude. More and more she is sounding like someone who will deserve Phil if she gets him. "I see you with someone else." Fern hangs tough.

"Look harder," Marsha says, with a bossy edge in her voice which Fern doesn't like, doesn't like at all.

By the time she has hustled Marsha off the phone, then logged out, Dolores is just a kimono left on the sofa and Harold is off to a rehearsal of his play. Fern heads home and on her way ties Lucky's leash to a parking meter and ducks into the Blockbuster to pick up a movie for herself and Jeanne. She is making a gesture of thanks. When Fern went out to the cottage in Michigan with her dad and Louise in July, she couldn't bring Lucky (Louise is allergic to everything but humans and fish). Her mother loves Lucky and can be counted on to feed him and take him on the slow, sniffing-opportunity walks he enjoys; she would never let him languish. Jeanne, though, throws herself into dog care with enthusiasm. She takes Lucky to the park, and on what she calls "happy rides," which are to the drive-thru at McDonald's. This time she took him so often that he was a little portly by the time

Fern came back. She had also — a minor miracle given Lucky's age and lifelong resistance to doing anything cute — taught him to shake hands.

Jeanne is all cultural on the surface, it's all Joffrey and Symphony and Yo-Yo Ma. She is also the mildest person, a pacifist both personally and politically. And yet she is a sucker for the most violent American movies, anything with mobsters or drug kingpins, and lots of resolution achieved with semiautomatic weapons.

A small bonus is that Nora hates these movies, has made a point of being above them, and is, Fern can tell, jealous in a small way that Fern and Jeanne have this trashy thing they enjoy together from which Nora has excluded herself.

In the Blockbuster, on her way to the Action section, Fern sees Cooper. All this time and suddenly there he is. Hunkered down in front of the lower shelves in Cult. He's wearing black jeans and a vintage leather jacket, although outside it is too warm for the jacket. Weather is not much of a consideration for Cooper. "Outside" is a brief area of transit for him between one interior and the next.

He neither looks up, nor turns. He's unaware of Fern's presence. He's reading, through tiny wire-rim sunglasses, the back of a video box. Probably one of the mondo bizarro compilations he enjoys — disturbing things done in remote areas of the world. Cooper is an anthropologist of an amateur variety.

She doesn't want him to see her. Then they would have to stumble through one of those phony "hi, how are you" things. She knows she couldn't bear it; she would buckle in some uncool way — something blubbery and collapsing or something eye-darty and anxious. The only possible good meeting would be the one following the two or three calls where he begged her to take him back.

She wonders how much time she has before she will filter into his peripheral awareness and he will look up and over. Anyone else would have by now. But Cooper stays pretty enmeshed in his own reality. She has time to imprint this image of him, like one of those long exposures required for photographs taken in caves. She wants to burn this one in, for future reference.

He looks a little different, more relaxed. She can't tell, though, what's new and what's always been there only she couldn't get enough distance to see it back then. Like when he broke up with her, it was supposedly about a Vietnamese girl his family approved of. And then, a month or so later when Tracy mentioned seeing him at a party with a blonde, Fern, instead of coming to the logical conclusion that he'd been lying, instantly concocted a Vietnamese girl with blond hair. She could see her so clearly, the child of a Vietnamese father and a Scandinavian mother. The mind, she can see based on personal experience, is an incredibly powerful mechanism, especially when it's hard at work against logic. But why not keep being stupid about Cooper? Now that he's gone, she doesn't have to be smart about him. It doesn't matter *what* she is about him, as long as she keeps it to herself.

She slips out of the Blockbuster without renting anything. She and Lucky stop off at the small neighborhood shop where they let him come in with her. Ron Video. Apostrophes seem to be disappearing a lot from signs around where they live, a no-nonsense approach to the English language by foreign shop-keepers. (There is also a Sue Cleaners a couple of blocks over.) Ron doesn't have a great selection, but with a little looking, Fern comes up with a copy of *Things to Do in Denver When You're Dead.*

Later, she and Jeanne sit in front of the TV, eating a pizza Jeanne ordered when Fern showed up with the video.

Lucky is raising his paw repeatedly for Fern to shake it. Now that he has this trick up his sleeve, he's trying to get some mileage out of it. The movie is up to the scene where Treat Williams has been lying in wait for the hit man, is now blasting him to smithereens. A huge bloodstain mushrooms on the wall behind the victim.

"This is such an excellent film," Jeanne says.

Fern is paying only the lightest attention. Seeing Cooper has run a rough, hot cloth over surfaces she has only just been able to cool down, smooth out a little. Her old juju thinking kicks in with a flutter of superstition that Cooper's presence in the Blockbuster was a sign that he would *not* be happy if anything happened between Fern and the skateboarder she met yesterday. This old line of internal chat gets interrupted, though, by a small, newer voice that says "So what?"

talk show

"AND TONIGHT'S SPECIAL GUEST, a show biz jill-of-all-trades — dancer, singer, actress, comedienne — let's have a big hand for Lynette Lambert!" As he shouted, Harold extended from behind his back a baseball mitt, to represent the big hand.

This bit cracked up their father and mother, who were the cohost and guest respectively on *The Harold Dennis Hour*. At eleven, Harold featured himself the world's youngest talk show host. All he needed to make it into the big time were a network slot, guests who weren't his relatives, and a sport jacket that fit. He was wearing one of his father's tonight, smoking a cigarette from a pack Art had left in the pocket. He was allowed to smoke on his show, because Johnny did.

Art was already on the sofa as Harold's overly appreciative sidekick. Lynette came onstage direct from the kitchen, where she had been cleaning up after dinner. She was still holding a dishtowel in one hand as she shook Harold's baseball glove with the other.

After refusing to make an appearance on the show, Nora had been relegated to the armchair in the corner, where she was serving as the sole member of the program's audience, also the only one in the room who thought Harold was tragic. The talk show was his latest foray into entertainment, following his puppet theater and, before that, a hapless collection of card tricks. Her parents' encouragement was relentless. Sometimes Nora would wake up on a Saturday or Sunday, go downstairs, and, simply from sitting, eating toast in the middle of all the optimism in the kitchen, become exhausted and have to go back upstairs and sleep two or three more hours.

The person Lynette most admired was Harriet Nelson, the way Harriet was able to parlay her singing career into a TV series with Ozzie and even bring her kids onto the show. This would have been Lynette's dream life — a total blurring of the line between onstage and off, a singing-dancing-acting family with Art for a manager. Harold had totally bought into this vision; Nora was the only one fighting it.

Nora often felt older than her parents, well beyond the corny, childish way they saw life as being either onstage, or backstage, waiting to go onstage again. Also, they didn't seem to see that their notions of entertainment had been superseded. That no one wanted to hear Lynette sing "Mambo with Mama." That the mambo was ancient history. Rock and roll had happened, and the war, and windowpane acid. People could see and hear a mambo just by closing their eyes. Her family was on a path to nowhere, a highway made obsolete by a new turnpike.

In the slightly wider world outside her home, Nora fared better. She was a junior in high school and was popular, mostly, she knew, by virtue of her looks. She had a small group of friends, smart girls in her class — "sharp" was how they thought of themselves. Also, she kept an eye on two seniors — Tory Latham and Raeanne Maggio. Tough girls. Nora didn't speak to them, their paths never crossed. She suspected they were probably morons, or high all the time; they had this trancy air about them in the halls. But she had almost nothing to go on in her efforts to decipher them — a little gossip, no hard information. Her total relationship to them was seeing them during change of classes, and imagining situations in which they would come to her rescue.

Like: She's mugged on her way home and they see her and rush over, chase the guy off, and Nora's bleeding, but only a little.

They take her to their apartment. In the fantasy, everyone's a little older. Tory and Raeanne have an apartment of their own, in New York, down in the Village. They clean Nora up, put her in a bubble bath. Wipe her face with a washcloth. One of them leaves, and Nora is alone with the other.

Things got vague from there.

Once she saw them shopping at Macy's. They weren't giggly or goofing off. They were, in fact, barely speaking to each other. They had reached a point beyond talking, some higher plane. They would pluck at various items hanging in the Teen Style department, and then nod at each other, or lift an eyebrow, making small judgments on what was cool and what wasn't. Macy's was at their service, offering up a selection for their approval or disapproval. For them, shopping was serious work. They carried the burden of their importance in their small kingdom of style. Also, they were definitely aware of how they would appear to anyone who might run into them.

And that afternoon, they did see Nora flipping through a circular rack of turtlenecks. They didn't say hi; that would have been way over the line. But Raeanne did nod slightly in Nora's direction, which was huge, given that they were seniors and she was beneath the level of them having to notice or recognize her at all.

Nora took this nod home with her, ran the scene through the loop a few more times, spun it into a few more vague fantasies about Raeanne and Tory befriending her, taking her on trips, opening before her their vaults of secrets.

None of this seemed to have anything to do with sex. It was more about a romantic version of friendship she couldn't imagine happening in real life, but which had evolved into a definite set of aspects and emotions inside her. Rescue was a large component. These girls would save her from something.

Sex was another matter entirely; it occupied her in a blunt, urgent way that she didn't hear in the conversation of her friends.

They either liked making out (or making out and more) or didn't, but it was more tied up with particular guys in a getting them/keeping them/losing them way. Nora wasn't interested in any of the boys they knew, not in any of these ways.

For Nora, sex seemed to occupy a side room beyond the walls of her regular life. There was the kissing that had happened with the girl in the motel on the way to Florida that time. Then, when she was thirteen, a girl named Cathy, whom she knew from having done a science fair project together ("The Labyrinth of the Human Ear"), took her to the Vogue Theater.

"It's a different kind of show," she told Nora and left it at that.

The Vogue was in a working-class suburb a couple of towns out from White Plains. They took a bus there. The theater was so decrepit outside that at first Nora thought it was abandoned. Inside, the seats were sprung, the fabric worn down and slick, the whole place overheated and smelling of butter and a flowery deodorizer. On Saturday and Sunday afternoons, the deal was that you would leave an empty seat beside you. Once the lights had gone down, a guy you didn't know would slide into it. One of the hoody guys who hung out there, skinny guys with long hair and cheap, black parkas. For the length of the movie, you could make out with him, and when the show was over you left with your friend as though nothing had happened. Everyone inside the Vogue seemed to play by these rules. To Nora, it was a perfect place. She went there other Saturdays, even after Cathy tired of it. She went by herself, which was better, in a way. Then Teddy Frey moved into the neighborhood and Nora didn't have to go to the Vogue anymore.

She visited Teddy after school while his mother was still at work at the hospital. They had plenty of time. His mother worked until eleven. There was no rush.

Teddy was a boring kind of regular — short and stocky. He wore wheat-colored Levis and John Lennon glasses with blue lenses. He had dirty hair. He looked like a fifth Beatle, on his way to see the Maharishi. Teddy was not particularly interested in the social life at school. He liked to read books on Eastern religions and smoke dope, neither of which was a very social activity. At school, he was a nonentity, lost in the shuffle. He wouldn't bother telling anyone that Nora came over to his house after school. There wouldn't be any point; nobody would believe him.

They would go down to the family room in his basement and smoke a little dope and watch TV, mostly sports — baseball, golf, whatever was on. Once it was a fishing show. They would turn off the lights and let the TV run, and, without saying anything, Teddy would stretch out on the sofa on his back and Nora would stretch out on top of him. They kept their clothes on. What they did with each other was suppressed and constrained, like sex in a monastery, or in some ancient Chinese dynasty. She pressed her face into the sofa arm, which smelled like dog. They made almost no sound, even breathed in a controlled way that produced slight shudders. Eventually, while she bit the arm of the sofa and he had his head turned to the side (she imagined his eyes open, staring at the golf match), they would bring each other off. They never discussed, or even referred to what they did in the basement. They were just watching TV.

scheme

NORA LISTENS to Mrs. Rathko pack up and go. Although from inside her office she can only hear what's going on, she can visualize each step. She knows each component of Mrs. Rathko's leave-taking by heart. The sighing as she drops weary and underappreciated into her secretary's chair, then pulls up a foot to change from businesslike pumps into running shoes for her brisk hike to the El. The gathering up of soiled Tupperware and her thermos, one of the last plaid wide-mouths in America. The nestling into her tote bag of one of the paperbacks she plods through serially — thick, hair-raising stories of bacterial plagues or nocturnal takeovers by secret cabals of now ancient Nazis. Rainy days like today, Mrs. Rathko's ritual substitutes the running shoes with the snapping on of galoshes (which she, of course, insists on calling "rubbers"), the fluttering open of a pleated rain hat. She prepares for her nightly trip home as though it will be a great journey across borders, travel that will require supplies and stamina, papers of transit.

It's nearly six by the time she has pulled the door shut behind her and Nora is left alone to scheme. It started small. At first all she did was look up Pam's application form, get her address, and drive by one night. It was a brick bungalow in Ravenswood Manor. There were no lights on, no clues to the life lived inside. Also from the application, she got Pam's birth date and started checking Omarr's horoscope for Pisces every day. In Omarr's opinion, something big was about to happen to Pam; Nora took this to mean herself. She was waiting for Pam to make the next move, to follow up on all that steamy flirtation at the steamy orientation.

Then it began to seem as if she wasn't going to make any move at all. Early on, she came by the office for the parking permit, but Mrs. Rathko was there to take care of it. Nora came out of her office at the sound of Pam's voice, offered a little chitchat, and Pam was friendly enough, but there was nothing freighted about her conversation this time, no more of that delicious eye contact. Still, Nora was left riled up. As though she had been surreptitiously tickled and, once Pam had left, needed to smooth down her skirt, open a window to let in some fresh air, go to the cooler for a paper cupful of water.

Since then — nothing. If there's a next move, Nora is going to have to make it. She sits inert at her desk, but within, she's a Greek drama in an ancient amphitheater — foible and folly paving the way for tragic consequences. She sat here last Tuesday night, watching this same play of bad judgment and horrible consequence, and ended up slinking home, grateful to Jeanne for her unwitting protection.

Tonight, though, she can't summon up this gratitude, and her restraint last week now seems like good behavior that should count toward a small dispensation. She gets up and grabs her jacket and a clipboard she finds on top of Mrs. Rathko's file cabinets. A clipboard — could she get any sleazier? How different is she from Claude Frolich down in his lab? He probably uses a clipboard to camouflage his overtures. She can picture it only too clearly. And, morals aside, is she risking being called on the same carpet as Claude? (She recently heard he hired a lawyer after his meeting with the ombudsman.) If Pam is not interested, if Nora is horribly mistaken, won't she be guilty of harassing a student? This prudent line of thought does not so much as break her stride on her way out the door as she heads over to the Fine Arts Annex.

She tracks down the ceramics workshop and finds a long table lined on both sides with hunched-over, aspiring ceramicists. Pam is one of them. While most of the students are painting spots on the backs of clay bullfrogs, or stripes on the haunches of unicorns, Pam's piece is a small pot with a narrow opening at the top. A vase, maybe, for small, short-stemmed flowers. Pam appears, however, to be transforming it into an antivase in which flowers might not feel entirely welcome. The background is black and, at the moment, she appears to be totally absorbed in painting over this a floating nonpattern of amorphous, ghostly shapes in colors from a cranked-up primary palette. Postmodern yellow. Insane-asylum green.

Clipboard crooked in her arm, Nora asks the instructor (Evelyn Fitzpatrick, who has been teaching basic art courses at the night school since forever, since before there was clay or canvas, when there were only paintings on the walls of caves) if she could please have a moment with one of her students. As though she is taking Pam by the ear down to the principal's office for detention.

When they are a ways down the corridor and Nora has been made a little goofy by all the noticeable aspects of Pam in black polo shirt and tight, faded, paint-smeared jeans and Pam is looking back at Nora with an expression that usually precedes laughter, only Pam doesn't laugh, just holds onto the look, Nora says, "I was wondering if maybe, maybe you could get out of here? When you're done?"

This suggestion gets Pam a little more serious. "I'm done enough. I'm at a drying part."

Nora waits in the hall, leaning hard against the wall as though she might buckle without its support, while Pam cleans her brushes and puts her antivase away on the shelves. Nora clutches her clipboard, which she only now realizes has no papers attached to it, and she thinks, *Okay. Here we go.*

This is the first cool night of the early fall. Nora rolls down the sleeves of her jacket and buttons the cuffs as they walk to the parking lot. Pam drives. She has a pickup (as opposed to a car), black (as opposed to nothing; whatever she drove, it would have to be black). The vanity license plate reads BLDR GRL. It turns out Pam is an independent contractor. She adds family rooms onto homes with growing families. She puts dormers in attics, updates kitchens and baths. She has also built two greenhouses and an artist's studio. She handles the carpentry and wall-busting on her own, wields — if she says so herself — a mean Sawzall. She farms out the beam work and electric and plumbing to subs, gets them to show up and stick to schedule even if it means hauling them out of bed or bar. She loves her work. The ceramics class is a sort of artistic outcropping of these same inclinations. She thinks in colors and shapes. She loves working with her hands.

Nora has nothing this good to trade.

"What you've got," says Nora, "it's what everybody wants. I'm one of the everybodies, I suppose. I don't have a career so much as a job that's about ten jobs down a straight line from a dumb job I took in a temporary way when I got out of college. I mean, it's not like I had a doll when I was little, and dressed it up as a little college administrator."

"I never played with dolls," Pam says.

"Me either."

"Do you think that's a dyke thing?"

There is something stunningly invasive about this question, with its tacit assumption that they are both dykes. Of course this is the whole basis for their presence in the suddenly close quarters of this truck cab. Still, as long as it wasn't mentioned, their quarters could feel roomy, their purpose on this ride vaguely social. By saying "dykes," Pam has ripped off her underpants and handed them over to Nora.

From the passenger seat, bumping along on the truck's springy shocks, Nora watches Pam's huge hands, fascinated by the way they dance a little over the top of the steering wheel, the way they are not quite cleaned up from class, are still painted green along the sides. There is also, peripherally, the way Pam's jeans tug around the muscles in her thighs every time she depresses the clutch, then the accelerator. Also, the place at which her forearms emerge from the rolled-up sleeves of her old gabardine bowling jacket. In these ways, Pam's immediate presence blots up most of Nora's thought processes, pushes out any memory of whatever clever conversation she was going to come up with on this ride.

Pam has decided, apparently, that they will go to the lake. There's a parking lot near the beach at Foster where there seems to be some gay guy cruising going on, but mostly it's just the usual nocturnal parkers — people waiting for drugs or brooding alone or finding a small patch of privacy with someone they've no business being with in private.

When Pam shifts in her seat and turns to Nora, the best Nora can come up with is, "I'm not sure why I'm doing this."

Pam doesn't bother responding to the lie. Instead she explains why she likes to keep the truck's heater on, but with the windows open. "In summer I do the opposite, run the a.c. full blast with the windows open. It's the blend that's so great, cool on hot, hot on cool. Like a hot fudge sundae."

Nora listens and stares at the floor mat beneath her feet and smells Pam from across the cab. She has a teenage guy odor, a mix of leaves and sweat cooled down after a scrimmage. Nora sits in the dark and enjoys the amount of sensation contained in this moment. Stars of fascination float around in the darkness of the cab. She could stay here all night with the engine idling, the heat eddying out the dashboard vents, the smoke from Pam's cigarette dragged up and out the window into the flue of the night. All Nora has to do is wait as time collapses in on itself, past and future folding inward onto this tiny patch of present in which Pam reaches over and drags the calloused tip of a middle finger along the hard right angle of Nora's jaw.

"I think, maybe, a few girls have hurt themselves on this," she says, then settles back into the driver's seat, tosses the lit butt of her cigarette out onto the blacktop, looks at Nora, shifts the pickup into reverse, pulls out of the lot, and heads back to the college.

When they are in the parking lot at school, idling behind Nora's car, Pam says, "Maybe I should call sometime?"

Nora nods. "But it would have to be . . ."

"At your office."

"Yes."

Pam finds a pencil and a scrap of paper in the glove compartment and Nora writes her direct number on the back and Pam folds it and slides it into a pocket over her breast while Nora watches, forming not so much thoughts as murky thought constellations. Pocket. Breast.

She parks a couple of blocks away from home. What she really needs is a decompression chamber in which she can adjust the pressure of the blood in her veins, bring herself down to ground level, room temperature. Maybe a short, secret session with a professional debriefer. All she has, though, is her car.

She's not sure who will be home when she gets there. It's a little after eight-thirty. Jeanne is doing an *intensif* at Berlitz, tonight and tomorrow night, but Nora can't remember how early it started, how late it's supposed to run. And Fern, Fern's schedule is absolutely impenetrable.

When Nora comes in, she is greeted only by Lucky. He is always happy to see her (or Fern, or Jeanne), but the overwhelming nature of his happiness tonight — not merely wagging and woofing, but an old college try at jumping up on her, his back paws slipping on the scattering of mail on the floor under the mail slot — tells Nora that he hasn't been out for a while. Lucky is Fern's responsibility and she's usually very responsible. But when she screws up — with dog care or cleaning up the kitchen or bathroom after herself — Nora is no longer comfortable with calling her on it. Although she is still Nora's child and still lives at home, Fern is also no longer a kid, and is only living at home because of circumstances beyond both of them. And so she has taken on something of the status of a roommate, a boarder. Someone whose housekeeping might disappoint, but not someone who can really be yelled at about it.

Nora opens the door to the backyard for the dog, then mixes some biscuits and canned food in his bowl and sets this out on the back steps. She picks up the mail and finds a postcard from her mother, who is apparently on a trip to the Bahamas with her bridge club:

Got my hair bead-braided in the old market. Back tomorrow. Mom.

She tries to remember if Lynette told her about this excursion. She tries to imagine her mother with bead-braided hair.

"Lucky!" she shouts out the door. At first she can't see him, then spots his shadow lurking along the back fence by the alley. "Forget the possums. Let's go for a *walk*." The magic word.

They are almost up to Cornelia — Lucky sniffing a particularly interesting weed along the parkway, Nora mentally replaying Pam's fingertip running along her jaw — when a cyclist careens around the corner and skids to a stop in front of them. It's Fern. Lucky is beside himself, his hind legs going out beneath him from the force of his wagging as Fern drops her backpack and rubs both sides of his head.

"Oh, Mom, thanks so much for taking him out. Did you feed him, too? I got stuck in the computer lab waiting for a printer. They have people in there who are printing out whole theses or phone books or whatever, and everyone has to wait. Somebody's going to blow up in there one of these days."

Fern is slightly flushed from her ride. At the college, Nora sees girls Fern's age every day, and by contrast understands that her daughter is shaping herself in an iconoclastic way. She is not going to be ordinary, but the ways in which she will set herself apart are still in formation. Although Nora has offered several times to help her get a used car, Fern prefers to bike around town. She came up with her interest in anthropology on her own with no counseling from anyone, and in the face of most of her friends going into fields more associated with graphics or software design than with huts and tribes. She wears odd gatherings of clothes, assemblages that really can't be thought of as "outfits." Tonight she's in parachute pants and a checked shirt under a plaid flannel overshirt. Her multicolored hair pokes out of a crocheted cap she got at an African crafts shop. She is breathtaking to Nora in the surfeit of potential she embodies, the directions in which she could take off. Nora sometimes looks at Fern, and at Tracy, and thinks, So, these are the new humans, the fresh replacements.

"I saw you at school," Fern says once she has caught her breath. Nora's heart drops with a small thud in its cavity. Before she can come up with a reply, Fern adds, "This afternoon. You must've been heading for lunch with Geri. I waved, but you guys didn't see me."

Geri from Admissions. Nora exhales. And when she is able to meet Fern's eyes, she sees she has been caught. Fern picked up on her small spasm of fear. She knows something, she's just not sure what.

For all the distance that has set up between the two of them, they are still linked by molecular structure. Lucky will drag Fern's clothes into his basket bed to sleep with. He does the same with Nora's stray laundry, but not with Jeanne's. It took a while for Nora to figure out that he perceives Fern as his master, and associates her with Nora by scent. Along these same lines, you could put Nora and Fern on opposite sides of the planet, let a decade or two elapse, and the link would still be in place. And it is this, Nora thinks, which allowed Fern, in the moment immediately past, to see the brief click of fear behind her mother's eyes.

"Did you just get home?" Fern says.

"I had a stupid meeting at school."

Fern gets off her bike and nods, absorbing the lie, which they then carry home together.

laundromat

FERN BIKES OVER to the laundromat against currents of slant-
ing rain and wind-whipped trash. She wants to talk with Harold.
He has Wednesdays and Thursdays off from the restaurant, but
Thursdays are devoted to canasta, which is really the whole day,
what with canapé preparation, martini glass chilling, the whole
business of transforming his apartment, warping it back in time,
to the forties. (Fern loves this whole scene, but especially the canasta itself with its multiple decks, so many cards that a crank-
operated shuffler has to be brought to bear. And the dealer with
her mitts full, dispensing the cards into fat stacks around the table, which are then opened into wide fans of possibility, all those
jokers and wild twos and black threes, all those melds ripe for
the making. It's such an optimist's game.)

This schedule leaves Wednesdays for Harold's business-of-life
stuff. He is terrifically organized. He has thirty pairs each of underwear and socks. Ten pairs of jeans, ten of black Dockers for
his waiter job. Ten T-shirts, ten polo shirts for work. A laundry
bag for each category (plus one for Dolores's "trousseau"), and
he brings two here each Wednesday. While he waits, he reads
Hollywood bios — the past few times Fern has seen him, he has
been deeper and deeper into a huge, scathing book about Marlene Dietrich, written by her daughter.

There's a sweet detergent tickle in the air as Fern enters, looks around, and finds Harold on one of the plastic seats against the wall. Laundry sloshes back and forth with a lulling rhythm, clothes take leapfrog tumbles — sock after shirt after towel — inside the dryers. It's a warm, comforting place and a safe one for gossip since no one can eavesdrop over the mechanical din. She taps the top of his head to make her arrival known. He looks up, startled and edgy. Then Fern sees that the owner, a small man in the back, is keeping a sharp eye on Harold. He is suspicious that Harold is using his machines for dyeing rather than for washing. When Harold sees it's not the tap of authority, that it is, rather, Fern, he lights up.

She peels off her slicker, gets a can of pop from the machine. While she's settling in — shaking the rain out of her hair, rubbing her hands along the fronts of her thighs to get some blood back into them — he starts in about Dietrich.

"She had romances with everybody. *Everybody.* Flirtations, one-night stands, affairs. Maurice Chevalier. Erich Maria Remarque. Edward R. Murrow. Edith Piaf. Frank Sinatra. Kirk Douglas. JFK. The troops in and out of her tent during those World War Two USO tours. Doing her bit for the war effort. Yul Brynner. She was nuts about Yul. He had to call her, like, ten times a day or she'd go into despair. Basically, I assume everyone had a thing with her unless they tell me otherwise." He fixes Fern with a probing stare.

"Not me," Fern says. "Cross my heart."

"Okay. She would have been too old for you anyway. By the time you were even born, she was heading into her decline. She stayed in bed the last dozen years of her life. So she could drink and not fall down."

Yellow lights begin to flash on his machines.

"Fabric softener," he says, then takes a giant sky blue plastic bottle over and pours a little, like a potion, into a slot in the top of each rusty, tilted machine. Fern looks at the photos in the bio.

"Until she gave up, though," he says, dropping back into

his seat, "she fought a long, hard battle for eternal youth. She had this specially made foundation garment, like a whole body sheath she sort of poured her sagging self into. She'd drop her tits into the tit holders, pop her nipples into the nipple slots and then stand up and someone would *zzzzzip* her up the back and she was twenty-five instead of fifty. She was also into instant facelifts — braiding the little hairs around her face into tiny twists, then basically bobby-pinning her face back."

"Man," Fern says.

"I know. It's a great book."

They talk awhile.

About his play. He practices being dead by lying on his sofa for an hour every morning.

About his job. There's a small uproar. The waiters used to get their dress shirts from the restaurant, which would also launder them. Now all the staff — even the singing bartenders, who are threatening a walkout — are required to provide their own shirts, and get them washed and starched on their own dime. This was a top-down policy change, directly from Gretel. "She's tough," he says, but it's a compliment.

About Tracy and Vaughn. He hadn't seen them for a while before Fern's dinner.

"What a dreamy little guy. Tracy as a mother, though. It's quite a concept."

"I think she has a little trouble herself," Fern says. "I mean, of course she loves him, he's her kid. But reality is settling in. You know. This can't be a passing interest like everything else. She can't say, 'Well, now I've *done* motherhood.' Like when she thought she was going to be a disk jockey and got Brad and Tina to buy her those turntables, and now they're pushed into a corner of the basement. Plus I think she's not all that crazy about being stuck with the mother image. When she brings Vaughn along, it cuts down on her old allure, and on her chances with guys. The diaper bag and all."

"Didn't she anticipate that her style might get a little cramped?"

"I think she wanted to do parenthood a whole new way, but now nothing that's happening looks all that radical or dramatic or new. She has a baby and problems getting a whole night's sleep and getting through Vaughn's colic. And her breasts hurt. I mean she's only my age. And I know where *I'm* at. Every day I'm, like, this total surprise to myself."

She's still flipping through the Dietrich pictures and puts her finger on one now. "Nice white tie and tails, Marlene. You know," she looks up at Harold. "Dolores might look good in a tux." Then she thinks this through for a moment.

"Tell me," Harold says, taking the book out of her hand and closing it gently, "about being a surprise to yourself."

"Well, like, in Observational Models last week, we videotaped each other interacting in groups and, of course it was sort of bogus because you knew you were in front of the camera, but still. The thing is, I was *amazed* at how I came off."

"You mean the accent?"

"Be serious." She thinks for a moment how to put it. "I'm always worried I come off loud and goofy."

"You're never loud and goofy."

"I think I must have extrapolated that from being tall."

"You take the tall thing too seriously. You're actually demure, reserved even. Which makes you look short, in a tall way."

"That's *exactly* what the tape showed. I seemed almost shy."

"You *are* shy."

"I'm not, really. But I think I might come across that way because I'm trying so hard to not come across loud and goofy. Harold. Do you have any idea who I'm turning into?"

He considers the question for a while; you can't rush him into an opinion.

"I guess I don't see you becoming anything you aren't already.

Which is to say wonderful, unique. You'll bring that to whatever comes along."

"Actually, I was thinking of T. E. Lawrence."

"Of Arabia?"

"We read a biography of him in a history class I took last year, and by the time he was eight or nine, he knew his mission in life was to save a captive people."

"Oh," Harold says, then whistles softly. "Do you think you might be setting the bar a little high?"

Finally, before she goes, she gets around to why she came over in the first place.

"I have something." Meaning something to tell. Not about the skateboard guy, James. He called, but it's too soon to talk about him. And when she does tell Harold, she'll filter the news through Dolores. What she wants to run by Harold today is something else entirely. She needs to try out her suspicion.

"Something's going on with Mom."

"Something like . . . ?"

"Something stupid is my guess. I mean, I don't have anything concrete, like that I saw her stumbling bleary-eyed out of one of those terrible motels up on Lincoln."

"I woke up in one of those once," he says, then looks for a second overcome by his past, then leans in, positioning himself for gossip. Fern starts in.

"Just in general she's been very distracted lately, with nothing to account for it, but when I'm talking to her it's as though she's kind of hearing what I'm saying, but at the same time listening to something much more important on a hidden earphone, like a newscaster. And then I ran into her last night. I got home late and she was walking Lucky for me. I asked her if she'd just gotten home. She said yes, she'd been kept by a 'meeting.' So I tried to call up a picture of this meeting, the way I do when my clients describe a scene or a person. I tried to gather up the details — a conference room, everyone tired, someone blathering on — blah, blah, blah. But it didn't jell and then I knew the meeting was bogus. It hadn't happened, the conference room had been vacant and darkened, or being vacuumed by a guy from maintenance. My mother was somewhere else.

"Harold, this psychic job is changing me. I'm developing something. It's not so much that I can look into the future. It's more a different way of seeing the now — like I can spy around corners, into private places. I see surprises all around me."

Today is the first time she's told anyone about these developments. She takes a swig of her ginger ale. The machine here gets the pop so cold it's like liquid ice. She holds it in her mouth, feeling the pinpricks, waiting, afraid of what Harold might say. But it's okay.

"Maybe you're developing your sixth sense. When you think about it, why should we be limited to five?"

Fern grabs his head from behind and plants a kiss on the side of his face. She is so relieved to have someone believe in this cockeyed (but exciting) notion along with her.

Harold thinks things over. "Your mother, on the cheatin' side of town. Hmmm. She hasn't said anything to me."

"But she probably wouldn't. She knows you adore Jeanne."

"Oh yes. I do. But still, she'd tell me." (Harold hates being out of the loop, will never admit when he is.) "Of course, it's something your mother's good at — getting girls. She had quite a run of it for a while. She's all settled in now, but she must have moments when she'd like to see if those old powers are still working."

"I don't even know why I care," Fern says. "It's not my business. I'm almost out of there. I *am* out of there in my head."

"It's an old sore spot for you, her tipping things over in her hurry out. But stuff doesn't usually happen the same way twice."

"But why *now,* when she's all tucked in?"

"If you read enough biographies, you begin to see a pattern.

There's often a great affair, a grand passion a ways along in life when nobody's expecting it — Dietrich was in her early fifties when she fell for Yul — or in the middle of some dull period of domesticity. People like to screw up a good thing. Happiness is hard to bear. Everyone's always worried about it running out, always nervous. And as long as there's bound to be trouble anyway, you might as well make it yourself."

Neither of them says anything for a while. Harold gets up and pulls a huge tangled wad of socks and jockey shorts from the machines and wheels the pile in a small wire cart over to a waiting dryer. Once he has them tumbling around, he sits back down. "Man, though, what *about* poor Jeanne?"

"I know." Fern nods. "She's a sitting duck."

tara

NORA AND FERN are taking the long way around to Russell's with Fern at the wheel. They drive all the way up to Evanston, then back down to Lincoln Park, drifting, building up steam for the evening ahead, which they are both dreading.

They are mostly silent, then Fern says, "You okay?"

"About tonight?"

"About anything."

Nora is positive Fern suspects she is up to something.

"Yeah. I'm fine. No problem," she says. In most of the ways Nora would like to be close, she and Fern are miles apart, and then there are these primal, subterranean connections that give her the willies. She can't really tell her anything. Fern would be deftly judgmental. Nora would lose what little respect she gets from her without gaining any sympathy in the bargain.

They stop at an old Dairy Queen on the way back into the city. They sit in the car and eat greasy burgers, then decide to have raspberry sundaes.

"The good news is that this is probably the last time we'll have to do this with Dad and Louise," Fern says. "Next year I'll be out of school."

"Well, you might fall in love and want a huge wedding with an ice swan and you coming down through a cloud of dry ice on a swing and nets of doves let loose all around you. But . . ."

"Probably not," they say, almost together.

When they've finished dining in style and Fern has stuffed their garbage in the can and they've dusted the crumbs off their jackets and brushed their hair in the rearview mirror, there is nothing else they can do but head on down through the wall of fire.

"There," Nora says, pointing up ahead, at an open space on the right.

"Nope," Fern says, not even bothering to slow down. "Hydrant." She picks up her father for dinner once a week. She knows this block by heart.

Parking is impossible here in Russell and Louise's neighborhood. There is never a free space, ever. Since she got the boot last year, Nora has been trying very hard not to park illegally. To get unclamped, she had to pay sixty dollars plus all her back tickets, including some she was in the middle of disputing, but there was no arguing at that point, what with her car languishing, undrivable, and twenty-four hours shy of being dragged, for another hundred dollars, to some remote lot off the edge of the earth. So Nora has stuck a Post-it, an advisory against illegal parking, to her windshield visor. It says:

DON'T EVEN
THINK ABOUT IT.

But after they have circled the block twice and found nothing, they tacitly admit defeat and Fern slides the Jetta into an illegal spot at the end of the block. If they get a ticket, it will just add insult to the injury of having to visit Russell and Louise.

"Don't you do any bowing or scraping," Nora says. "Particularly not the scraping. I'll do it all."

"I hate that you have to do this for me," Fern says. "It's Louise, you know."

"Some of it's Louise." Nora leaves it at that. Fern's hatred for Louise takes the heat off Russell. And it's true, Russell does honor his financial obligation to Fern. And of course, he wants her to finish college, and he can afford to help. Since he has stayed in advertising all these years, he brings down a nice, chunky salary. But recently the Louise factor entered the equation on one end, and on the other, Fern seems to have entered an academic area that will almost surely require graduate school. Plus, next summer she wants to do a month of field study up in the Arctic, with some tribe on the tundra. At least she is making her own decisions now, mapping out some future for herself. The only solace Nora had until just recently was that Fern wasn't making any conspicuously bad choices. She wasn't doing major drugs or gambling on casino boats or heading toward a peculiar line of work, like embalming.

Now, though, she is interested in anthropology, and although Nora worries this will lead to a job teaching for a pittance, part-time, at some obscure college, waitressing nights at Hooters, still it's a path (actually, very nearly the academic path Nora herself was on before Fern's arrival prompted a change in course). So Fern has her path, plus good teeth and a wry sense of humor. She is well worth the small trouble of this evening.

"Sometimes I wish," Fern says.

"What?" Nora asks.

"Nothing." Her jaw is doing the little grinding-popping thing it does when she is upset.

"Come on."

"Just that it wasn't like this, that things could be like they used to. Like they were before."

Nora has to think a moment to get that what Fern means by "before" is when she and Russell were still married and the three of them were a family.

"Oh, honey, that's ancient history."

"To you. To me it's like a giant scrapbook. Everything's still inside for me to look at. You'd be surprised what I remember. Like, Dad used to wear those cool vintage bowling shirts to work. He'd cook us Szechuan food, making that huge mess in the kitchen. He set up that little room in the attic. So you could write your poems."

"Oh, those poems. I put them all in the Weber one night and torched them. My contribution to the survival of literature."

Neither of them says anything for a while, but they don't get out of the car either. Finally Nora says, "How can I find an apology big enough to cover everything?"

Fern looks straight ahead, but not at anything; her jaw is still making the little twitches.

"There wasn't going to be a happy family if I stayed," Nora says. "There was only going to be the ironic shirts and the Chinese food and me smoking up in that attic, thinking how I was going to get through another week."

"And that was the key thing, after all. Getting you through."

Nora takes this slam and sits with it. What Fern is saying is true. In the crunch, Nora saved herself. She never wants to try to defend that to Fern. She could, of course. She could point out that her unhappiness and restlessness were going to bring the whole thing down one way or another. And while all of this is accurate in a large-picture way, it could also be said that Nora fled her marriage, grabbing Fern on her way out, in order to — and in that particular moment this was really all there was — in order to sleep with a security guard named Sugar.

She is both not guilty, and guilty as charged. Defending herself further will only turn this conversation into a fight. And so she tries to sidestep.

"Even though father and I aren't together, you still have both of us."

Another statement that is both true and not true. By busting up her marriage, Nora jeopardized Fern's relationship with Russell. She left Fern slightly displaced, and vulnerable to further change. When Louise came into the picture a couple of years ago, Fern became Russell's ex-kid, opening up a more central space to be filled with the baby Louise and Russell are (according to gossip from Fern) busy trying to have. Russell's attention to Fern has ebbed. Sometimes he calls off their weekly dinner on short notice with a flimsy excuse. He forgot her birthday last year, a horrible day. Nora knows she bears some of the responsibility for all this. But there is nothing she can do about it now, nothing she could do about it then. She failed her child and can't find her way either backward or forward to a place of succeeding for her.

What is love? she thinks. Fern guilt-trips her, and Nora allows it. Is this a variant of love, some blank space in the Hallmark rack? Whatever, it's what she has. (Sometimes, in these hard moments, Nora escapes by imagining an alter-Fern who is devoted to her. They paint each other's toenails on a raft on a lake.)

"Come on," she says, getting out of the car, taking on the small task at hand. "Let's go see if we can get you some moola."

On the phone, Louise tried to expand this visit to include dinner, and Nora haggled it back down to a cup of coffee. She doesn't know why Louise is being so atypically social, given her opinion that Nora is a lesbo-weirdo freak and Fern is spoiled and should be doing more to support herself.

Nora had hoped Louise was not going to be a player in tonight's discussion. She can still remember when Russell told her he'd met someone, and she had cast this development in an optimistic light. She started imagining they could be friends, put their failed marriage behind them and in some hip, contemporary way be cordial, occasionally go out to dinner together as a reconfigured foursome — Russell and his new partner, Nora and Jeanne. Maybe even little group vacations that would include Fern, too.

Then Russell's new partner turned out to be Louise, who added fresh contempt for Nora to Russell's long-simmering anger. He is too civilized, or perhaps too passive-aggressive, to hate

Nora in a straightforward way. Instead he comes up with a certain level of congeniality so she has nothing to complain about — to Fern, to whomever — while beneath the surface, she's pretty sure he's as filled with anger as those stalking ex-husbands in TV miniseries. There should probably be creepy, nervous-making music, a soundtrack underlying all her encounters with Russell. Of course, Louise might be the real-life equivalent of creepy background music.

He is totally justified in hating her, even Nora sees this. She betrayed him, then left him in such torturously small stages that he didn't actually get it until she was out the door.

At first, when they were married, he liked that she was different from the other wives in their social sphere — more independent and freethinking. "Scrappy" was the term he used to describe her to their friends. Then, gradually, she was a little too different. He didn't like the women's reading group she joined, was sarcastic about their selection being limited to books written by women. If they were shipwrecked, he pointed out, forced to choose one of the two books that had washed ashore with them, by these rules they would have to read Jackie Collins over James Joyce.

After the group met at their house and he saw the actual women in the group, he had more ammunition. First it was about Sara, who was huge. Russell, a quick study, began referring to her as a "woman of size." Then Betty was a "woman of red hair color." There was a lot of this sort of funny but not really funny commentary.

Then one afternoon at work, he broke a finger at an agency lunch-hour softball game and was taken to the emergency room. Which brought him home with a tiny cast on his pinky at one-thirty in the afternoon, left-handedly fumbling his key in the lock. This was the first signal of his unscheduled arrival, the door opening too quickly for Nora to disengage from Chimera, one of the women from the reading group, but not the only self-named one. With whom Nora (having taken a personal day off from work for something personal) was not quite naked on the living room sofa, Rod Stewart rasping from the stereo, sandalwood incense smoke twisting up from a charred nub in a saucer on the coffee table.

Tonight, all these years and miles later, Russell greets them at the door and drapes an arm of fatherly appropriation over Fern's shoulder and leads them back through his apartment to the kitchen. He still has a very good butt is Nora's line of thought until she gets distracted by the apartment, which has undergone new onslaughts of decorating since Nora was last here. She used to think she and Russell shared at least a superficially common view of the world. And so it depresses her to come into this patch of maroon and azure, decor reminiscent of Tara, which must surely spring out of Louise's Confederate imagination. But what sort of chameleon is Russell that he lived so comfortably in what Nora always thought was their funky, ironic style and now seems equally content amid white furniture with gold edging, velvet drapes, a lighted cabinet in the bedroom showcasing Louise's collection of cotillion dolls?

Louise is setting out mugs by the coffee maker. She wears her clothes extremely tight — tonight a stretchy striped T-shirt and exercise shorts. Nora doesn't suppose the intent is sexy so much as a longing to show off the peculiar muscles she has acquired. Louise is fascinating to look at, in a sideshow sort of way, to see what she has been overdeveloping. Tonight, it's her neck — thick as the trunk of a small tree, circled by a thin chain with a small heart pendant. The message being that she might be built like a little brick shithouse, but underneath, she is one hundred percent woman, strictly a female female.

She looks up from her bustling to acknowledge Nora and Fern with a marvelously false smile, not masking in the least her weariness with having to deal with them. Nora doesn't care if Louise gives her this look, but hates the way she looks at Fern — as though she is a troublesome piece of everything Russell dragged into their marriage, like an elderly cat with a skin condition or a giant Budweiser poster.

"Decaf?" she says brightly. She says everything brightly. She has the beady eyes and scary inner glow of the zealot. She is radiant with her beliefs. The wattage in any room with Louise in it always seems to be pumped up.

"I'll only be a minute," Nora says and ducks into the bathroom to get out of the glare. While she's there, she goes through the medicine cabinet — an old and reliably fun activity. Russell's taking Rogaine, now that's interesting. There are many prescriptions for Louise, nothing Nora recognizes. She guesses these are fertility potions. And there's lots and lots of floss. Louise would, of course, be a serious flosser.

Everyone brings a coffee mug into the living room, and Louise sets out a plate of sliced banana bread. Nora and Fern settle into the plump sofa, readying themselves for the bumpy ride ahead. Nobody touches the banana bread.

Russell starts off the conversation by being generous about the academic path Fern has chosen.

"I was too plugged into the job thing when I was her age," he says. "Let her have this time to explore. And I like the idea of the field study thing. She should be doing all the stuff we couldn't, or didn't." Who's going to pay for it is a question that floats around in the air above them, a lazy balloon.

Then Nora notices Louise giving Russell the hairy eyeball, which cuts short his praise of the broadening influence of travel.

"What we were wondering was why Fern isn't contributing more to her education herself," Louise says, shouldering the burden of this less pleasant topic.

Fern sits like a closed clam, taking Nora up on her offer to do all the dirty work.

"Well, give her a break," Nora says. "She was only able to get something part-time this summer." She is not sure if Russell and Louise know the exact nature of Fern's job. She herself has described it only as "telemarketing," but who knows how revelatory Fern has been. Nora is protective of Fern, and in these sorts of bad moments, she puts Russell into the camp of those from whom Fern needs protection. Then there will be other moments when she feels herself shifting into an old, familiar parental alliance with Russell. Like when she first saw Fern's tattoo, her impulse was to pick up the phone and call Russell, to figure out what they should do. (As if there was anything they *could* do.) She didn't, of course. She has no idea what Russell thinks about the tattoo.

"I had a savings account, even when I was a little girl." Louise reminisces on the money issue. "I saved almost all my allowance. Plus I held on to all the savings bonds I got for birthdays. I was quite a little Scrooge."

"Well, that was a different time and place," Nora says. "Louise, I don't think you can expect thrift to be a compelling notion to a twenty-one-year-old. You can try talking to her. I mean, you're welcome to that conversation." She reaches over and ruffles Fern's hair, as though she does this all the time, as though they are always teasin' and joshin'. Fern goes along with this charade, smiling shyly. She is a good actress when necessary; it's all that show biz in her gene pool.

Louise isn't interested in persuading Fern, though. She is a dollars-and-cents girl; she oversees budgets for all the ad agency's campaigns; that's how Russell met her. She has gone over their finances with the same ruthlessness and has a dollar figure at the ready, the extent to which she and Russell are willing to help. This amount has clearly been arrived at before Nora got here; they have just been making her dance.

Nora tries to pull out of this sinkhole into some Zen place of larger vision. Instead she winds up fiendishly craving a cigarette.

Russell interprets her brief silence as concession, and hands her a check — for a little better than half of what Nora had been hoping for. He says, "Now, Louise has something she wants to talk with you about. And while we leave you girls to your little chat, I want to show Fern my new laptop. Humongously powerful. I have to strap myself into the chair before I launch onto the Web."

Fern sits tight and looks at Nora as if she knows her mother needs to be rescued (and that she owes her something for tonight), but Russell takes her hand and pulls her off the couch and down the hall and all she can do is look back over her shoulder at Nora, which Nora interprets as a silent wish for good luck.

When they are alone and the room is silent, Louise leans forward across the coffee table.

"What's this about?" Nora says, not giving Louise a chance to lead up to whatever is coming. She tries to suspect the worst, but can't really see what that is going to be.

Louise clasps her hands together and fixes Nora with a look of synthetic sincerity. "I wanted to apologize."

Nora knows enough not to ask "for what?," but lack of a prompt is not going to stop Louise.

"My faith teaches us to hate the sin but love the sinner. But sometimes, well, sometimes I'd get the two mixed up. The truth is I had a hard time dealing with your perversion, and, of course, at first I had to cope with my personal concerns. That I was, perhaps, being regarded in a, well, an unsavory way by you, the way a man might look at me."

Nora doesn't know where to begin. Sarcasm, usually a tool close at hand, eludes her. Which leaves Louise free to continue cataloging her fears.

"And of course, Russell and I worried about Fern's development, that you couldn't provide a role model that was, well, healthy."

Nora sinks deeper into the sofa. She can't imagine Russell actually shares any of these crackpot notions, but she supposes it's possible he lets Louise *think* he does, which is almost worse. She knows that in a few days she will come up with knifelike replies to Louise's remarks, but in the moment she seems to have fallen into a chasm of silence she can't climb out of. All she can come up with is "Are you nuts?"

"Well, you can insult me, Nora, but I'm only voicing concerns you must realize are shared by most people, *righteous* concerns."

"Basically," Nora says, "I have trouble dealing with any line of chat that includes the word 'righteous.'"

"Well, then I'm sorry for you." Louise is on a roll. "Righteousness comes from having God and Scripture on my side. Leviticus tells us —"

"Oh please, Louise. Don't even start thumping that Bible with me. Doesn't that homo thing come in some passage that also forbids putting two fish in the same oven and riding an ox to market?"

Louise puts up a hand, like a Supreme singing "Stop in the Name of Love." "Please. You're taking this the wrong way. Let's start over. I'm only trying to bring you good news. My church has a new ministry that's very exciting —"

"I am not interested in being accepted by your religion. I think being shunned by your religion is the best possible relationship I can have with it." Nora has to get out of here. The air in the room is beginning to thicken and become cloying, as though those little air freshener things are plugged into every wall socket.

"I think you're only defensive because you haven't felt welcome before. But now we have an outreach specifically directed toward your needs." Louise's eyes begin moistening. Nora's discomfort is nothing to her; she's a Mack truck with a mission, bearing down, ready to run Nora over if that's what it takes to get her message out. "It's called Healing Waters. You see, it's a beautiful program that uses the power of prayer for change. And we've been so successful. It's been wonderful to see all these happy people who used to be sad and sorry, trapped in perversion and a godless lifestyle, and now they're freed from all that through prayer, free to live a normal life again, to find serenity and be in God's grace. Think about where it could take you. You could even remarry, provide a healthy atmosphere for Fern. Now we even have scientific studies to back us up. It's been proven that if you try hard enough, you can make it work for you."

"Or maybe," Nora says, belatedly finding her full voice, "we could take care of your concern from the other direction. Maybe they could come up with a program for you. You know, if you tried hard enough — with God's help, of course — *you* might be able to turn queer. Think about it. You could be in the Pride Parade. I could get you a rainbow bumper sticker."

Louise closes her eyes for a long moment, clearly praying for strength. When she opens them, she has nothing more to say, only sits with her hands clasped in front of her, prayerfully poised fingernails pointing at Nora, aiming enlightenment at her over the banana bread.

As Nora gets up from the sofa (more awkwardly than she would like, as the deep cushions don't relinquish their occupants easily), she senses the heat in her face and hopes it doesn't show. "Louise," she says as she goes to find Fern, "don't ever talk to me like this again."

In the car, she turns up the radio, then lets Fern change it to a station she likes, which has a playlist of songs that seem to be mostly amp backlash and guitars about to be slammed against the wall. If she lets Fern have her station, she won't have to talk. The tactic doesn't work, though.

"Something really bad happened, didn't it?" Fern says, turning off the radio.

"Really. Bad."

"I think I know. I saw some pamphlets lying around. When I was at the cottage. I figured she was going to unload on you sooner or later."

"Then why didn't you warn me? So I wouldn't get ambushed."

"What difference does it make what she says? It's just another stupid thing she believes in. I mean, she's against Halloween because it has witches and goblins and they don't believe in that. She also thinks there was Adam and Eve and then us, no monkeys. She's a moron. I couldn't even talk to her tonight. It's like I just locked up."

"I know. I was there."

"Don't blame me. Please. I mean, how was I going to defend myself in the face of that noble little picture she was painting. Thrifty little Louise standing with her piggy bank —"

"I saw it as a cookie jar full of quarters."

"In line at the bank —"

"The East Bumfuck Bank," Nora fills in.

"Yes, the First National Bank of East Bumfuck," Fern says, and rolls the radio back up, but switches it to XRT for Nora. Sometimes, rarely, and only in little spots like this one, in blips on the verge of dissolving even as they are formed, but still, the two of them align and ally and sit in soft grass on the same side of the fence.

At home, upstairs, Jeanne is curled up on the sofa in her study. She is the picture of domestic contentment, of constancy and faithfulness. Nora has been out the entire evening, and all Jeanne has done with this time alone is keep the home fires burning. She has not been sitting out by the lake in a pickup truck with a stranger. She is right here with a glass of wine and a short stack of travel magazines.

Jeanne enjoys these not so much to plan vacations, or even to travel via armchair into the luscious photo spreads, but rather for the columns that relate readers' horror stories. Travelers stranded in airports for days with all their luggage lost or passports stolen, subjected to cavity searches for drugs. Tourists who wind up in Greek prisons for going over their Visa limit in a gift shop. Bus group stragglers lost for days in the maze of some ancient medina.

"Anything gruesome?" Nora asks, slumping into the easy chair opposite the sofa, envying Jeanne her uneventful evening.

"Nothing. This month, they are all whiners, babies." Then she adds, very casually, not looking up, "I was surfing the Web for a while before. I found a fantastic fare to Paris." She really means Tours, where she is from, but can't say the word; it's too incendiary. In lieu of real vacations these past few years, Nora has visited many chateaux, and suffered through three visits with Jeanne's provincial, judgmental family — two sisters and a mother. They never fight, but gang up on Jeanne in chillier ways. They are particularly adept at pointed silences and ill-natured teasing. Nora drives from chateau to chateau while Jeanne cooks for her mother, shops with her sisters, and by the late afternoon when Nora returns, Jeanne is up in the guest room crying, but pleads with Nora that her family mustn't know they have driven her to tears, and so dinner is always tense and hideous and cloying with reduced wine sauces. Nora thought she and Jeanne had already agreed that she wouldn't have to go over again until somebody died. And so Nora doesn't feel she has to ask how cheap the fare is, even just to be polite. Plus she knows Jeanne will tell her anyway.

"Two hundred sixty dollars *aller et retour.*"

"How could it possibly be that cheap?"

"Well, it's not a nonstop. That is where you find the very deep savings."

"Where's the stop?"

"Phoenix . . . first." Nora doesn't ask if this plane is going to Paris the long way around the planet, or doubling back from Phoenix and stopping in Greenland. She's too downcast to work up even the mildest sigh of exasperation, and her silence on this normally touchy subject prompts Jeanne to put down her magazine and really look at her.

"Oh! Tell me please what has happened," she says, sitting up, reaching to pull Nora down beside her.

Nora relates the worst of the conversation with Louise. "If only Fern had tipped me off, I could have had my dazzling retorts prepared, or headed Louise off at the pass. Instead I cowered, then got in a few licks, but really, she won. She made me feel as bad as she could have hoped to. As it was going on, I realized that I've almost never had to deal with head-on contempt."

Nora starts crying. She almost never cries. Jeanne knows enough not to offer any sort of facile consolation. Instead, she sits with the information for a while, then says, "We're too insulated. We live in a small place where everyone is understanding and tolerant of differences, where everyone *is* different, our little neighborhood of oddness and peculiarity."

"I should laugh it off," Nora says gloomily. "Why can't I take Fern's position, say Louise is a moron and forget the whole thing?"

"It is difficult being challenged, even by fools."

"At least I refused to defend myself against her stupid accusations. Like that I'm a vampire, that I want to suck the blood of schoolchildren and seduce housewives."

"Well . . ." Jeanne says.

"Well, not *all* housewives anyway," Nora amends. "They don't know we're very fussy about our housewives." From there she takes the folded Kleenex Jeanne has pulled from the pocket of her sweater, wipes her nose, takes Jeanne's arm, pulls it over her shoulder as she leans into her sofa-warmed body, and allows her sadness to be blotted up.

This is what the long run is about, she thinks, the deep comfort furrowed out by time and endurance. This huge and important thing is what she is putting in jeopardy. She fills with good sense and firm resolve. She will put an end to the nonsense with Pam. Now she sees it is simply a test to pass.

salad

FERN WAS HOT AND ITCHY inside her crouton costume, which consisted of a black leotard, dancing slippers, and a box with no bottom and a head hole cut in the top. The outside of the box was covered with roughed-up burlap, tan and scratchy.

She was standing in the wings, waiting for her part in "Dancing Salad," the *grand finale* of the "Food Friends" show at her school. The point of the program was that it's important to eat good things, not just candy and junk food.

She had only a little while longer to wait. The lettuce wedges, tomatoes, and cucumber slices were onstage now. Next would come onions, carrots, then herself and the three other croutons, then the bottles marked VINEGAR and OIL with their squirt guns.

She found a gap in the stage curtain and looked out into the audience. Her father was away in Ohio, making a presentation to a tire company for a campaign. "Tires that grip the road." The tire in the picture turned into a glove grabbing a snow-covered stretch of highway. The glove was his part of the idea.

Anyway, she was not looking for him because she knew he wouldn't be there. She was looking for her mother, who was against children being forced to perform onstage, even though Fern had sworn she hadn't been forced, that she loved being a crouton.

The lights were off in the school auditorium, but there was enough light spreading out from the stage to see into the audience. There were a few fathers, but it was mostly mothers and brothers and sisters, a few of the kids from the show who were in the proteins dance, now sitting down in their costumes — which made them look like primary-colored worms — to watch the end of the show. She dragged her gaze slowly over each person, to put off the moment of surprise when she would spot her mother.

She was still looking when Miss Elmquist put a hand on the top of her box, by her shoulder, gathering her together with the other croutons, telling them all to remember that they are tossing themselves into the salad, not walking into it. Fern had heard this before, had her tossing movements inside her, stored up, waiting to burst out from behind the curtain into the jumble of somersaulting, cartwheeling vegetables.

She took a last look into the shadows of the back rows, beyond where the light reached. She picked a shape that might be her mother, probably was, was for sure. She could, with only the slightest pressure of imagination on reality, see her mother there among all the others, hands together, holding back her applause until she saw Fern burst onto the stage, toasty and scratchy, tossing herself — perfectly — into the mix.

bump

WHEN SHE PRESSES HER FACE into the slight depression at the center of James's chest, the smell is dry and slightly salty, like a potato chip. The taste of the place behind his ear is tart. There is a lot about him naked. The woolly hair on his chest. The deep, freckled tan, especially on his shoulders. The scars, mementos of various mishaps — a pencil-thin line under his chin (diving board), a squashed star shape on his elbow (skateboard), a raised curve above his right knee (bike). His fingers spatulate, his toes so peculiarly long.

"You're quite an oddball, really," Fern tells him, leaning on an elbow as she makes her diagnosis.

"Well, let's see who's talking," he says, turning onto his side to make his own examination.

A few days after the day in the park, while she was still working up elaborate plots for running into him again, he asked Tracy for her number and called. The conversation didn't go totally smoothly. He meandered so aimlessly, for so long, that she began to wonder if he'd lost track of whom he was calling, what he was calling about. But then eventually he said maybe she'd like to get together sometime, it didn't have to be soon, and she said it could be soon as far as she was concerned, it could be that night for instance, and it turned out this was fine with him.

He is someone who needs to be steered a little in the right direction. She has to do most of the calling and planning, but he is always happy to hear from her, as though he was expecting her call, is already nudging the rest of his life over to make a space for her.

He worries a lot, about a lot of things — the future, the environment, greenhouse gases, the meaning of things and the possibility that they don't mean enough. He riffles through her anthropology texts and seizes on the grimmest examples of existence. Nomads in arid parts of Africa who spend each of their days searching out a cup of water, a few bits of grain, a little shade. He fears that, stripped of music videos and new ways to distress denim, human enterprise would quickly be reduced to nothing more than scavenging for water and shade.

Fern, by nature an optimist, thinks she provides a counter to James's pessimism. She thinks it's a good thing he ran into her.

The only hurdle she had was right at the beginning. She tried to tell him that she was "sort of" involved with someone. He asked what that meant. She had to admit she hadn't seen this person much in the past few months. Not at all, actually. And that maybe it was more like a year.

"Then," he told her, "I think it's okay to see me."

They are on the mattress on the floor of his apartment, which is above a large garage behind a house on Barry. The apartment is made up of dormers and ceilings that slope with the roof above them. You have to stoop a lot walking through the place. James, who tops even Fern by several inches, uses a lurching gait as he ambles from room to room, like someone with a peculiar limp. The gravedigger in an old monster movie.

The place has a red kitchen and a lot of dusty sunlight and is given over to the boxes he makes (something like Joseph Cornell's, but really very different) and to his collections. His skateboards rest in a set of slotted shelves. Globes litter the floor, a drifting galaxy. The few vertical walls are hung with the opened boards of games from before their own childhoods. Rich Uncle. Chutes and Ladders. Pillow Fight. James is three years older than Fern, but he seems to occupy a different geography, a place less edgy and future-oriented than hers, more relaxed and suspended in childhood.

They have each blown off what they are supposed to be doing with this back half of the day — Fern is skipping her Peasants seminar and James has knocked off early from his messenger job. They have been making love, off and on, for a couple of hours. Sex with James is very different from sex with Cooper, which she used to think of as Big Sex (although her experience was, is still, pretty limited). With Cooper, she would go around the day after, sore in the obvious places, but also at her elbows, in the muscles at the back of her neck. When he disappeared, the sex bore the weight of everything he hadn't said, held the meaning she needed to counter her constant disorientation.

With James, what happens in bed is more easygoing, sometimes even comic. In a purely physical sense, their height, turned horizontal, becomes a matching of lengths; they are two long creatures of their species tangling in a graceless way, looking for a shortcut, as though if they learn each other physically, they can skip everything else that's going to be necessary. Necessary for what, Fern can't say.

He pulls her flat on top of him.

"Let's pretend we're missionaries," he says.

"The part where we go out and convert natives," she says, "oppressing them with our cultural assumptions?"

"Actually, I was thinking about the part where we have sex in the missionary position."

"Then I think you'd have to be on top."

"Sssh," he says, shifting beneath her. "Just let me in. I'll tell you later about our religion."

*　　*　　*

Lucky is growing restless. He has been napping on the window seat of the dormer in the front of the apartment, but is now pacing in and out of the bedroom.

"He needs to go out," Fern says.

When they get themselves dressed and outside, dusk is settling in; the sun has taken along with it any warmth that had been adhering to the afternoon. Fern clutches her jacket at the front and waits while Lucky pees luxuriously on a bush and James finds his car keys. He has an ancient Datsun, older than either of them. They open the hatchback for Lucky. He gets as far as standing with his front paws on the bumper; James hoists him the rest of the way in.

There is an affinity between Lucky and James. They both have expressive eyes that give them an air of being in on some terrific joke. They are both happiest when they are in motion — Lucky ambling along on a walk; James on his skateboard, on his bike.

Fern has begun to see dotted lines between certain people and animals, between certain events — indications that the universe is ordered, but in a way that has yet to reveal itself. This universe holds particularly significant friends. Lucky is one, and now James. Others are still out there, waiting in places as snug as tree forts, stockpiled with the laughter of running jokes. The trick will be to find them. They are part of Fern's suddenly expanding view of the space her life will occupy.

"Watch out for the floor," James reminds Fern as she gets into the car, referring to the fact that there isn't any on the passenger side. She props her feet on the dash for the short ride up to Welles Park, Lucky's old stomping grounds, from the days when he was a pup and Fern lived with her mother and father close by there.

The park is brilliant in the midst of the falling night, its playing fields and basketball court, the horseshoe-pitching pits, all bathed in a false day created by the gang-busting floodlights.

Lucky totters over to the fence by the baseball diamond, his favorite pooping place. Fern heads over to pick up after him.

"He knows this park like the back of his paw," Fern tells James a little later, as Lucky herds them from behind, some working-dog hard-wiring. There's another dog out, a hobo with no apparent owner, no collar, fur of many colors and directions — the sort of dog for which Lucky has always had a mysterious affection, maybe from his early days on the rocky road of life, before they got him. What begins with a burst of hilarity — the two dogs throwing themselves against each other's shoulders and chasing each other back and forth — winds up with Lucky losing sight of his buddy, and then, before Fern can do anything to stop him, he is blearily heading out of the park, straight into four lanes of traffic gunning up and down Western.

Even in the mildest hours of morning, Western is a route of serious, lightly menacing drivers in beat-up vans and high-wheeled trucks. At night, these vehicles are driven by the same guys, now with a few beers under their belts. And so when Fern loses track of Lucky as he slips into the surly stream of fenders and headlights, she panics. All she can do is stand bolted to the curb screaming, "No!"

James jumps onto the hood, then the roof of a parked SUV.

"I see him!" he shouts down and leaves Fern on the curb as he scrambles down and leaps into the traffic. Cars honk and begin slowing down, then stopping altogether. Humanity swells up around Lucky; nobody wants to hit a dog. Fern sees, when she unfreezes and heads into the street herself, that, amazingly, a few people have gotten out and cordoned Lucky off. When she finally gets there, Lucky is on the ground. He has been hit.

"No," she says. He cannot be dead. He just can't.

"Hey, man, I'm really sorry," a huge guy with a mullet haircut and a plaid shirt with the sleeves cut off in a ragged way is telling James, who tells Fern, "It's not that bad. See. He's only been bumped."

And it seems to be true. Lucky's name has carried him through. He only has a cut over one eye, a little blood. He's disoriented, Fern can tell when she crouches down to hold him. He comes up with a brave look. This is the part that kills her and she starts crying.

They drive down to the emergency vet where it's expensive just walking in the door, but after hours it's the only game in town. They wait for a few minutes on turquoise plastic chairs. Lucky rests on Fern's lap, her arms bracketing him, one hand tapping a beat of comfort on his haunch.

"You are a fabulous dog," she tells him, and then tells him the story of the day they got him at Anti-Cruelty so many years ago. He loves hearing this story, which she embellishes a little every time she tells it. She also tries to stick his name in every couple of sentences, so he knows the story is about him. "You were showing off in your cage, wagging your tail and smiling. You needed to do some big-time public relations. You'd been brought back twice, Lucky. Yes, you had such a long rap sheet tagged to your cage. *Eats furniture. Barks. Chases cars.* My dad thought you were homely and a pack of trouble and wanted us to take this little dog that looked like a fuzzy football, but of all the dogs there, Lucky was the one I wanted. Only you weren't even called Lucky then. The name on your cage was Kool. Anyway, I cried and pitched a fit and finally my dad said we could take you, 'on probation.' On the way home, he said you were one lucky dog and that's how we came up with your name. Lucky."

By the end of the story, Lucky's tail is thwapping a slow beat on the seat of the chair next to them.

The only other people in the vet's waiting room, aside from the receptionist, are a mother and a boy about seven, who is holding something motionless in his lap, something wrapped in a dishtowel. Fern looks away, presses her forehead to James's shoulder, and says in a low voice, "Oh, man. What do you think — parakeet?"

"Hamster," James says, and turns to kiss her temple.

They have to wait; the mother and kid are next, but they emerge in no time at all, without the dishtowel or its contents.

The vet on duty is incredibly nice.

"Hey, big guy," he says to Lucky, squatting in front of him, kissing him absently by the ear as he checks out the damage. Then James lifts the dog onto the table and the vet stitches up the cut, which gives Lucky a jaunty, devil-may-care look.

"He's going to be fine," the vet tells them, "but his eyes have pretty heavy-duty cataracts. He probably only sees shapes now. His hearing might be going, too. What I'm saying is he's not navigating with as much info as he once did. You might need to keep a closer watch on him."

When he leaves to write up the visit and James goes to find a cash machine so they can pay the bill, Fern crouches in front of Lucky.

"The doctor says you're doing great," she tells him.

They bring the dog home. Fern figures this is as good an opportunity as any to filter James into the house in a nonchalant way. She wants him and her mother to meet, even though she can imagine every moment of this meeting. How Nora will be gracious and seem welcoming and interested in James, and totally cool about his life at the moment being lived in the middle of nowhere. No college or real job. Nora will draw him out about his artwork and seem so fascinated he won't have a clue that he's being dismissed, dispatched way down in her pecking order. For Fern, the visit is over in her mind before it has even begun. But keeping James a secret, which is what Fern has done for nearly a month now, seems like giving her mother way too much power.

Before they go in, she briefs him on Nora's situation with Jeanne. She should have told him before, but there hasn't really been a right moment. When she tells someone, she likes to just slip it in, by the by. As opposed to dropping her mother's sexual orientation as if it's a bombshell, which she doesn't think it is, really. Now, though, she has to make it a bombshell. Otherwise, she risks bringing James in and finding her mother and Jeanne necking on the couch, which, amazingly, they still do sometimes. And so she just tells him. He doesn't act like it's a deal, only asks if it's a deal for her.

"No, of course not. Not now anyway. When she first told me, though, I was maybe twelve. She had a talk all prepared. I'd sort of figured it out by then anyway. But even then I wasn't so much weirded out about her. I was mostly just mad that she'd left my father, and this new thing was a part of that. But it did make me have to think about why I liked boys in that way, and not other girls. What it was about them that I liked. What it was about me that was different from her."

"Piece of luck for me, you being straight," he says, turning off the ignition, then, "Hmmm. Your lesbian mother." He goes around the car, opens the hatchback, and lifts out Lucky, who is totally into being injured and helpless. "Let's go meet her, then."

They come in the front way and are immediately hit with a wall of noise. Jeanne is watching *Payback,* one of her favorite junk movies. Mel Gibson is clinging to the bottom of a careening car, shooting through the floor to kill the Asian gangsters inside.

"Do not mess with Mel," she says to Fern when they come into the living room, but then she looks over her shoulder and sees that Fern is not alone. She politely grabs the remote and stuns the screen to a silent solid blue. First, there is a great flutter of concern and explanation over Lucky. Then, when the dog is sitting like a potentate on the futon sofa, which is usually forbidden to him, Fern introduces James, then asks where her mother is.

"She had an appointment with the dentist after work."

In the same way she couldn't call up a picture of her mother's after-school meeting that other time, Fern now can't see Nora in the dentist's chair. There is no appointment; the dentist is gone, the office is closed, dark and silent and smelling of mint and metal.

"You two would like Cocas?" Jeanne says. You can't tell her they're Cokes, Fern has tried. In France they are Cocas, and come in tall glasses and with a slice of lemon. Everything is just a little better in France, a little classier. This running line of Jeanne's conversation can get a little tiresome, but tonight it stops here. She is only charming.

While Jeanne is slicing the lemon, pouring the pop, Fern has a little time to wonder where her mother really is.

And then, in the very next moment, Nora bursts breathless through the back door. She almost immediately grows a little flustered — seeing Lucky with his shaved, stitched forehead, and then tuning in to James. The scene would be a tough one to piece together with no information; anyone might be a little bewildered. But Fern caught her mother a beat earlier, caught her expression at the instant of arrival, before she had to start focusing on what she was coming into, and yet even then she was flustered, by something left behind, beyond these walls. And she drags a little bit of it in with her, the way kids drag in the snow or cut grass in which they've been playing, along with a spillover of mood from whatever they've been up to, and now have to come down from. Fern picks up on this mood spill, and knows she has her mother dead to rights.

Fern holds off explaining Lucky on the sofa, James in the kitchen, and tackles her mother before she has a moment to get her guard up. "So, are you numb?"

Nora's eyes flicker, as though she's been blindsided.

"From the Novocain." Fern amplifies, prompting Nora to put an actor's hand to her cheek.

"Oh, you know it." Nora flicks a finger against her cheek to illustrate the deadness. "Go ahead." She laughs, and says to everyone, "Sock me."

job site

NORA IS SUPPOSED TO BE at the dentist, the latest appointment in a phantom after-hours schedule. She writes these ghost events into her datebook, in case Jeanne should ever flip through its pages.

The time she is claiming to be at Dr. Gerber's will actually be spent in a small house in Ravenswood. A small house, but a big job for Pam — a kitchen and bath renovation plus a sun porch to replace a rotting deck. The new owners won't be moving in until all the work is done. When Nora arrives a little after six, the house, with its uncurtained windows and harsh work lights within, is a jack-o'-lantern, brilliant against the backdrop of nightfall. She stands out front for a moment, breathing in the graveyard smell — leaves expiring into the bottomless cold and damp, the vast hollow that is the winter to come. Once inside, she flushes as though with sudden fever, but it's only that the heat is so cranked; radiator thimbles hiss and sigh all around her.

She finds Pam in the kitchen, conferring in fast (theirs) / bad (hers) Spanish as she writes a check and gives it to the head guy among the drywall mudders, a circus act of small Mexican men on stilts, shadow-dancing between the fresh white walls and the high light of their work lamps. Nora has seen this ballet before, at another job site, also at night, when the crew was folding up their tents as these guys are now, leaving Nora and Pam to their own devices in these vacant, darkened places. This is the housekeeping they do.

"Upstairs," Pam says. Outside, the drywallers' van is pulling away from the curb.

Always there is an aura of ambush at the start, Pam shutting a door behind them, locking it if possible, even if they are alone in the house, as they are now. Her moves are fluid, assured, as though she possesses a past lively with the practice of secrets — girlish diaries with locks, clubhouses with branch-covered entrances, and into adulthood, into other rooms with other women before Nora, situations in which locking the door would be the first bit of foreplay.

The bedroom door has no lock and Pam gently presses Nora against it. In the few weeks of their affair, they've had little opportunity for anything languorous, or even properly between sheets. They have to take whatever opportunities present themselves; neither can offer a bed free and clear. Nora lives with Jeanne. Pam lives with Melanie, who, according to Pam, is a "hothead." Melanie is an emergency room nurse, her everyday is filled with saving lives, which Pam finds impressive and fascinating. Not quite so fascinating to Nora, who hopes never to meet Melanie. Nora listens for another sort of detail. Such as that, in an unfortunate combination with her hotheadedness, Melanie is apparently also the jealous type. Pam is nervous about cheating on her. Nora infers that something cautionary has happened before along this avenue.

If Nora wants to scare herself, she only has to calculate how little she really knows Pam. In the narrow patches of time when they're not grappling around naked on a paint tarp, or coming out of their clothes across the bench seat of Pam's pickup or (twice) in the middle of the afternoon on a king-size mattress at the Heart O' Chicago motel, they talk, but not in any reasonable or efficient way, not with the purpose of exchanging the hard information they ought to be. Most of their talk happens over the phone. These calls come into the office from Pam on the phone in her car.

Nora feels overexposed taking these calls at her desk; they seem much more like calls she should take *under* her desk. (She can hear Mrs. Rathko puttering in a phony way in the outer office, surely eavesdropping.) These calls have a breathless quality to them; there is never enough time available to explore their small repertoire of inexhaustible subjects:

how they really shouldn't be doing this
how they are managing to get through daily life in a constant
    state of distraction and exhaustion
where they ache
what they would do if they had a whole day or a whole night —
    the dinner Pam would fix for Nora, the movie they'd go to.

Even as she is held in thrall by these chats, Nora also understands that they are common currency in the realm of the illicit — small, easily spendable change dropped into the palm, enclosed in a fist. Their conversations are probably no different from those of the salesmen and secretaries who occupy the other rooms at the Heart O' Chicago.

As for Pam and who she is and where she comes from, Nora knows only this and that. She is blue-collar by redefinition; her parents are both high school history teachers. Her small rebellion was to drop out of college and into the building trades.

She is fond of extreme sports — deep-water scuba diving, freefall parachuting. This is how she met Melanie; they took their first jump together. She has a three-tooth bridge on one side of her mouth and a scar up the side of her left calf, both from the same bad landing. The ceramics class fits into another cache of interest — artistic pursuits. She has also taken courses in collage and watercolor painting. The ring she wears she made herself in a metalsmithing course. She is thirty-five, but seems younger for all these lively interests, still bursting with all her potential. There is something enormously appealing about how Pam sees life as a blank to be filled in any way she wants with no constraints, is so dashing and adventurous, and now Nora is part of the adventure.

She has never met anyone who operates with such confidence, with so little regard for the hurdles that stop most people. Which makes her admirable in the abstract, dangerous in their particular situation. If Pam decided that Nora was a next step in the big adventure that is her life, she would probably be able to work up the nerve to dispatch the incendiary Melanie, as well as tromp straight into what Nora has with Jeanne. She can too easily imagine Pam getting to a point where everything in her way would be just so much fragile china on a glass shelf.

Nora can't help but observe that Pam is so very different from Jeanne, whom she envisions sitting up in her study, buttoned into her cardigan, in a muddle of three-by-five cards, or sulking after a call with one of her bitchy sisters. Nora tries to apply checks on this sort of thinking, tries to recognize that if the situation were reversed, if she'd been with Pam for years, she might well find all her swashbuckling grandiose and tiresome by now, might find Jeanne's quiet, cultured charms refreshing. She tries to keep in mind that a great part of Pam's appeal is simply her newness, that she is as yet ungotten. Ungotten but possibly gettable.

And she can come up with a few such sensible thoughts on the matter when she is alone, or at the office, but these then completely evaporate the moment she is with Pam, like now — naked on a crumpled canvas paint tarp, wrists pinned to the floor next to a rusted radiator, sweat rolling off her everywhere as Pam lies hard on top of her, mouth at Nora's ear.

Later, Pam sits naked except for her flannel shirt hanging open. Her body is a sketch composed of planes and darkness, propped against a wall that was a Floridian pink when they came in and the overhead was still on. In the dim, referred light of the street-lamp outside, it's a rosy gray.

She asks Nora, "What's it like, to look the way you do? Do you go into the john late at night, turn on the light, and hang out in front of the mirror and say, 'Man, it's great that I'm so good-looking'?"

"I don't think about it that much."

"Right."

"It's not as big a deal as you think. I guess it smoothes things out a little, situations. I walk in and I can feel the smoothing."

"But that *is* big," Pam says. "Huge, actually."

"Maybe. But huge in a subtle way. And with limits. Like, maybe it's part of how I got you to here. But it would probably take something else to get you any further."

Pam doesn't say anything. Then she says, "Further would be trickier."

"I'm not pushing for further," Nora says.

"Right."

Of course, in her worst moments Nora does want further, without understanding exactly the shape it would take. When she begins thinking about further, her imagination, mercifully, shuts down.

"Right now is the best part. For me," Pam says, bringing Nora back to their present. She takes a deep drag off a filterless cigarette, some additive-free brand made by Native Americans, and stretches forward to pass it to Nora, who is still supposedly a nonsmoker, but has been taking hits off Pam's, and now keeps a pack of Camels in her glove compartment for moments when she is wired, of which there have been a few lately. "You'd think the best part would be the fucking, but it's not. The best part is the having fucked. It's now, when I get to sit here and — even though out there we don't exist, out there you and I are *nothing* — in here, in this little space where you're so grateful to me, I own you."

When she says this stuff — so bullying and appropriating —
Nora is appalled and thrilled. The fine hairs on her forearms
stand up. Sometimes it seems Pam is someone she has made up,
the woman in the roadside restroom, the woman in the motel by
the tracks.

Nora doesn't need to look at her watch, which lies on the crumpled edge of the painter's tarp. She knows it's getting late. She
can feel the pressure of misspent time bearing down on her,
without creating too long an absence, which she is going to have
to account for with a tire she found flat when she got out of the
dentist. A flat and a bumpy drive to a gas station, where they
took forever to patch it. She concocts its details the whole way
home. Hearing these lies when Nora gets there, Jeanne will sit
blinking in a way that will make Nora worry that all her malar-
key has only made her sound more suspicious.

This isn't what happens, though. Instead, while she has been
out of the loop, something has happened inside it. The kitchen is
startlingly full when she comes in. Jeanne is there, and Fern, who
asks Nora about the dentist, a lie she has already half forgotten.
There's also a boy in the kitchen. Lucky has been hit by a car, but
he's all right. He sits on the sofa like a welcomed-home war hero
with his wound stitched up. Fern has brought him from the vet,
along with the boy, who is tall and sleepy-looking. He and Fern
stand close, tilting in a little toward each other, totally unaware
they are doing so. They are in love.

It was the boy who rescued Lucky. James. Who is beautiful in
his youth and in the easy way he moves and the slightly sorrowful cast to his expression. His other immediately distinctive feature is hair so thick it seems at first that it must be a wig. Nora
tries to make a determination without appearing to stare.

Cokes, wouldn't they like something to drink? And then Nora
sees they are already holding glasses. Then what about a pizza?

They could order one. Should she call Pete's? She rummages through the junk drawer, then waves a carryout menu in the air, trying to generate a mood that's fun but casual. What's important, crucial even, is that she makes Fern understand that she can bring this lovely, hairy boy here, that this house is open to him, to them.

Unfortunately, she doesn't have enough time to get this strategy rolling in the couple of minutes before Fern politely declines the pizza offer, and ushers the boyfriend outside to say goodbye. Then comes back, picks up Lucky, and takes the patient to her room. On her way, she shoots Nora a look with a thin edge, like a blade. Not dangerous, only incisive. To show she knows Nora was not at the dentist.

Nora usually casts the geometry of their relationship as one in which the distance all belongs to Fern, but this isn't really true. Tonight, for instance, Fern brought her boyfriend home, stood him squarely in the middle of her life, while Nora left a lover behind in an uninhabited house. She thinks back to all the women she used to meet in darkened spaces, or brought home late and ushered out early, before Fern was up — a ghostly third shift of characters who populated Fern's childhood even though she never saw them. Over the long haul, Nora has, in a spirit of protecting Fern, tried to keep her from knowing the whole of who her mother is. And yet she somehow knows anyway.

Nora makes herself something to eat to fill in for the dinner she missed. They need to go shopping. The cupboard is pretty bare. She has to settle for a sardine and ketchup sandwich. She is hungry and not hungry. What she really wants is to be alone and in a tub soaking Pam out of her pores, but also thinking about her. Jeanne comes up behind her, pushes Nora's hair out of the way, and puts her mouth on the back of Nora's neck. "You smell smoky," she says absently.

"Oh, I'm so weak. I got upset with Mrs. Rathko and went down to Geri's office and bummed a weed off her." She is flooded with huge relief in being able to confess anything at all, even something she has made up.

At first, Nora doesn't tell anyone about Pam — how can she? The whole thing is so purely wrong. Telling would be like mentioning that you had someone chained in your basement "for observation." That you liked to set out tacks on bus seats.

But of course she can't stand *not* telling anyone, and so decides to tell her friend Stevie, whom she has always been able to tell anything. She is setting up the easiest possible test. Stevie will have to be understanding; she can't throw any first stone. When they were in college together and everyone was smoking a little marijuana and considering themselves "into drugs," Stevie was shooting heroin. She dropped out to become a housekeeper for a professor and his wife and was soon sleeping with both of them and wound up destroying their marriage. Then she left Manhattan behind and became a Buddhist nun and lived several years in a convent in Boulder, but got excommunicated in some dramatic casting-out ritual that meant she was barred from the convent and the order and the whole Buddhist religion, and she has never been able to tell even Nora the reason and so it must have been pretty bad. Currently she is in a relationship with a woman twenty years younger whom she met in her therapy group. If there is anyone Nora can tell, it's Stevie.

They go for coffee and Nora finds them a table in the back and scans the café. She doesn't want to run into anyone she knows. She feels guilty even so much as talking about Pam. But she finally manages to pour out the whole story, placing herself in the most sympathetic light possible — helpless, felled by unexpected passion — in hopes that Stevie will be able to counsel her in a nonjudgmental way. And so it is disconcerting that her response is how can Nora possibly be doing something so morally bankrupt.

"I mean," Stevie says, *"how!?"*

Nora looks into her coffee and becomes lost. She tries, but can find no answer at hand, nothing important or crucial, nothing weighed and considered, nothing of substance and merit that she can hold up with conviction and say, "Because of this."

fever

VAUGHN WAILS. He's internally amplified, an impressive screamer, a sorrowful, miniature James Brown. Please, please, please, he's trying to say.

He has an ear infection. Tracy took him to the pediatrician, started him on an antibiotic; now they're waiting for the fever to break. Fern has come over to help, even if helping means only waiting along with her. Tracy looks beyond exhaustion. She has greenish circles under her eyes, from lost, longed-for sleep. The eyes themselves have a bad gleam, a madness-in-the-jungle cast, as though she's hearing the beating of drums from over the mountain. She has dyed her hair a strange mauve. She has been in the house too long.

"At first I thought it was his colic coming back, then maybe that it was only another cold, but then he started getting red and hot so I took him in. Man, this kid comes down with *everything.*"

Fern cups Vaughn's forehead with her palm: definitely warm, but not fiery.

Tracy's mother comes into the bedroom, looking persecuted. She stands just inside the doorway. She doesn't want to be drawn into the situation, only to critique it. Vaughn has been in this house half a year without having as yet received any real welcome from Brad and Tina. What is their problem? It has to be more than disappointment in Tracy. Fern suspects it's an image thing. They are clinging to their flower childhood, which now requires the assistance of cosmetic surgery (Tina's nose and eye jobs, Brad's jowl rehabilitation) and spa vacations, and of course part of the reason they want you to first-name them is they don't want to be Mr. and Mrs. Meyers. Or Mom and Dad. For sure, not Gram and Grampa.

"You could quiet him down if you wanted to," Tina says. "With the kids at the commune, we used to dip a rag in tequila and let them suck on it."

"You also ate my placenta," Tracy says. "Life has moved forward from the seventies. The seventies are a period piece."

"Oh, shut up."

But Tracy is not interested in shutting up. "Your commune is a roadside historic attraction."

"What part of 'shut up' didn't you understand?" Tina says. She talks like this a lot, in bumper stickers. She's still standing in the doorway to Tracy's room, her hands on her hips like Wilma Flintstone, mad at Fred. Since her nose job, when Tina gets pissed off her nostrils flare in a horsey way, as though she's about to snort. The nostril-flaring always lends a comic air to her fit-pitching, and it's hard to take her seriously.

Still, Fern doesn't particularly want to be in the middle of a blowout between Tracy and her mother. And the fight won't even be about anything other than the further thinning of their already worn good humor going into this millionth hour of Vaughn's wailing.

Fern gets a washcloth in the bathroom, turns on the tap, and waits for the cold. In the meantime she picks lazily through the contents of the medicine cabinet, an idle pursuit she picked up from her mother and Harold. Tina is apparently on Zoloft, and there's a little stack of Viagra samples on the top shelf. From a pharmaceutical standpoint, things around here should be sailing along on smooth seas. Everything else on the shelves is extra-

or maximum-strength. Fern helps herself, popping a couple of Excedrin Migraine and a Valium, little hedges against the stress levels in the air.

She gets the washcloth as cold as she can, wrings it out. She knows a little about babies, from sitting jobs in high school. The thing now is to help Vaughn over the hump.

Tina has disappeared to some more tranquil quarter of the household. Vaughn is still wailing, like a siren, ebbing a little, then getting louder again, pausing only to inhale. His hands and feet are fists. Tracy is looking down at him in a way that troubles Fern.

"Basically, this is getting a little old," she says.

"Let me take over for a while." Fern lifts Vaughn off the bed, wipes his face with the washcloth, then presses it to his forehead. "Go take a walk or something. Chill."

"Yeah. Right. So I can come back and listen to this for a few more hours."

"I can stay the night if you want. You can crash at my place. Just tell my mom what's going on. Take Lucky out for a walk. Then get some sleep."

"I can't leave him."

"Of course you can. He's got a fever is all; it'll break pretty soon. I'll be here the whole time. Take the cordless into my room; I'll call you if anything happens. I'll call the doctor if anything gets worse, or doesn't get better. I'm totally on top of this. And you're too nuts to be much good to him anyway. So get out of here."

Tracy nods, as though she is in third grade and being sent home with a small scrape and a Band-Aid on her knee. Trying to look as though she's only taking orders, but is secretly euphoric at being sentenced to freedom.

Once Tracy is gone, Fern focuses all her energies on calming Vaughn down. He is red — maybe from the fever, maybe just from all his crying. He has small round patches on his cheeks of a deeper red, like the stain of beet juice. She brings him into the bathroom, lays him down on his back, on his cotton blanket, in the empty bathtub while she fills the huge old washbowl with cool water. She takes a couple of cotton balls from a jar on the back of the toilet and stuffs one in each of her ears, the way she does before concerts. Vaughn's cries move a slight ways off. When the bowl is full, she picks him up and sets him gently into the water. For a moment, he is startled into silence, then begins crying again, but he is at least looking outside himself. His eyes open and he stares in a panicky way at Fern. She tries to get all his unsubmerged parts — his head and shoulders and chubby chest — with the washcloth. It's then that she notices the small marks on his upper arms. Bluish. On the back and front of his left arm, a fainter set on the other. Fern clicks into cognitive dissonance. She tries to come up with a benign scenario. Vaughn wiggling his arms a little too enthusiastically between the rails of his crib. Falling onto, running into, something, what?

But of course he can't be running into things or falling down onto them since he doesn't yet run or even walk, isn't really up for there to be someplace to fall down *to*. The only picture that would explain these marks is the one Fern is trying to keep at bay. Someone holding him by these arms, just below his shoulders, a bit too firmly, perhaps shaking him a little, maybe to stop him from crying.

She wants to think the bruises are Tina's work, but can't imagine her getting participatory enough to hold Vaughn. They have to be Tracy's doing, a byproduct of carrying too much fatigue, moving into yet another dark hour of last night. But probably also fatigue in a larger sense, a dark brooding rolling in along with the realization that even when this crisis is over, this fever broken, she is not going to be released. She will only be stuck with a well and happier Vaughn. There is no place she can see to where she won't be with him. After zooming through her teenage years with agile moves, Tracy is now carrying the weight of another human through a seemingly endless series of uninteresting but arduous tasks, an absurd picnic game — one leg strapped to someone else's while holding an orange between chin and shoulder, balancing in front of her as she goes an egg jiggling in a tablespoon. And no finish line in sight.

As Fern gets Vaughn out of the bath, into a dry diaper and terry cloth shirt, his infected ear begins seeping out a thick discharge, yellow and viscous, like the snot she has been wiping from his nose. And instantly, with no tapering down, he stops crying. He opens his eyes and tells Fern, "Ba-ba-ba," then falls softly to sleep with several fingers of his left hand in his mouth.

His vulnerability is excruciating.

crouton

SITTING IN HER CAR, in the school parking lot, Nora noticed she was in the space marked RESERVED FOR VICE PRINCIPAL. She kept the motor running, for the heater, also because she was not sure she was going to get out of the car. She was still trying to make herself, but had so far been unable to go inside.

Nine years of shielding Fern from tap lessons, flute lessons, choral group, and yet somehow this school pageant — Food Friends — got by her. By the time it popped up on her radar, Fern had already been cast as a crouton in the salad number, was already gluing burlap onto a box she found in the basement, already practicing her terrible song, which rhymed "lettuce" with "get us."

Someone, a portly guy in a car too small for him, who had been idling behind her for a while, now pulled into the space next to her and gave her an indignant glare before getting out of the car and locking it, then coming back and checking to make sure it was locked. Probably the vice principal. Fuck him.

Nora had never been in the auditorium of this school, but could see clearly its hardwood stage, its heavy velvet curtain. She carried inside her a full catalog of stages. The small, black box stages on which Harold tried to find his motivation as one supporting character or another. The high-gloss stages on which her mother yanked the microphone out of its stand, threw the cord behind her, and began her beguine. The larger, more lavishly lit stages on which Vicki Ashford tossed back her signature blond mane. Back even further than that, into legend, to the stage at Radio City, to her mother and Fern Lawler, younger than Nora ever knew them, their bodies perfect, their as-yet-unveined legs kicking in unison with all the other Rockettes. All this energy pumped into insignificant moments of connection with strangers sitting beyond the footlights. She couldn't face that same earnest supplication she knew she would find on Fern's face this afternoon as she was giving her all for the approval of the audience inside.

Still, eventually, she turned off the ignition and got out. She repeated to herself what Russell had told her a couple of times this past week, that this show was nothing, augured nothing, was not about Nora and her philosophical position on all things theatrical. It was only about Fern being part of a salad.

She came in at the back of the small auditorium. Everyone was either applauding in a lunatic parental way, or snapping pictures of the dancers in the salad number as they left the stage, apparently having taken the last of their bows. She scanned the backs of a tomato and a lettuce wedge before she spotted Fern — even from behind Nora recognized her immediately, from the little skip-steps she took when she was especially happy or proud of herself.

She tried to wish her into turning around one last time, so she would see her mother standing here, not being a jerk. But she didn't turn. She just kept following her fellow croutons, heading in the same direction, away from Nora, preoccupied with having to shove a little to get herself and her costume through the parted curtain.

misty

NORA AND HAROLD and Lynette and her old friend Fern Lawler, all of them dressed up for the occasion, are shooting out from the Intracoastal to the open sea on Art and Lynette's old inboard, a mahogany-hulled Sea Skiff, its huge engine rumbling away beneath them. As in their early days, Lynette is at the helm, her children in the back. Nora trails her hand overboard and turns to look at the wake — sunlight pulverizes the spray to glassy dust. She thinks Harold looks quite captainish in a white linen suit until she catches the slight blue blush of shadow on his lids, the yellow tinge to the suit, from its long time hanging in the back of someone's closet, then on the rack at Value Village.

They are here this afternoon, following the coastline south from Fort Lauderdale to put Nora's father to rest. He died two days ago, a middle-of-the-night heart attack. Lynette phoned 911, but by the time they arrived, there was nothing to be done.

He has left them instructions; he had everything written down. No funeral or memorial service, just a simple cremation, his ashes scattered on the waters in front of the Tiara Hotel on Miami Beach, where Vicki Ashford hit the peak of her (hence his) career in the mid-seventies. It takes them awhile to motor down from Lauderdale, hugging the coast as they pass Hollywood and Dania, Golden Shores, North Miami, to where the hotels start pumping up, finally arriving at a patch of ocean in front of the huge pink and white absurdity that is the Tiara in its gentle decline. Lynette cuts the engine, and the boat slows, then sidles among the light, lapping waves as Nora twists off the top of the container, which is about the size of a coffee can. They all look inside. The contents are lumpy — ashes and chunks. Lynette reaches in and takes out a piece.

"Bone," she says.

"Something to think about, isn't it?" Fern Lawler says, her small face half-hidden behind huge sunglasses. "All those grapefruit diets and collagen creams. The eye lifts, the tummy tucks. In the end, you wind up chunky in a can."

No one has brought along any words to read or recite, and at any rate, their gathering is too small. Besides, a big eulogy wouldn't be Art's style. He was a quiet man in a noisy business. Elegant posture, beautiful socks — even his *Variety* obit mentioned the socks. He was an earnest man, devoted to his family, and to the business of entertainment, which fascinated him.

They all look at one another for a next step, but they're stuck, stunned by the impact of sudden event.

Lynette takes charge. "Look at me," she begins singing quietly in her thin showgirl voice, joined mid-line by Fern Lawler, an octave lower.

"Misty" was Art's favorite number. Nora overturns the canister and the contents spill onto the surface of the Atlantic as Lynette and Fern continue in ragged harmony, as helpless as kittens up a tree, never knowing their hats from their gloves.

"I called Vicki," Lynette says when they are back inside her deeply air-conditioned house, overlooking one of Fort Lauderdale's Venetian canals. Lynette adores air-conditioning, finding it an unequivocal improvement on previous concepts such as "fresh air" and "outdoors." She keeps the rooms as chilled as a florist's display case. "Vicki's not well — ghastly diabetes, I think they just sawed her feet off — but she still sent these." Lynette gestures toward a lavish arrangement of Casablanca lilies in a cut crystal vase.

"She was always a bitch," Fern Lawler says, "but a classy bitch."

Nora loves, has always loved, everything about Fern Lawler. The long string of husbands, the spaniel dogs, the major jewelry, the hacienda in Beverly Hills, the fortune built on the wealth and financial advice of the husbands. After her brief years in show business, she took up painting and has made a small reputation for herself. Somewhere along this road of art, entertainment, and money, she took off for four years in the Peace Corps teaching English in Nigeria. Fern Lawler has always lived large, acted on impulse, and shrugged off regret. Nora hoped to pass along some of her spirit along with the name she gave her daughter, whom Fern Lawler still calls "Little Fern."

When the two old buddies have gone into the kitchen to get drinks, Nora, shivering lightly, goes to the hall closet, finds an old terry cloth beach jacket of her father's, and puts it on. In the hallway mirror, she can see that her lips have turned a little blue. When she's back on the sofa, facing Harold, she says, "That's so sad. About Vicki."

"I know," Harold says. "She hasn't been doing so well lately."

"How do . . . ?"

"Well, we keep in touch, of course."

Nora doesn't pick up on whatever he's trying to tell her, but understands it is something specific, that she is sitting inside some small comfy foyer of ignorant bliss, an instant before the door at the other end blows open.

"You know," he says, as though he is amplifying the information, and Nora fears that Harold has been moved by their father's death to make some dark, horrible confession.

"I don't," Nora says. "I don't have any idea. And to be frank, I'm not sure I want —"

"She was my first, my, well —"

"What can you be talking about!?" Nora says, lowering her voice even though her mother and Fern Lawler are two rooms away. "We were *children*."

"I was fourteen. It's not as though she took advantage. Basically, I just thought I was extremely suave for my age."

"Oh, man. Please. Don't tell me about this."

"Okay," he says.

"How could something like that even start? I mean, I'm trying to get a picture."

"The big pool at the Tiara? The one that was shaped like a harp with the strings made of tile stripes on the bottom of the pool? She had her own cabana there. She had this mix of iodine and baby oil for tanning. She was a major tanner — do you remember? — a semipro. Those little eyecups, the reflector thing under the chin. Anyway, it was, you know, could I spread some on the back of her legs, and it pretty much went from there." He pauses, staring into the miniature rain forest of their mother's terrarium coffee table. "Her suite at the hotel was like an apartment. There was a closet as big as a bedroom. She had the most amazing lingerie. Special-order stuff."

"How long did this go on?"

"Well, it wasn't 'on' exactly. Or off. It was more catch-as-catch-can. I guess I was in college when Dad stopped managing her."

"Years?! You're talking about years?!" Nora is whispering and shouting at the same time.

"I thought martinis," Lynette says as she comes in from the kitchen, followed by Fern Lawler, both of them walking as though in a traditional procession of their tribe, carefully balancing a tray of cocktails, another of snacks — olives and Goldfish crackers. Their arrival pulls the emergency brake on Nora and Harold's conversation.

Nora tries to regroup. As she takes a glass from the tray, she looks up at her mother. Lynette is still an attractive woman. She has not given in to the reductive mechanisms of aging. She stands out among the other old ladies around here for not having cotton candy hair, for not having defaulted into the determined cheer of pastels and floral prints. She looks only like a slightly worn version of her signature self, the persona she designed for stage and screen. She still has her black pageboy, is slim in her version of mourning clothes — black capri pants and a caftan top. She still has most of her height, which set her apart in her heyday. Now she would be somewhere down the chorus line. Her legs are shot, she'll tell you that, then add, "But I've still got my dancer's back, they can't take that away from me."

Like Fern Lawler, who also dyes her hair (in Fern's case, a shiny auburn), and bleaches her teeth and gets her eyes done every few years, Lynette has taken on aging as a sort of modernization process. A little cosmetic surgery, a multitude of sins hidden behind large sunglasses, a devotion to European body wraps. She has also performed minor renovations on her lifestyle, to keep abreast of the times. She no longer smokes, although she says, "Existentially, I'm still smoking." She has given up red meat, cut back on her cocktails. Even her addiction to ginger ale is behind her; she now drinks spring water and sautés vegetables in a small wok. As she will tell you, she keeps active. She's into aquarobics.

Although up close Nora still finds her mother oppressive, with her inexhaustible supply of friendly suggestions for how Nora might live her life, or raise her child, or cut her hair, from a distance she is still fascinated by Lynette, particularly by the arrogance with which she has traveled through a life that probably wouldn't have given anyone else much confidence at all. She did some film work early on, pictures where the plot called for a good-looking, feisty secretary. She was a minor dancer, first at Radio City, later in dinner theater. And then there were the three years on her TV show, *Glenda's Girls*. In spite of this smattering of response to her looks and talent, Lynette has always seen herself as a star, and lived up to this inner image.

"To my dear husband," she says, clinking the rim of her glass against Nora's and Harold's.

"*Dearly* departed," Fern Lawler says, offering her own glass for clinking. She travels with a flask and so is usually a couple of cocktails ahead of everyone else.

They sip until Harold lifts the silence with a short chorus of fond memories about Art. The time he brought home two dogs as prospective pets, rejects from Cynthia and Her Capricious Canines — Pinky and Blue — four-legged vaudevillians who could jump through hoops and over the sprinklers of all their neighbors, who could stand on each other's backs and bark out an off-key version of "Happy Birthday," but who also pooped casually and with no sign of remorse on the laundry room floor, a habit acquired through their years of confinement in a backstage kennel.

Then there was the time he tried to take Lynette and Nora and Harold on what he thought would be a regular American family vacation at a rented cottage in the Adirondacks, then spent half of every day driving to and from the pay phone at the gas station at the crossroads, booking an entire tour for the Harmonicuties.

"Your father was born for the cell phone," Lynette says, gesturing with a toothpicked olive. "He just showed up a little too early, technology-wise."

Nora doesn't say anything. She knows she should be offering some charming anecdote from her own stack of memories, but she is too busy trying to push away an image that has crept back, this time in more detail — her brother, pubescent and pumped with hormones, on top of Vicki Ashford in some ludicrous bed, something with a round mattress and a satin headboard. She can smell the Chanel vaporizing into the hotel room air above them, can see the seams of borrowed fishnet stockings running up the back of Harold's long calves as he services the Purring Kitten.

They wait for their ranks to fill in. When everyone is here, Lynette will take them all to the Moonlight Carousel, her favorite romantic restaurant. It occupies the top of an old hotel and overlooks the ocean near the harbor at Port Everglades and serves sole amandine and beef Wellington and cherries jubilee with lots of tableside theatrics — decantings and debonings, tossings and flamings. The restaurant itself revolves slowly with hydraulic creaking, providing diners with a panoramic view of the marina at Bahia Mar, the ocean, the high-rise condominiums out of which most of the patrons have come to have dinner. Nora will pop a Dramamine before they leave the house.

Jeanne and Fern are flying down together after their respective classes. Fern's arrival will prompt a feast of adoration. She is adored competitively by Lynette, because she is her granddaughter, and by Fern Lawler, because she is her namesake, and by both of them because Fern is who she is.

Jeanne is not adored, but is genuinely liked by the old gals, although with Lynette, it was rough-going at first. In principle, she curls a lip at the notion of lesbians. The only ones she has known personally were a couple of Rockettes. Tough characters, but also tragic — so off in the wrong direction, suffering terrible heartaches without the ultimate payoff of husbands.

Although Nora knows her mother loves her, and even likes her in the sense of enjoying her company, she also understands that she is a disappointment for having squandered her legacy by not even trying for some rung of stardom, and also for being sexually peculiar, an oddity Lynette cannot present in an uncomplicated way to her friends.

At least, as Lynette told Nora in the past, Jeanne is "normal-looking."

"Whatever *that* means" had been Nora's response, but of course she knew. Jeanne wears dresses and make-up and a stylish (but not too severely stylish) haircut and earrings (but only two, as opposed to sixteen in one ear). Lynette can, with some measure of comfort, refer to Jeanne as Nora's "friend," can cast the two of them in a domestic situation together without ever having to picture them naked.

A thought flickers across Nora's consciousness: as opposed to Pam, who is precisely the sort of woman Lynette could *only* imagine in bed with her daughter.

Pam hasn't called. Nora left a message on her cell phone yesterday about her father dying, and has checked her own several times last night and today, but there is nothing in the mailbox. (The cell phone is a recent purchase. At home, she hides it beneath the seat of her car. Pam is the only person to whom she has given the number. She buys minutes on a card so there won't be a bill.) This isn't the first time Pam has ducked out of reach; it has happened a couple of times before. She will be suddenly, startlingly incommunicado. Meaning she doesn't call Nora, doesn't respond to Nora's calls. For a few days, Nora will go crazy inside while trying to act normal at work, or at home, or here in her mother's living room. And then Pam will return as casually as she departed, and it will turn out that Pam and Melanie went to Starved Rock for a few days of hiking, or Melanie's parents came to visit. And Nora will sink with these reminders that Melanie has the whole of Pam except for the little compartment in which Nora waits. Like her unanswered messages in the mailbox of the cell phone in Pam's glove compartment.

Nora tries to climb out of herself and offer something to the moment she is supposed to be inhabiting. She asks her mother, "Are you going to be all right, down here by yourself?"

"Oh, I have my friends, too many really. My bridge group, the aquarobic gals, my Thespians." Lynette is involved in a theater project out at the city senior center. They cast their productions from the pool of themselves and so wind up with Stanley Kowalskis and Sally Bowleses in their seventies and eighties, which gives the plays a whole new spin.

"Money's not a problem," she adds. "Your father and I have gone through all the papers and accounts together, a few times. Like little fire drills. I just wasn't expecting widowhood so soon."

"I know," Fern Lawler says, weighing in with a second opinion. "I thought he had real golden-years potential."

"Exactly. I know he was a little overweight, a little sedentary, but still. He was only seventy; I'm only sixty-eight. I thought we'd have a longer run of it is all."

Harold suddenly starts weeping, his head in his hand, his shoulders shuddering. Nora's emotional state is dry, but dark. She thinks, a little angrily, about how soon into her childhood she had to get used to her father leaving, how he was a receding character for the whole of her life. When she was little, he was always going on the road with Vicki or some other client. Art's idea of being a good father was being a good provider, which meant working most of the time. When he retired, Nora was already long gone from home, raising her own daughter. She had fleetingly thought that perhaps, with some of his new free time, he and Fern might form the friendship Nora had missed out on.

Instead, with no deals to close or calls to make, Art settled back into the quiet, remote person he must have been by nature. He took up deep-sea fishing, spending long days — even those of Nora and Fern's visits — on rank-smelling boats with other quiet old guys in squashed hats and clip-on shades. Other guys who felt they had talked enough for a lifetime, now they'd fish.

His having left so early and often should make his death easier to bear, but Nora instead finds herself in a place where facts can't touch feeling. She sits freezing in her mother's living room, shrugging deeper into her father's beach jacket, falling while no one notices, into a small moment of self-pity for having lost a father she'd still been vaguely hoping to gain. She thinks how death shuts even the unopened door.

Across the living room, Lynette has gone over to hold Harold as he weeps. While she's doing this, she apparently is also softly nudging him out of the spotlight.

"I'm a widow," she says, holding her son and shaking her head in disbelief. She sounds as though she has read the line on a script, then the gesture in parentheses beneath it.

Nora can see that her mother is beginning to transform Art's death into the latest in her lifetime string of dramatic moments. She speaks, not so much in direct reply to anyone in the room, but as though she is being interviewed by an invisible television personality who has asked some terribly sympathetic question about where Lynette will go from here — courageously, of course — and what she will do to fill the emptiness.

"I think I'll get a cat or two," she says. "Your father was allergic, but now, what the hell."

offer

WHEN THE COMPRESSOR on the refrigerator shuts down with a sigh, it's as though this exhalation is the last sound in the world, now sucked into the powerful and complete silence of the kitchen.

"You don't know what it's like," Tracy says finally. "You're only around in little bursts. Happy, fun bursts. You're not here for the hour-after-hour part, the day-after-day part. He was a colicky baby, and now he's a fussy baby. He needs his mommy all the time. He's Mr. Personality, but sometimes at four A.M., I could do with a little less personality since I already got an hour's worth of it at two-thirty."

"I know," Fern says. "I'm not making a big judgment. I love you and I love Vaughn and I'm trying to figure out how to get things to a better place."

"It's not going to happen again, if that's what you're worried about. I must've just lost it when he was crying for so long. I wanted him to stop is all. I yanked him out of his crib. A little too hard. It wasn't great, what I did. I'm not saying it was great."

As though he knows this conversation is about him, Vaughn is watching them intently from his swing, which is set on the table amid their cups of coffee and a bag of doughnuts Fern brought with her. The microwave pings. Vaughn's bottle is ready. Today is the first Fern has seen of him with a bottle.

"The breastfeeding thing," Tracy says. "It's over."

"Where are your lovely parents?" Fern says. She has noticed that they don't seem to be rattling around anywhere.

"Out at the factory. They're never here anymore. They've got a new herb. Tree bark from some Himalayan valley, it's supposed to give you earth-moving orgasms. They can't ship the stuff out fast enough."

"They're part of the problem." Fern wants to spread the blame a little, so Tracy won't feel like Fern is beating up on her. "Where are they when you need them? You don't have enough support. Like, if you lived in a small Sicilian village you'd have generations of extended family handy. Or even in Idaho. You'd have an old farmhouse and a reliable husband and a kindly aunt who'd take the baby while you went into town in the pickup on Saturday night for the hoedown. You don't have any kind of bigger situation that can absorb a baby. All you've got is you."

"All you ever have, really, is you."

Fern doesn't want to listen to Tracy go existential.

"Hey. Let me give you a break. I can take Vaughn days I don't have class, maybe bring him to Harold's when I work over there, see how that goes. I could keep him over some nights."

"Oh, man, your mother would love that."

"She'll be cool." Fern has no idea how Nora will be; she'll worry about that later.

"I saw her last week, by the way. Before you all went to Florida. She was coming out of Selmarie." She punctuates this piece of information by lowering her head and raising her eyebrows, so Fern will get her drift.

"Not alone," Fern says. "I knew. I knew something was going on. I *know* her. I am not fooled by her disguises. She fluffs up those throw pillows, all comfy on the sofa, reading a book with Jeanne's feet on her lap. Jeanne's feet with those fuzzy sock slippers on them. The picture of domestic bliss. But I saw through it!"

"I was out with my friend here." Tracy has him out of the

bouncer. He is latched onto the bottle. "We were hanging out in the little square. They were coming out, heading to cross the street."

"Where were they going, do you think?"

"The apothecary shop. I waited to see. But that's not the crucial part. They had to cross the street, and your mother was going to lunge out without looking, but the girlfriend stopped her, and this is the thing — the way she did it was putting a hand down in a restraining way on your mother's thigh."

"So?" Fern says.

"Well, try thinking how many times I've put my hand on your thigh."

"What'd she look like?"

"Mmm. Scary. Crewcut. Skinny. Black jeans. Long black coat. One of those things the Marlboro Man wears when he's getting the herd in from the snowstorm."

"Oh boy. Just her type."

"But Jeanne's not like that."

"Jeanne makes a nice presentation. Jeanne is who my mother *wants* to want. But who she really wants? You should have seen the babes before Jeanne. And the ones I saw were probably the more presentable babes. There were others I think she brought in at night, after I was asleep. But even the ones I met were sullen things. That's what I think she really wants — sullen and impossible. Someone who'll push her around a little. Maybe a little on the dumb side. Someone she can't really bring into her life. I can't believe they were out in broad daylight. She must be totally lost. Oh, my poor mama. I could almost feel sorry for her."

There's a long pause during which Fern assumes they are on the same page, thinking about her mother's ridiculous affair. But then Tracy says, "You haven't told her, anyone, anything, have you? About me, about this Mommy Dearest thing?" Tracy gives Vaughn a kiss on his furry head, a protective gesture, although she is the one they are trying to protect him from.

"Of course not." The truth is she hasn't told anyone except James, whom she told right away. But she can't let Tracy know that. Tracy has been tentative about accepting James's arrival in Fern's life. If James is Vaughn's father, that would account for it. Tracy hasn't come forward with that piece of information, and Fern hasn't pressed. It could just be that Tracy sees James as someone on her pile of discards and isn't comfortable with him turning up again in her life. Whatever the snag between them, Fern is hoping it will eventually smooth itself out. In the meantime, she tries to downplay the intimacy she has with James.

When she told him about Vaughn, about what she'd discovered and what she thought she — which means they, really — was going to have to do, he listened and rubbed Lucky's ears with his thumbs for such a long time that Fern thought he was going to say this was more than he'd bargained for. (They are so far "together" in only the loosest way.) But then he said they should definitely help, but that first she needed to talk with Tracy, to get her cooperation, make her part of the new plan. Fern had intended to follow up immediately, but then she had to go down to Florida, a delay that made her nervous, but also gave her time to fine-tune the conversation — supportive and nonthreatening — that she's having now.

Tracy has a good poker face. You have to look hard to get what's going on beneath the blankness. Today, though, there's a new element. Fern pays attention, tries to figure it out. It's not only that Tracy has lost her bad-girl look, her attitude, her weird signature make-up with all that sixties eyeliner. Or that her home dye job is that unfortunate housewife mousy mauve, now with roots. What's new about how she looks is something more fundamental, the tracks of hard times.

"You must think I'm such a loser," Tracy says.

"I think everything is hard. I think what you're doing is especially hard. I don't know that I'd be doing much better."

"But you would. Of course you would."

"Maybe," Fern says, but they both know she probably *would* be doing better. They are both capable of fucking up, but Tracy's potential along these lines has so much more range.

"Let me show you what he can do," she says to Fern as she hands Vaughn over. He is making funny faces; he thinks he's the pinnacle of wit. Tracy goes to the living room and fetches a bolster pillow from the sofa, sets it down on the floor, and then takes Vaughn and props his stomach on the pillow.

"We play wheelbarrow." She picks up his feet and starts rolling him gently back and forth. He starts laughing.

"You try it," she says to Fern. "He loves this game. I take him for rides in the car, too. We drive around. Lots of walks. He's a guy who likes to be on the move. Mr. Mobile."

Mercifully, the phone rings, saving her from any more of this pitch. Fern doesn't want to watch Tracy selling herself as a good mother, a flawed but improvable human. She shouldn't have to do this.

Fern takes over the wheelbarrow operation while Tracy gets the phone. She holds Vaughn by his fat ankles and tries to imagine the weight of the responsibility Tracy bears, as well as the huge connection that must come with shepherding someone through the beginning of his life. Then she imagines being Vaughn, pinning all his hope on Tracy, on her coming through for him.

It's a guy on the phone. Fern can tell. Tracy has a whole other voice she uses for guys. There is suddenly a little challenging element in her tone. And then she has hung up. She'll save this call for later. She doesn't want to have this conversation with Fern around.

"How was Florida?" she says instead.

"I feel like I was only there for a minute. I hardly knew my grandfather. I mean once he read to me from a picture book. I was like four or something. The main point was trying to be there for my grandmother. My Fern was there, too. The two of them — she and my grandmother — are total characters together. They've been friends since they were our age. Inside, I think, they're still the chorus girls they were all that time ago. They have tons of stories." She pauses, then asks Tracy, "What do you think our stories will be?"

Tracy hardly has to think at all. It's as though she had stories at the ready, as if there were going to be a quiz. "The time we were in Michigan with your dad and Louise and we were skinny-dipping at night and that boat of fishermen puttered by and we had to swim like crazy to get to our clothes." She pauses to think some more. "When you had appendicitis that summer in high school and I drove you to the hospital and you were in agony and the thing was about to burst and then they gave you that huge pain shot in the emergency room, and then you wanted me to get you out of there and take you to the beach. Don't worry. We'll have plenty of memories for our golden years."

Fern pauses, then says, "So. Okay. You'll let me start picking up some of the slack? When you can't do it, you'll know I'm there, ready to step in." She doesn't want this conversation to turn bad. She just wants it to be over with, behind them. And so she doesn't say anything else, only waits until Tracy shrugs and picks Vaughn up off his bolster and holds him and says, "Sounds like a plan."

madame x

NORA IS PUTTING TOGETHER a "Crying Jag" party for
Jeanne. Two pricey bottles of Bordeaux and a video are riding on
the passenger seat next to her. She has just been to Facets, where
she tried to get *Imitation of Life,* but it was out. (How could it be
out?) So she settled for a second-best weeper — *Madame X.* Lana
Turner is a little older in this one, a little more doughy in the
face, thicker in the waist. Her age works against her in the setup
scenes, where she's supposed to be a blushing bride, but *for* her
in later scenes, where she's down in Mexico in the Cucaracha
Hotel, on the long lam from her past — the suspicious-looking
death of her playboy boyfriend, the child and husband she was
forced to leave in order to spare them scandal. Now reduced to
drinking absinthe with a blackmailing Burgess Meredith. Destroying her mind, marbles all but lost.

From memory, as vibrant as though it happened only the
night before, Nora can see herself and Harold and their mother
in front of the television, sharing the box of Kleenex on the big
round coffee table in the den of the house in White Plains. The
three of them watching one of these movies, all favorites of
Lynette's. The tragic figures in these films are always women —
mothers cast off because of their class or color or indiscretions,
forced to hide themselves away, watching their children from
afar. Barbara Stanwyck as Stella Dallas. Joan Crawford as Mil-
dred Pierce. Lana Turner as Madame X.

In Harold's case, these stories seem to be another element in his peculiar imprinting. (He is not invited tonight. If he came, he would give everyone the benefit of his expertise. On the movie; on Lana Turner's entire filmography; on her life, which was as lurid as her movies — the multiple marriages, the teenage daughter killing the gangster boyfriend, the late-life devotion to the nightclub hypnotist. No, Harold will not be coming tonight. He's probably already watching *Imitation of Life* anyway. Who else could have rented it?)

Nora's next stop is Pete's up on Western. At Pete's, they put pizza on an industrial scale with long rows of stainless-steel ovens manned by sweating guys with huge biceps, their torsos bound in white aprons smeared with tomato sauce. These guys shuffle pizzas in and out of the ovens with spatulas of the gods. In front of them, closer to the counter, is a shorter line of order-taking women of similar heft. They sit facing a bank of wall phones, a notepad and a small raffia basket in front of each of them. A sign on the wall reads:

ALL GIRLS ON 7–11 SHIFT *MUST* PEEL GARLIC

From Pete's, Nora heads home in a vapor lock of greasy cheese and cardboard. The pizza, the movie, the Bordeaux, this whole evening is a satin pillow plumped up under Jeanne, everything arranged as a small pageant in her honor, showing off Nora's encyclopedic knowledge of her lover, combining elements guaranteed to please. Nora can already see Jeanne weeping at the end of *Madame X*. Of course, she understands that she is proving something.

Arriving at their house in a half-hour will be Nora's friend Stevie and Stevie's girlfriend, Lauren. Although Lauren is twenty years younger than Stevie, they seem to be a perfect match. They don't even joke about the May-December thing, and when you're with them, it does seem about as insignificant as Lauren being a couple of inches taller.

Since Nora has told Stevie a little about the thing with Pam, and since she always assumes any secret you tell anyone is tacitly telling her partner too, she supposes everyone tonight but Jeanne will be holding the same soiled scrap of information. Jeanne will be the only one in the room whose enjoyment of the pizza and the good Bordeaux and *Madame X* will be wholehearted and unburdened. Nora joins the chorus of everyone who would hate her in this moment.

"Oh, lovely," Jeanne says when the pizza box has been opened, the wine uncorked and poured.

Fern slides in with Lucky at her heels, both of them scouting for pizza. Fern takes a slice, tears off a strip of crust for the dog, nods hi to everyone. Then stands looking at the scene in the living room as though the sofa and the TV are props on a stage, as though she and Jeanne and their friends are actors in a small, domestic drama staged by Nora.

Nora has been getting a lot of these penetrating, ironic looks from Fern. At first Nora was sure she was being judged harshly, but now she suspects that what Fern is actually doing is pitying her. She can't decide if pity is better than disapproval, or worse.

"Why don't you stay and watch with us?" Nora says, trying to get in the way of Fern's look, also to get her to join the group. Lauren is also in her twenties; Fern would fit right in. Even as she offers it, though, Nora is confident her invitation will be rejected. Fern is already backing out the doorway.

"Yeah, well, I've got a little sleepover buddy tonight. I think I'm just going to hang out with Vaughn and work on my presentation for my seminar." She gives Lucky a nudge forward and slips with him back out of the room before anyone can delay her with polite conversation. Tonight is the third or fourth time in the past couple of weeks that she has kept Vaughn here. She's trying to give Tracy a break. She's a good friend, Nora thinks. And although she and Jeanne have been woken a few times by Vaughn's middle-of-the-night longings for contact or food or changing, it is also nice to have a baby in the house again.

"A toast," Jeanne says, lifting her glass, and Nora thinks how beautiful and lovely she is, small and still, even after all this time a little mysterious for being from another place. Then she thinks how the wine looks like liquid garnet in their glasses and how full her home is tonight and how this is her real life, the life she is meant to be living.

Jeanne's toast is to Stevie and Lauren, who have bought a house. It's an awful house — too far west and in a gang-riddled neighborhood. The owner lives in Saudi Arabia and has rented the place out for years and was only selling to avoid the long-distance legal hassles that would have come up if the property were condemned. But now — as opposed to the years ago when Nora and Jeanne bought their house, which was merely dowdy and paneled everywhere — the only houses any of their friends can afford are in distant neighborhoods, requiring a map to find them, or terrible houses, which will be years in the reclaiming.

"There was shit in the corners of one of the bedrooms," Stevie says. Something like pride reverberates under the statement, a Swiss Family Robinson dauntlessness.

"Human shit?" Nora asks.

"We didn't get a lab analysis."

Madame X is fabulously terrible. Stevie and Lauren find it hilarious. Lana and John Forsythe, old as Methuselahs but gamely impersonating young newlyweds, new parents. Ricardo Montalban, heavy accent notwithstanding, wedged into the role of Connecticut hunt club playboy. The special credit for "Gowns by Jean-Louis." The gowns themselves. The Technicolor dialogue.

Best of all, the tearjerker ending. After years spent in boozy reclusion, Lana has returned to New York, shot the blackmailing Burgess Meredith, and is about to be tried for his murder. To protect her identity, she burns her passport and signs her confession with a spidery X. In the years she has spent going downhill, her husband has become governor of New York. He comes to her trial to see the young public attorney assigned to her case — the music crescendoes — their son!

Stevie and Lauren are in a state of high hilarity, tossing wadded-up paper napkins at the TV screen while Jeanne remains impervious to these peripheral hijinks; she stays firmly enmeshed in the movie's trumped-up tragedy. She yanks Kleenexes furiously from the box on the coffee table, snorts, and wipes her eyes.

Nora is neither laughing nor crying; rather, she has slipped into a niche between the two. The movie has given her an opportunity to crawl into this place, where she currently spends quite a bit of time. What she does inside is listen to Pam. Replay is all she has available at the moment. They have agreed to a hiatus, to cool things down, like the shower with a chain pull they used to have in the chemistry classroom in high school. If anything blew up, they were supposed to rush over, stand under, and pull the chain.

Of course, nothing at the moment is going to cool down anything. Surprisingly, Pam is new to passion. Up until now, romance has been more cut and dried for her. And so she tells Nora she is floored and baffled by the intensity of what has happened between them. Whereas Nora, from benefit of slightly more experience, recognizes this strain of fever, malarial in nature. Once you've been struck, you may recover, but always carry a susceptibility. In a weak moment you can be felled again, a quick swoon to the ground, then the lovely, terrifying incandescence that is the hallmark of the condition. And as you lie there, you have to wonder, is it the other you want, or the other as agent of the incandescence?

This afternoon Nora found a message waiting on her cell phone voicemail. Now she neither makes nor receives calls on this phone. It is now purely a vessel for messages. In not talking with Pam, only replaying the messages in her car, in the basement while she is doing laundry, Nora feels she is at least technically adhering to the hiatus. Pam is having less success. According to her latest message, she's going crazy, has to talk with Nora, has to see her. She wants to talk about a future for the two of them, a life beyond Melanie. "She's not going to be easy to get away from, but I'm prepared to run through the wall of fire."

Hearing this declaration is terrifying. Nora has said nothing to Pam about a life beyond Jeanne. She doesn't want a life without Jeanne. Still she replays Pam's message a few times, listens as though something more must be done with these words of desire, as though they must be eaten, swallowed, inhaled. What, she has begun to wonder, is this — obsession or actual love, and what is the difference between the two? Does one merely disguise itself as the other? Here is the very scary part, the idea that you might think this huge, invasive force is love and too late see it's only obsession in a cheesy costume, with a zipper up its back.

boogeyman

FERN AWOKE on the outskirts of a nightmare. At eleven, she was still dogged by the same bad dreams that went back to the earliest parts of her childhood, populated with the same creeps and boogeymen. Dark, never quite revealed figures, lurking around corners, behind doorways, or as in this one, waiting behind the trees of a dense forest.

She dragged herself awake. If she fell back to sleep, it could well be back into the same dream, which would only pick up where it left off. This apartment, still unfamiliar, especially in its night shadows and shapes, was only a little less scary than the dream.

She was sweaty under her covers, also thirsty. She had to pee. She was going to have to get out of bed. It was a little after two; she could see the face of her clock in the watery light of the alley streetlamp. The greenish glow, which filled her small bedroom, was one of several crummy features of their new apartment. The apartment was the latest in the small steps down her mother had taken since she and Fern's father split up, and all of them moved out of their house.

Her mother tried to turn these moves into an adventure, as though they were pioneers in a Conestoga wagon, or circus performers in a colorful caravan. But there was no caravan, just the two of them opening and retaping the packing boxes they'd moved in with the year before, heading for some place her mother was convinced would have more reliable heat, or less noisy neighbors, or better pest control.

Her father now lived in a loft apartment that was really just one huge room and a bedroom and a bath, but no space set aside especially for her. When she was there — most weekends — she slept on the foldout sofa in the big room. During the week, she was here with her mother. A visitor would think Nora and Fern must be very close. They ate little dinners together, sometimes only apples and cheese and crackers, but with everything arranged on plates as though they were having a small party with no one else invited. Then her mother helped Fern with her homework. They watched TV together. Sometimes they went to Kmart late and bought paper towels and underpants, little frames for photos they set out along the windowsill.

But the apartment had another life. Fern could feel this life drifting around when she came home from her father's on Sunday night. The place smelled different, things had been moved around a little. There were new products. Honey with a honey dipper in a kitchen cabinet. In the refrigerator, a jar of something powerful-smelling called "mango pickle." And in the bathroom, candles, a whole new category of odd item, had just started showing up recently. Tonight, when she went into the bathroom to pee and drink the glasses of really cold water required as part of getting rid of the nightmares, she could tell that one of the candles had been lit earlier, leaving an apple scent hanging around in the moist air. The moistness meant the shower had been on. Fern had become a detective assigned to the case of her mother. Because although her mother was here, she was also somewhere else, sometimes even while she was here. When Fern wasn't looking or listening, or was asleep.

She checked to see that both the front and back doors were locked. Lucky was on the overstuffed chair in the corner of the living room, guarding them all. In this way, he was totally a joke. He always settled in as though positioning himself to keep an eye on everything at once, like a sentry on the Great Wall of China. But the one time there really was something to watch — someone breaking into their old garage by prying open the side door — he didn't make a peep, not a woof. Totally off-duty. Now, as she passed by his chair, he opened an eye, then closed it and flipped over onto his back with a wheeze.

She knew she was too old to go looking for comfort, but went to find her mother anyway. If she woke her up and told her about the dream, it would go away. This trick always worked. When she got to the door of her bedroom, though, and pushed against it lightly, the darkness was clear enough to see that the bed was too filled for it to be just one person. There was talking that wasn't talking exactly, and a rearrangement of shapes under the blanket. A long, muffled sound that went "nnnnnnnn." The room smelled, too, like a tent at summer camp — filled with too much breathing in and out.

Fern left unseen, unheard, her presence unfelt as she backed out softly and retreated to her room.

messenger

FERN FINDS JAMES lying next to his bike, flat on his back on the quarried rocks along the lake, north, up past Foster. His eyes are closed, his hands clasped across his chest. He looks as though he's waiting to be beamed up.

She has biked around the North Side for a couple of hours trying to find him. He has an assortment of brooding spots. This is one. There's also a toboggan hill up in Rogers Park. The roof of one of the office buildings where he delivers packages and to which he has a key. Places that are deserted in their off-hours, or off-seasons.

Today, although sunny, is also one of the first really cold days of the fall, the signal day for winter. The water is the fierce blue of northern seas. And so, even though it's Saturday, James has this stretch of the lakefront nearly to himself, sharing it only with a trio of gang guys a short ways off, the wide legs of their pants snapping in the wind like black sails. And a little closer, a brawny older woman, one of the population of Russians up here at the north edge of the city, leaning back on her elbows against the first level of rocks, coat and sweater and blouse piled beside her as she offers her enormous, brassiered chest to the sky.

James's usual gloom sometimes bottoms out in chasms of desolation and despair. When this happens, he goes back on an antidepressant that lifts him out of the abyss, but also flattens him in ways that, after a time, become uncomfortable.

"It's like the med installs a floor," he has told her. "It will only let me go so far down. Which is great. Without it, as you know, I can take some pretty headlong plunges. But the other part is that there are no highs. And it's terrible for sex. You go, like, 'Sex, what's the big deal?' And that wasn't so important when I was alone, but now that we're together, well, making love is one of the best things about us."

He thinks the depression comes, one way or the other, from his mother.

"I mean, I could have a chip of my mother's DNA, or I could be this way from having been raised by someone who was smoking and on the sofa through most of my childhood."

James's depression, Fern has begun to see, is a fundamental part of who he is. In addition to being enormously kind to everyone (but especially to Fern), and in possession of a wonderfully oddball point of view, he is also someone who needs to be on medication a good deal of the time. He has a therapist he sees once a week, a psychopharmacologist he checks in with every month. Even on his sunniest days, deep cold currents run through him.

Today, though, life has dealt up something to which he can apply his vast reserves of sorrow. His friend Kevin, another bike messenger, has died, a road rage hit-and-run, some guy in a van. Somebody got the license number and the cops tracked the guy down.

Fern stands and watches him from a few feet away. Even after all her efforts to find him and make sure he's okay, she briefly considers getting back on her bike and leaving before he sees her. She has moments when she doesn't feel quite up to the task of keeping James afloat, when flash cards of Cooper flip into view, and she gets slammed with a nostalgia for those long, languid months of being in love with someone who, by virtue of his absence, required no maintenance at all. Then, the thought flips away as quickly as it flipped in.

"Hey," she says as she approaches. She is drowned out by Canada geese, making such a racket as they group into formation overhead that she has to repeat herself, this time shouting a little, before he sits up and smiles, happy to see her even though he is sad about everything else. She drops down next to him, and falls into a groove of bumping lightly against him for the next little while, to show him she's there. *Right* there.

James has his own tattoo: little wheels on his ankle, little wheels with speed lines and clouds of dust behind them. He and his friends are boys in motion. (Fern suspects that for James, movement provides flight from the sorrow that can accumulate around him if he stands still too long.) Mercuries with wheels instead of wings. Some, like James, are couriers. Others do something more stationary for a living, then spend their time off skateboarding or in-line skating. They are free agents in the treacherous traffic of the city. The risk is part of the thrill. Dodging and weaving among the too many people getting places via too many transportational modes, in too many separate hurries and private fogs, in the midst of too many cell phone calls, juggling too many lattes.

This is different, though.

"It's not only this guy. It's like, if this guy in the van is even possible, then there's some terrible breakdown in the human circuitry. Did you meet Vik — Vikram? He's from India, and he says in Calcutta when someone gets run over, they just leave the body there. There are too many people to bother about just one person anymore."

Fern tugs at the sleeve of his jacket and says, "You can't go global. Global is the wrong direction. You'll wind up way too far down. You have to go small. Come with me. We need to find something small and really good to do."

"Okay," he says, but his voice is numb.

"We'll go take Lucky down the alley where the big scary black dog is locked behind the gate, and Lucky can bark a bunch and get him all lathered up."

"Okay."

"Then we can pick up Vaughn at my mom's and let him throw his soft blocks around. You know, how he thinks it's a game with a big point and he's winning."

"He *does* like that an awful lot," James says, but it still takes a while longer before Fern can unglue him from his rock and get him up and going again.

Tracy has been gone for over three weeks. She hasn't disappeared exactly; she phones Fern every few days. She is up north, in Wisconsin, way up. Scenic as shit, she says.

Her being up there is because of a guy named Dale. He must have been the guy on the phone, the one Tracy wouldn't talk to in front of Fern. Tracy met him in the park. He was fishing in one of the ponds. He's big on fishing. He had a job as a mover, but that got dropped pretty quickly in favor of taking Tracy up to spend some time in a place called Otter Lake, in a double-wide trailer that belongs to his father or stepfather. He comes from a family amorphously extended by divorce and remarriage and sex in the parking lots of bars, really more of an extended town than an extended family. Everyone's at least an "uncle" or a "cousin."

The guy who is Dale's father or stepfather wears a baseball cap that says LIE DOWN HONEY, I THINK I LOVE YOU. Dale's whole family lives in trailers, or prefab houses that are really just trailers without the wheels. Friday nights they have a fish fry and everyone eats hearty. Good manners is spreading your napkin over your unzipped pants while you digest. The guys work in construction, when they do work, but mostly everyone hangs out in the kitchen of one or another trailer doing a lot of slow, all-day drinking, which picks up speed in the evenings. That's when the back-seat sex and the jealous rages kick in to liven things up. For added entertainment, there is apparently a lot of falling — off docks, down stairs — that, along with hunting mishaps and ice-fishing frostbite, accounts for a steady parade to hospital emergency rooms, where the drinking and fighting often continue.

Tracy reports every couple of days from a gas station pay phone. "You want to do an anthropology paper, get your butt up here. Bring a notebook. *Definitely* bring a tape recorder. Except for having a satellite dish to pull in the Packer games, Dale's family is your basic primitive tribe." If Fern didn't love Tracy, these stories would be hilarious. As it is, though, they are pretty harrowing to listen to.

When she handed Vaughn off to Fern, Tracy was going away for a "long weekend." In every call since, she's coming back "soon," but this return remains vague, holding its place firmly in the near future. Every few calls, she talks about coming down to "fetch" Vaughn. Fern understands that Dale's family isn't the Mansons, but it doesn't sound as if it's a "family values" sort of family either. Fern doesn't like the way "fetch" has crept into Tracy's vocabulary. No one's going to do any fetching of Vaughn if Fern can help it.

This protectiveness toward Vaughn followed improbably out of a moment soon after Tracy left, when Fern panicked in the face of what she was taking on. She and James brought a car full of stuff over to his apartment and then James had to rush downtown to work and there she sat in the middle of an encampment of highchair and bouncer and crib and a short stack of Pampers boxes. Cans of formula. Bottles with nipples. Plush toys and a mobile of cartoon birds. All of this stuff sat silent while at the same time emitting a low reverberation, like a faulty stereo speaker when there's no music playing. Here, the reverb said, was her immediate future, a replacement future for the one she had thought she was heading into. Because of someone else's mistake compounded by someone else's irresponsibility.

And then the silence was broken by Vaughn, in the bouncer, adding his own bit of commentary.

"Ba!" was what he had to say, a small explosion of joy, about what, Fern couldn't be sure. But there he was, happy with his immediate situation, not asking Fern for a thing. And it was this realization — that he wouldn't ask for anything, that he couldn't be his own advocate for anything — that made it crucial to give him what he needed, whatever that was going to be.

She was not the only one to respond in this way; Vaughn has become a new element in many schedules. Fern has morning classes this semester (a piece of luck), while James keeps the baby at his place. ("Like John Lennon" is how he has characterized this arrangement, and Fern has taken this casually dropped comment as his low-key acknowledgment that he is Vaughn's father.) Fern takes over in the afternoons, and if she's working she brings Vaughn along to Harold's. She leaves him in the living room while she takes her psychic calls. Harold has a calming influence on Vaughn. He finds records at the library, songs about ducks and trucks and such — many look from their covers to be songs Harold might have listened to during his own childhood — that bring Vaughn down from the rowdy, toy-banging boy he typically is to a mellow guy. The only big switch Fern has had to make is giving up her Thursday shift and keeping Vaughn while Harold has the canasta girls over. The canasta girls are feminine, but they are not maternal.

Most nights Vaughn stays with Fern at James's apartment, but Nora and Jeanne have been surprisingly eager to pitch in. They take Vaughn a lot on weekends so Fern and James can have some time alone together. They are being generous, but they are also goofy over Vaughn. One time Fern came to pick him up, and

Jeanne and her mother had gelled his hair into a mini-Elvis, while the real Elvis was on the stereo singing "I'm a hunka hunka burning love." All this good nature has forced Fern to revise her opinion of her mother upward a couple of notches. Her good-naturedness, plus the fact that Nora is having this stupid affair, which makes her look tormented so much of the time. How can Jeanne not see this? Or is it only Fern, with her newly heightened perceptions, who can see through to her mother's strained conscience?

Brad and Tina are not part of the Vaughn picture. At first it looked as though they were going to be terrible villains. Tina called Fern with some talk about alerting child welfare that Vaughn's mother had abandoned him and he needed to be adopted by someone more responsible. Basically, Tina would like to close the file on Vaughn. Since this original outburst, though, they haven't made a peep. Fern heard through Tracy that their orgasm herb has been causing irregular heartbeats, and they've stopped production. They're staring down the barrel of a few nasty lawsuits, much too preoccupied to bother with Vaughn.

That night, Vaughn is fussing, so Fern takes him for a walk in the papoose sling, a trick that usually works to settle him down. But as soon as they are back inside and she has taken him out of the sling and his quilted jumpsuit, he starts crying.

"He's driving me crazy. He wants to go out again," Fern tells her mother, who has come in from the living room, a paperback dangling from her fingers. Nora does not like to be disturbed when she's reading. Tonight, though, she doesn't seem to mind. Actually, what she seems is already disturbed, already distracted.

"Maybe you can *pretend* you're taking him out. Babies are pretty easy to fool."

So Fern puts the baby back into his quilty suit, then into the sling, puts her own jacket back on and starts walking him back and forth from the bedroom into the kitchen and back again, with Lucky following as though they are all on a real walk through the neighborhood. And Vaughn is quiet within a minute. He looks around at everyone, pleased with the situation and with himself.

Nora drops into the old, sprung, overstuffed chair by Fern's bed.

"Did you use cheap tricks like this on me?" Fern says, still walking, just in case.

"Yes, this one, and cheating to beat you at checkers."

Her mother is such a different person lately, an extremely modified version of her usual self, subdued and agitated at the same time. Instead of going around looking smug and confident and cocky, as she usually does, as if she has swallowed the canary, she now looks more like the canary that understands it is about to be swallowed. She has the desperate, exhausted-but-overstimulated look of something hunted. Her eyes film with starter tears; underneath there are pale violet shadows. Of course, where all this ravage would make anyone else look worse, it only makes Nora a little more beautiful.

When Fern was a kid, after they all moved out of the house when her parents split up, but before Jeanne came along, during the stretch when Nora had a stream of women coming through, Fern thought of her mother's attraction to women as an aspect of her power. Only with this recent thing has Fern seen that under Nora's seamless confidence, she is actually weakened by her desire, disadvantaged in wanting someone so badly. And, in a larger way, Fern suspects there will always be these women for her mother; that she will never be able to get out of their way. In this position, Nora seems so fragile and ordinary.

"Where's Jeanne?" Fern asks.

"Upstairs. Working on the 'a.'" They don't call it the "article" anymore.

"I'm going to stay here tonight. James is having a little memorial thing for Kevin at his place. He needs room to wail with his buddies. I've got to hit the books anyway."

"Are you getting enough time for your school stuff?"

Fern tries to find the barb couched in this question, but there isn't one. One of the disconcerting new aspects of her mother is that she carries no concealed weapons. It seems completely safe to answer, "Yeah. Mostly."

"I worry a little. You seemed to be on a real path. It was the same with me. And then you came along. Which was a different kind of good. But, well, you have to be aware that a baby changes a lot in the way of plans."

"The path thing might be giving me too much credit. I've really just been fumbling my way through. And Vaughn, well, what can I do? He's my friend. If he was in college and I was in a stroller, he'd take a little time out for me. He's that kind of guy, you just know it." What she doesn't add, because it is both too personal and too unformed as yet, is that taking care of Vaughn is what the person she would like to be, the person she hopes she is becoming, would do.

doorbell

THE DOORBELL RINGS. It's Sunday afternoon. Nora has spent the past couple of hours in the backyard in a bone-chilling drizzle, pulling up the garden, filling recycling bags with tangles of spent tomato plants, stalky sumacs, limp clusters of impatiens, their summer colors now an indeterminate pinky gray.

Her reward is this nice soak in a hot, hot bath, a cup of tea with milk and sugar on the edge of the tub. She has plucked off the shelf an old favorite novel, *Housekeeping*, set in the Pacific Northwest. She needs a mournful landscape to match the day outside, a narrative enveloped in dank mists. She becomes absorbed immediately, and so the ringing of the doorbell occurs in a distant outpost of her awareness. She is expecting no one. Jeanne is downstairs, in the kitchen, cleaning up after a baking experiment, trying to replicate her mother's famous baguettes. She'll answer the bell.

She does, and the small conversation being held at the front door drifts up the stairs, into the bathroom, then runs the length of Nora's immersed body like an electric current. The other voice is Pam's. Nora can't hear the words. The tone is flat, questions asked and answered; the rhythms of information being exchanged. After a few minutes, Nora hears the front door shut and, a second later, the storm door sigh with its own closing.

Jeanne doesn't come up afterward. Nora waits until there's no more hot water when she turns the tap with her toes, until the bath is inarguably over. She dries off, pulls on sweatpants and an old jersey, comes down to the kitchen, where Jeanne is not packing her bags or setting fire to the furniture, merely rubbing olive oil into the butcher block cutting board. Two misshapen but wonderful smelling loaves sit cooling on a rack on the counter.

"These smell great," Nora says. Then she adds, by the by, "Did the bell ring?" She has to ask. She pokes through the cabinets for nothing in particular, making her expression unavailable to Jeanne.

"Oh, it was nothing. Nobody. A builder, a carpenter. A lady carpenter. She came to give us an estimate on some remodeling. She had our address, but another name entirely. Somewhere she was mixed up."

Nora waits for more.

"I asked for a card. Maybe when we fix the bathroom, we can give her a call."

"Right," Nora says. "Good idea."

She still hasn't called Pam, has not seen her in three weeks, although she has wanted to see her during nearly every one of the several thousand minutes in these weeks. She has one of Pam's work T-shirts, which was sweated through when Nora stole it from the boot of the pickup. She keeps it in the bottom of her gym bag. Whenever she pulls the shirt out to press her face into it, she knows she is taking the measure of her derangement.

Her symptoms go beyond the mental — her joints ache and her mouth dries out, her eyes water. When she thinks about Pam touching her, Nora is moved in some symphonic way, as though she's in France, hearing Bach played in a cathedral. Huge, corny emotion. Pam saps her wit, makes Nora dull, reduces her to a scattering of aspects — lightly bruised, needy, grateful. All of it horrible, and she wants more.

Still, she has — in a feeble attempt to be a decent human being — not contacted her, not returned any of Pam's increasingly agitated voicemail messages. And this restraint made Nora feel that she was taking charge of the situation, holding the line, that her "no" was the deciding vote. That she and Pam were playing by some tacit set of rules, some code of emotional etiquette. Today, though, she has been brought up sharply to understand that either there are no rules, or that they won't be hers, or that Pam has toddled off the game board entirely.

She stands at the counter, facing the cabinet, even though she should probably be moving along, saying something else to Jeanne, something about the dinner they are making tonight for a couple of Jeanne's friends from Berlitz. But she can't. Instead, a new and terrible version of herself surfaces and asks Jeanne, simply for the pleasure of picking up the topic again, fondling it lightly, getting a second opinion:

"What did she look like? The lady carpenter?"

famous

"THIS IS A GREAT ARTICLE," James says, tapping the *Reader* profile on Harold that is taped to the refrigerator door. Harold has become famous in a small way. In one of the early performances of his play, he drifted off and began snoring in the casket. He was afraid he was going to be fired, but the audience liked it so well that the director kept it in as a regular thing. Now when he starts snoring, the audience shouts, "Hey! Wake up the dead guy!"

The whole play, in a similar, campy, cultish way — so bad it's good — has turned out to be popular. Extra midnight performances run on weekends. The kids who come have been before, some several times. They dress up like the characters onstage, also talk back to them. Fern has been four times. The last time, a couple of weeks ago, she brought James along.

"You were terrific," he tells Harold. "Very dead. *Muy deadado.*" And Harold turns from the stove, smiling, catching the praise as though it were sunshine. Fern loves the easy way he takes a compliment.

Harold is fixing dinner for Fern and James. He wanted to let Dolores do the honors, claiming she was the better cook, but Fern put her foot down. "Later. He can meet Dolores on another visit, a *future* visit."

And when he opened the door to them, he was his most manly self in jeans and a white T-shirt (no bra), and only the slightest bit of lipstick. You couldn't even tell unless you were looking for it. Harold has a sinewy build from working out in the gym he has rigged up in his back bedroom. He has a collection of exercise equipment bought for a song at garage and yard sales, from people whose best intentions have drifted off, leaving them happily pushing back in their recliners. In addition to recognizable items you'd expect, like a Bowflex and an exercise bike, he has gear and appliances from the distant past of self-improvement. A Jack LaLanne Glamour Stretcher. A machine with a belt that slings around your butt and jiggles the flab off when you flip the switch. A steam cabinet you sit in with your head poking out the top. Fern has hung out and watched Harold use all this stuff, which is weird and hilarious at the same time, but as he says, it all worked for somebody sometime, and it's true that he is totally buff.

When they sit down, Fern recognizes the meal as Harold's "Always Affordable Dinner," a scheme he has worked out to be able to do a bit of home entertaining beyond the canasta club. The menu is:

> home-made linguine marinara (one box linguine, two cans
> tomatoes, garlic, olive oil, oregano, Parmesan cheese)
> Caesar salad (romaine lettuce, more Parmesan, one egg, one
> lemon, one can anchovies, Worcestershire sauce, croutons)
> French bread (Pillsbury dough loaf)
> hot fudge sundaes (ice cream made in antique hand-crank
> freezer, fudge sauce by Hershey).

Wine, if you want to bring it, would be delightful. If you don't, there is always the default bottle of red from some emerging wine nation, someplace that has recently moved from the potato to the grape.

Tonight, there is the extra cost of one banana, mashed, for Vaughn, who sits on James's lap and opens his mouth for the spoon, then takes a very long time working banana around with a look of deep concentration.

Meanwhile James and Harold are looking for a conversational intersection. James tries to explain why he loves to skateboard, but, as usual, he is inarticulate on this subject and defaults into doodling a complicated move called an Ollie on the back of an envelope.

"It's about leaving earth behind" is as close as he's able to get to anything anyone else could understand, then adds, "You also have to not mind falling."

Gamely trying from his end, Harold gets up and puts an LP on the turntable. *Teresa Brewer's Greatest Hits.* "I'm gonna sit right down and write myself a letter," Teresa warbles in her excited ingénue voice, followed by other optimistic numbers, as though leading some pep rally of romance. "Button up your overcoat," she cheerily advises her beloved.

Fern feels an ache in her jaw as she is reminded of some slides she once saw in class. Early British explorers in Africa, standing awkwardly in a jungle clearing, meeting a group of tribal elders, each side bearing enormous goodwill, trying with little hope of success, to find so much as a square inch of common ground.

So when Harold wants to talk about Tracy, even though she is a touchy, difficult subject, Fern is just grateful to have any subject at all. Except her mother. She talked with Harold (actually, with Dolores) about her mother's affair, after she'd confirmed it with Tracy's sighting of Nora and the Other Woman. But she doesn't want this topic to come up tonight. She hasn't told James about it. She wants to present her mother to him as a model, the Good Lesbian. Monogamous and stable, having offered Fern a nurturing alternative family unit with her life partner. As opposed to someone slouching through the night, trolling for a little action. So Tracy is a better subject of conversation for tonight.

"She was back in town last week," Fern says. "For a little visit, I guess. But not to us, not to Vaughn."

"You didn't tell me," James says.

"I just found out. I ran into Deena, and she told me she'd talked with Tracy and Dale at the Radiohead concert. Tracy told her they'd come down to pick up supplies. Which I guess translates as scoring recreational drugs." Fern thinks for a minute. "This is one of the worst things she's ever done to me. I can sort of see the twisted path of emotional logic she's gone down. She couldn't handle Vaughn, and James and I picked up the slack, and we're managing to do what she couldn't. So, instead of being grateful, she's pissed off at me and alienated from Vaughn. Which explains why she's behaving badly, but it doesn't make me happy with her. I mean, she can't even stop by for a guest appearance in her kid's life?"

"On the other hand," Harold says, always ready to smudge any black-and-white situation into a gray area, "there's this new guy in the picture. Worse than Tracy disappearing would be Tracy showing up with him and taking Vaughn into those deep Wisconsin woods and raising him to be a drunken fisherman. You know, it's probably time to stop thinking of your situation with Vaughn as a holding pattern, and start considering whether you're up to a permanent commitment."

Vaughn, who doesn't know temporary from permanent, stays pretty squarely in the moment. In this one, he sucks on a plastic teething ring that Fern has pulled from Harold's freezer (wall-to-wall, Fern noticed, with packages of lima beans).

"I'm not saying you have to take Vaughn on," Harold says. "I'm not even sure you should. Just that if you're not, maybe we'd better think about finding someplace he can settle into for his upcoming childhood."

Fern takes a little while with this thought. The truth is, she hasn't made any long-range plan around Vaughn. A plan hasn't seemed called for. She has taken this sequence of days each as it has come. And so James takes her a little by surprise.

"I think Fern and I *are* the plan," he says. "We've made a

groove in our lives that fits around him. He's happy. We love him. We'll work the rest out as we go along."

Fern looks around for a few words but can't find them.

For the ride home, she has Vaughn bundled up inside two jackets. James's car is freezing on account of a busted heater, but much easier to ride around in since he cut a piece of plywood to make a floor on the passenger side. Fern took the floor as a gesture of love.

"When you and Tracy were . . . you know . . . together . . ." Fern says.

"That would have been for a short part of one night."

"But still. It could have . . . you could be . . ."

"Well, yes. I could be Vaughn's father. I suspect a few other guys could say the same. But, really, what does it matter? Those guys aren't here. I am. I mean, clearly it's not mattering much who his mother is, so it doesn't matter if I'm his 'real' father or not. What's 'real' anyway?"

"This?"

"Yes," he says. "I think it is."

A little further along, he says, "I like your uncle."

"It would have been okay if you didn't, but, well, I love him so much . . ."

"Does he have a girlfriend?"

"I don't think so. I think he has a crush on Gretel, his boss at the restaurant, but I don't think that's really going anywhere." Fern finally met Gretel backstage, the first time she went to see Harold's play. She had been expecting flaxen locks and an operatic build, tall with a huge bosom. Instead, she was beyond hip with Cleopatra hair and red leather jeans, glasses with turquoise frames. She was scary in a way Fern hadn't anticipated, witheringly serious. She wanted to discuss the play in terms of its semiotics. Meeting her, Fern thought she was going to have to go home and reconsider Harold's romantic inclinations.

"It's just that when I was using the john I noticed . . . I mean I couldn't help notice that there was a lot of Victoria's Secret sort of stuff hanging from the shower pole."

If James were a snoop like Fern (or her mother, or Harold himself), he would have found a lot more.

"Oh, that. That's a little complicated. I guess you could say, in that way, Harold is sort of his own girlfriend."

James takes this in without pressing for more. One of the most excellent things about him is that he is able to let conversations roll to a comfortable stop on the side of the road. He gets the general idea.

When they are almost to her mother's house, where Vaughn is scheduled to sleep over tonight, Fern notices Nora's car parked at the end of the block. The engine is running, the window open with a light veil of smoke drifting out. James is driving slow enough that Fern catches more than a glimpse. She can see that her mother is deep into a call on a cell phone. A cell phone that Fern wasn't aware Nora had. A cigarette, which she thought Nora didn't smoke anymore.

lipstick

NORA, in a moment emblematic of where she had arrived at twenty-one, stood waiting for an elevator, holding a paper sack from the bottom, her hand warming a little from the grilled cheese inside. She had a large vanilla shake in the other hand. So far, bringing the exact same lunch every day to her boss appeared to be the most important duty of this job, a job to nowhere. She had hoped by now to be a little further along toward somewhere.

The school part was a breeze. Taking a degree in literature was, for Nora, like a pie-eating contest at an old state fair — being rewarded for doing something purely fun anyway. For years, reading had been her refuge from the limelight in her parents' house, from their disappointment in her refusal to join the fun. Then the books provided her with a graceful way out, a fond farewell for all of them. Nora slipping off to college, Lynette and Art and Harold making up for their lack of understanding with abundant goodwill, as though they were flicking straw boaters over their heads, canes tucked beneath their elbows as they bid her goodbye.

Not that she had gone all that far away. She had great grades coming out of high school; she could have gone to college anywhere. Yet she had traveled only as far as Manhattan. Forty minutes by train from the house in White Plains. A short cab ride from her father's office on Forty-seventh Street. It was as though she didn't want to look back but wanted to be able to reach around and still feel them there. After a childhood spent setting herself apart from her family, she seemed to be entering adulthood already nostalgic for them.

At the same time, they appeared to be moving away from her faster than she was able to leave them. Lynette, now in her late forties, past her dancing days, had snagged a small but steady role in a TV series, *Glenda's Girls*. She was Glenda, the head of an all-female detective agency. She had about five minutes in every episode — at the opening, when she gave the girls their assignment, and at the end, when she affectionately scolded them for risking their lives to get the job done. For this work, Lynette lived in L.A. for thirteen-week stretches, staying with Fern Lawler, who was now an abstract painter living on the wealth of past marriages (four), while Lynette was bringing home the largest paychecks of her long career. The two of them were accomplices in recapturing their youth and glamour. Lynette even had a fan club. There was a board game for the show with tiny dolls to represent the characters. Lynette had given Nora a Glenda doll.

Nora's father still managed Vicki Ashford, who had a long-running gig in the lounge at the Tiara on Miami Beach. He also had a new discovery, a folk-rock duo called Hammer & Nails, and spent time on the road with them. He was going to bring Harold along with him next summer, teach him the business. Harold wasn't really interested in the biz aspect of show biz. Nor did he care much for the road, or for rock. But he adored Miami and seemed to enjoy being around stages in general, and so was going along with the plan.

He had pretty much given up on high school. He didn't like that they chose what he had to study. He found it oppressive. There had been meetings — Art and Lynette and the school psychologist. When Nora's parents were out of town and she called Harold at the house, there was no answer. Then, on some impulse Nora couldn't figure out, he would come to the city to stay the night with her, and seemed happy for her company, but he revealed little about what was really going on with him. If she asked direct questions, he would dodge and weave. He was "thinking about things," or was certain that "everything was going to work out." He was beautiful and confused and totally unable to talk about whatever it was he was sorting through.

Neither of them mentioned it when he used her make-up. Once, Nora got up before him and, coming through the living room on the way to meet Mr. Coffee, looked over at him lying tangled in a sheet on the sofa, and saw that his bony ass was snug inside a pair of flowered cotton Carter's Spanky Pants.

She loved Harold ferociously but wasn't up to dealing with everything there was to deal with about him. It was enough just trying to find her way into her own future, which in her more optimistic moments she envisioned rolling out like a rug before her — college, then graduate school, a thesis on the evolution of the novel of manners, an assistant professorship at a small college. In reality, though, she seemed to have already veered a bit off the carpet, or rather it kept getting tugged out from under her. This nowhere job, for instance, was the result of just such a tug.

Technically, it was not even a job; it was an internship for the spring semester of her junior year. She had been hoping for a spot at an old and famous literary journal, something that would have typed out as a nice, chunky line on her CV when she applied to grad school. Instead, she was only able to get something at a fashion magazine, which seemed enough of a comedown, but was actually a little worse in that *Elan* was not even a very good fashion magazine. Nora was assistant to the beauty and make-up editor, a thrillingly severe woman named Celeste, soon to be the recipient of the grilled cheese and shake.

Celeste was extremely thin; the rumor around the office was that she was addicted to laxatives. She consulted a tarot reader every month and ran her life by these readings. She seldom wore an outfit that wasn't all black; in rare cases, for contrast, she added an earth tone. She had distinctive hair — long and coarse, wavy, and made up of several shades of brown and blond. Kind of Joan Baez with highlights. It was hair that had its good points and its bad days, as did her eyes, which were sometimes recessed in dark hollows. But even on the worst days Celeste was extremely attractive in a way Nora hadn't encountered before. That is, she suspected the attraction existed in the space between them, that it ran both ways. She wasn't sure what to do with this magnetic field, which didn't seem to give her any particular power over Celeste, who mostly manifested her side of the attraction by averting her gaze from Nora whenever the job called for them to interact.

Today, when Nora brought her lunch in, Celeste looked out the window of the office and Nora followed her gaze. The window faced a warehouse that now held artists' lofts. The loft directly across from Celeste's office was usually brightly lit and sometimes occupied by a portly man who wore bright (yellow, Day-Glo orange) bikini shorts. It was always worth a look to see if he was there; at the moment, he wasn't. Whenever they did see him, each of them claimed dibs on him. This was pretty much their only joke.

"I'm going to give you a chance to prove yourself," Celeste said (to the window). As though they were in the brain surgery department of a teaching hospital. As though anything Nora could do here would prove anything. "I want you to do the fall lipstick roundup." She said this with a totally straight face. Everything was straight-faced and dead earnest around the offices of *Elan*. They couldn't afford to laugh at the ultimate purpose of all their enterprise and long days and pressing deadlines. If someone started laughing, it was all over.

"Roundup," Nora said, nodding, trying to look as though she was accepting a challenge, had precisely the article in mind, understood the concept and was ready to run with it. Celeste wasn't fooled.

"You have to find a new angle, some way our readers can think about lipstick and how it can work for them, and how it has to be particular to them. Specific."

"Like choosing shades based on your blood type?"

"We could all position ourselves ironically here," Celeste said, and took her gaze and tucked it down amid the proof sheets scattered across her desk. "But ironic detachment doesn't really work. It starts seeping into the pages of the magazine. Our readers are not ironic. They are young and desperate to be stylish and attractive. Because of this, they need to know what's happening with lipstick, and how it directly relates to them. They await our guidance."

Nora didn't know how to respond and so wound up standing silent across Celeste's desk from her until Celeste said, "You'll see. You step into this version of reality, and everything starts to fall into place."

Throughout that same spring, Nora had also been dating Russell Koenig, from her poetry workshop at school. Her poems, she was pretty sure, were third-rate Sylvia Plath. Maybe fourth-rate. His were a combination of corny and sentimental and rugged. She attributed these qualities to his being from the Midwest, which she imagined as a place of good intentions and plainer emotions. Russell was also an English major, but with a commercial bent. He had been working part-time for the past couple of years at an ad agency. He hoped they would keep him on after graduation. Nora liked him. Also, she liked that he didn't like her too much, that whatever he felt about her fell short of passion. There were training wheels on their romance. No one was going to fall off and get hurt.

On their dates, they went mostly to films at revival houses, and to author readings. So far they had been to hear Grace Paley and Joseph Heller, had seen *Notorious* and *Double Indemnity*. They had had dinner once at an Indian restaurant in a basement on Sixth Street, and twice at an Italian place in the Village. It was as though they were following some plan, ticking off events and accomplishments, acquiring merit badges.

They busied themselves filling in the blanks with a running sequence of questions, small revelations, fresh beats of one of the private jokes they now shared. She had already brought him out to meet her parents. (Lynette let Art "persuade" her to sing "Volare" while Harold accompanied on the piano. Nora was excruciatingly embarrassed in the moment. But over the weeks since, "Volare" had become a kind of code word between her and Russell for her family's idiosyncrasies.)

She would meet Russell's family at the end of the summer. He was going to take her home with him to Illinois, to Decatur. His father ran a hardware store there. Russell had three brothers, two sisters — some already with children of their own. They all gathered at their parents' house for Labor Day, no matter what. His mother put out a ham. She had a small smokehouse and was locally famous for her bacon. Nora dreaded meeting her, being confronted with her pioneer spirit, and with all of Russell's siblings, who apparently whiled away the long holiday afternoon with a rough and tumble lawn game — contact badminton. This was part of the tradition. Nora's family had no traditions. When she thought of going into Russell's tradition-happy family, she feared she wouldn't be up to the task, weathering all the hale-and-heartiness. And she couldn't imagine Russell shielding her from any of it. He was too congenial, and would expect congeniality from her as well.

They had waited to have sex until after the two movies and one of the readings. With Russell, it was a wordless, industrious affair, reminiscent of her afternoons on the basement couch with Teddy Frey, and satisfying in the same down-to-business way.

Now, on Saturday nights, they stayed in. They watched old movies on TV. He went downstairs and brought back carryout. He had a studio in Chinatown, above one restaurant and across the street from another. There was always a heavy current on the air that drifted up and through his windows, a Morse code of oil and meat, pepper, fish. Nora was hungry within minutes of arriving.

Sundays, they got up early and went running together. She enjoyed the weight of him beside her in the universe, the soles of their sneakers hitting the asphalt path in syncopation. She wanted a boyfriend, wanted that slot filled, and now it was. Now she didn't have to worry about not having one.

"How's the roundup going?" Celeste asked one morning, a few days after she had given Nora the assignment.

"I have a concept."

"A concept is a start."

"'Read My Lips — What Your Lipstick Says about You.'"

Celeste looked up from a layout. For once, she actually looked directly at Nora. The look had absolutely nothing to do with business, even as she said, "Liner. No matter what those lips are saying, they have to be lined. Our three largest cosmetics advertisers want us to feature lip liner."

Nora stood, listening and not really listening, noticing that as Celeste was casually looking at her, she was also assessing, taking a reading. It was a look that was both saying something and asking something else. Nora went a little wobbly.

A couple of weeks later, artwork for the lipstick roundup had come in late, by messenger. A lot of the shots — a few too many in Nora's opinion, but no one was asking her — dealt with how to use a brush to outline the lips before filling them in with the color that would most succinctly telegraph the wearer's personality.

"This peach looks a little weird," Nora said when she and Celeste had the slides laid out on the light box.

"Maybe," Celeste said. "Let's get a better look." She went

over to flip off the overhead fluorescents. The light coming up through the slides was the only light in the room. In this moment, Nora learned something about how it was with women, how it could happen in a brief series of seconds. The way time elided, transformed from something tocking between marks on a clockface into pure liquid, something to slide along on. How long did they stand there, hands flat on the translucent glass, almost touching, both of them listening, like pulmonary specialists, to each other's breathing — an hour? half a minute?

Beyond that, how long before one of them made a defining move? How long did they stay in Celeste's office, first on the sofa, then on the industrially carpeted floor? The fat man came home, watched TV in his briefs (electric blue), went to bed.

"I hope you understand, tonight changes nothing," Celeste said much later, when they had both signed out in the lobby in the middle of the night.

Nora wanted to believe her. She wanted to believe nothing had changed. Celeste didn't know that she had just brought Nora out, and Nora didn't want to give her that piece of information. Neither did she want to make a big deal of what had happened. After all, this was Manhattan, and it was the seventies — way into the sexual revolution. Tonight was not about being gay. She didn't want it to be about that. That looked way too hard — the social stigma thing, but more the boundlessness. Stevie, her closest friend at school, was a lesbian, and Nora didn't want to be that wide open, that tragically earnest, that annihilated by desire. The music Stevie listened to was also earnest, and ghastly — campfire songs only about women loving women, sisters leaning on sisters, instead of about cowboys on the range.

Nora didn't want to care as much as Stevie did, to bleed that way. But this was precisely what happened with Celeste through the rest of the spring and into the summer when her internship ended and Celeste hired her on as a part-time assistant. This arrangement gave them a couple more months through which they took afternoons out of the office — ostensibly to visit model agencies or scout locations for shoots. In reality, they headed straight for Nora's apartment, where they pulled the shades and slipped out of their clothes within moments of arriving, like firemen in reverse.

Like the job, the romance led nowhere. Celeste lived with a famous TV journalist. She was not going to put that relationship at risk, she had been candid about this from the start. And even if Celeste were available, she was not someone Nora could imagine as a partner. Celeste thought fashion had real importance. She talked seriously about accessories. She was vain and shallow, ruthless. Her highest aspiration was to be promoted to senior fashion editor for the magazine, a bigger stupid job. She would cut a deal with the devil to get the current occupant of the position to drop into a manhole.

But in these long, hourless afternoons in bed together, fashion was rendered temporarily irrelevant. In this context (which was really a retreat from context), Nora found she had the power to soften Celeste, to make her leave her datebook in her bag across the room, make her not call the office for messages, make her forget her next appointment, her famous girlfriend, and focus tightly on what she wanted from Nora, what Nora made her ask for, politely, made her say please.

Nora's sexual experience was limited; she had never been naked with anyone the way she was with Celeste. And so she made the mistake of translating this nakedness into more. There were wide flat stretches of pillow talk and afterglow during which she opened herself in ways that seemed extremely foolish later, when Celeste backed off suddenly.

She had to let Nora go at the magazine, and was simultaneously no longer available outside the office.

"It's just starting to be a very busy time for me" was how she put it. "I'm going to have to tighten my focus. It's nothing personal."

Nora was stunned. All she could do was stand there looking at Celeste's perfectly made-up face and see clear through to her vacant soul, unable to make any use at all of the knowledge that Celeste was utterly worthless as an object of affection.

She went back to her apartment, reviewed the affair, and came to a rough understanding that this eventuality had been on its way all along. Nonetheless, she behaved badly for a while. A little petulant stalking, a scene on the sidewalk outside a bookstore. From there, she behaved better but felt just as bad. She never wanted to feel this bad again; at the same time, she suspected she had just wandered onto the edge of a vast landscape of pain.

Through all this, her romance with Russell glided along on cruise control, staying on the same slick surface of old movies and Chinese food and earnest chat sprinkled with references to a future that implicitly included each other. Nora acquired the skills necessary to seal what was important away from the rest of life — the practical, daylight part. In September, as planned, she drove out with Russell to visit his family, and got through the long weekend, his smokehouse mother, even the rough and tumble badminton. She ascribed her nausea on the trip to too many hours in the car followed by four days of country cooking — breakfast biscuits with cream gravy, dinner ham with cream gravy, fritters, shortcake with whipped cream. When she continued to throw up after their return to New York, she went to the doctor, who took blood and urine. Nora's fears were clenched around a murky diagnosis of something malignant. And so she was totally baffled by an unequivocal diagnosis of pregnancy. In the first seconds after receiving this information, she inhabited a small flurry of confusion, linking the baby with the high-voltage connection to Celeste. Actual thought had to be brought to bear on the matter before she saw that, of course, this development was about Russell, with whom the sexual connection had the approximate wattage of a toaster. Still, somehow, that sequence of quick, industrious gropings had been enough to break a rubber and reset her direction. Nora saw in a telescopic way that she would tell Russell and they would get married and have the baby together and everything else that had happened this summer would be consigned to a private, unopened album.

hostage

NORA HAS BEEN TAKEN HOSTAGE by the new terrible version of herself. Today, instead of going home after work, she fabricated a chiropractor appointment for a fabricated pulled shoulder (from yanking out renegade sumacs in the back of the yard the other day) and drove down to Hyde Park. With some winding around, she found the address, a brooding, ivy-strangled six-flat, then the apartment where Pam is putting in a new kitchen. The owners have taken off to avoid the dust and disruption, so once again she and Pam are alone in someone else's home, like bad babysitters.

Nora finally caved in to Pam's voicemails and agreed to meet her. She gave herself a dispensation for this meeting by telling herself it would be their last. On the drive down, she prepared her side of the conversation: They simply have to stop. She has thought things over. The time-out has helped clear her thoughts, given her room to see that where she really belongs is with Jeanne.

And this speech is exactly what the better, more reasoned, and responsible version of herself truly believes, and so it should have been possible to say these prepared lines straight off. And so she has only the hostage theory to account for not having said any of it, even though she has been here more than an hour. Instead, she is naked on the primitive-print sheets of strangers. She is lying on her back with an arm draped over Pam's shoulder while Pam, with an ear to Nora's breast, listens to her heart beat.

They are both quiet. They are keeping the communication physical. Talking has become more complicated. If Nora were saying anything, it would have to be her carefully worded extrication, which, given the circumstances, would sound a little ridiculous.

She shouldn't be fucking Pam. She should be furious with her. That little visit to the house the other day to rattle Nora's cage. The explicit message yesterday, and not on the cell phone, but on Nora's work voicemail, to which Mrs. Rathko has the password, which means she probably played it for herself before Nora got to the office. Pam understands she is supposed to be totally circumspect in what she says in any messages she leaves at work, encoding everything as much as possible. Any message with the word "pussy" in it is not encoded.

But, instead of feeling angry, Nora, in a weird way, admires Pam for taking this affair with long, bold strides, while she herself crouches in a corner, afraid of everything about it, even (especially) the happiness it has brought her.

The two of them sit up. Pam goes to get a couple of beers from the refrigerator, while Nora pulls a cigarette from the pack on the bedside table — *her* smokes. Pam has quit; she's wearing the patch. Now Nora is the only one smoking. On the table, she notices a small bedside clock. She sees with a slight sinking sensation, but with no real surprise, that she should have left here at least half an hour ago. Behind the clock is a framed photo of a couple on a hiking vacation, leaning in toward each other on a boulder, backed by a photogenic vista.

"Oh boy," she says as Pam comes back into the bedroom. Nora props herself on an elbow, reaching over to pick up the picture. "I know this guy. Jeff Fanning. He teaches at Berlitz with Jeanne. Eastern languages, Himalayan dialects."

"They're in Tibet," Pam says.

Nora falls back against the pillows, takes a better look around the room. "I left my coat on this bed. We came for dinner. Maybe five years ago. They made something incredibly ethnic. A little grill on the table. Something on skewers. We drank out of wooden cups."

"She wants a clay oven put in the kitchen," Pam says, as though she's trying to help Nora reconnect with these old acquaintances.

"We're in their bed. I'm here with you sweating up the sheets of Jeanne's colleague. Someone I'll have to chat with at the school cookout next summer."

Pam doesn't see the problem. "They're not going to pop in on us. It would take them about five days to get here if they left right now. They'd have to start out on a yak."

"It's not being discovered I'm worried about. It's not them knowing I was here. It's *me* knowing. I don't want to have these sorts of secrets."

"Me either. I want to drive around with you. Go to a restaurant. A movie. Be happy when we run into friends. *Have* friends."

Nora tries to imagine who their friends might be. Pam's friends? The two or three friends of Nora's who won't have abandoned her after her breakup with Jeanne? Stevie and Lauren? They would stick with her no matter what. Probably.

Pam goes on. "I want to take you for dinner at my parents'. Make love in *our* bed."

"We don't have a bed."

"We could. Beds are obtainable."

Nora doesn't respond. She feels as though large items — marble sculptures and grand pianos — are moving around inside her. In the room that is her, there isn't space for everything and so the individual pieces keep shoving, jockeying for position.

With Pam she was only prepared for something that didn't

take up any space at all. She didn't go in looking for a whole new life to replace the one she was already living. Her life was already in place, already satisfactory, requiring at most a few small improvements. New windows in the spring. Jeanne finishing her article. And nothing about that life has changed. The only problem is that, at some critical point when she wasn't looking, she fell in love with this woman she had thought she was merely sleeping with. The elements of initial attraction have expanded in directions she hadn't anticipated. She loves the large way Pam inhabits her life, the long strides with which she moves through it. And now, the way she wants to be with Nora free and clear (while Nora is still looking for places to hide).

Another thing is that having Pam, even though she has her for only an hour or two at a time, has become such a huge part of her internal life. Without her, she would have a sequence of days, a schedule of activity, that was sufficient before Pam's appearance, but that would now be terribly diminished by her absence.

"I have a Christmas present for you," Pam says. "Wait a minute." She stretches off the bed to tug something out of a pocket of her jacket on the floor.

Nora closes her eyes and thinks, *Please don't give me a present.* Even though she has brought something for Pam, a pair of socks she has knitted herself, the first knitting she has done since the earliest, domestically ambitious days of her marriage when she knitted socks and scarves for birthdays, cross-stitched pillowcases for wedding presents. These socks are irrefutable evidence of premeditation. She has had to work on them over several weeks' worth of stolen moments. Nights when Jeanne was teaching and Fern was over at James's. When time grew short, she would sometimes knit and purl in her car at the far edge of the parking lot at school, the heater running, the engine idling, the dash light on so she could read the instructions.

Pam's gift is also premeditated. It's an old silver ID bracelet, scratched and nicked by its previous owner, polished by Pam, nameless on the front, but on its underside, in small, lowercase letters, Pam has had engraved "trouble."

"Oh man," Nora says, and folds her hand around the back of Pam's neck and kisses her.

Still, the socks remain across the room in her shoulder bag, wrapped in red tissue, pushed beneath her wallet and cell phone. Giving them would be a response — to Pam's present, which at the moment hangs heavy as an anchor on her wrist. The bracelet is not just about sex or mischief; it is recognition of a level of emotional content that has begun to assert its presence. And so Nora can't give her the socks, which would be a reply she is shy of making. Shy and cowardly.

"What about Melanie?" Nora says. Might as well bring her into the dialogue.

"She knows," Pam says. "About us."

Something icy shoots through Nora.

"You told her?"

"I told her there was someone else. I didn't say it was you."

Nora wonders how much time she has, closes her eyes and sees the sparks running merrily along the fuse.

elves

WHEN LUCKY STARTED PACING through the night, Fern would get dressed and take him for three-thirty or five A.M. (or whenever) walks. When he started hiding in closets, the vet, Dr. Sanders, told Fern that pacing and hiding are animal attempts to get away from pain. Lucky's joints are cemented with arthritis. The vet prescribed something that worked for a few months, but now the dog is bad again, this time lying in the same spot most of the day. Fern and James have to carry him up the stairs, not only to James's apartment, but even just up the front steps of Fern's house. He has been on cortisone for four days — a last-ditch shot at buying him some more time — but Fern can see the stuff is not kicking in. Lucky is practically immobile, and now one side of his face is swollen from an abscess in his mouth.

"He's crashing," Fern tells her mother on the phone. "I've been hanging out with him. Just to be around. He looks at me and I know he needs help, but there's nothing I can do to make him suffer less. Except one thing."

"It's Christmas Eve," Nora says.

"They're open until four. I called."

"Where's James?"

Fern sighs.

"That came out wrong," Nora says. "Of course I want to help."

"He's out at his parents'. They've got a tree-trimming thing they do every year. It's not like he deserted me. We didn't know

Lucky was going to go downhill so fast." This is a lie. The truth is that James couldn't handle the situation. Hanging out for the past couple of days with Fern and Lucky, he had eventually gone completely silent, buried beneath the weight of his grief, forcing Fern to feel bad for him as well as for Lucky. James's sadness used up all the available space for emotion in the room where Lucky was dying. Still, when Fern said maybe he should just go out for a while, leave the rest to her, she expected him to rally and say of course not, that he'd see this through with her. Instead, he nodded and said she was probably right, threw a change of clothes in his backpack and took the train up to his parents' so she could have the car. Fern watched him hold Lucky's paw for a moment, then kiss the dog's head, then head out the door, and it was as if she was seeing not only this particular departure but ahead to all the other clutches in which James wouldn't be able to be with her.

"I'll take him to the vet's myself," she tells her mother now, trying to let Nora off the hook, too. "It's okay. I only need for you to keep Vaughn while I'm gone."

"No. Let me come with you. I can get out of here anytime. Everybody's leaving. Most people didn't even come in today." Nora's voice goes to a muffled murmur; Fern can tell she's wrapping her hand around the receiver and her mouth. "Except Mrs. Rathko. She informed me this morning that '*half* holidays are not *whole* holidays.' She gave me a Christmas present for you, by the way."

"I'm really looking forward to that," Fern says. Last year Mrs. Rathko sent along a self-help book of tips on improving posture.

"I'll call Jeanne and get her to come by and stay with Vaughn," Nora says. You and I can go over to the vet's together. You don't want to do this alone. Plus, he's our dog, really. All this time."

"Do you remember when we got him? How the card on his cage at Anti-Cruelty said he'd been brought back twice for bad behavior, but Dad and I told you it only said 'Likes to look out windows.'"

"I remember he ate the sofa the first time we left him alone. He was a lunatic when we got him," Nora says. "*Tons* of personality, but a lunatic. I'll be right there. And I'll send Jeanne to stay with the baby."

"Can you pick up a Hershey bar on your way?" Lucky has a long history of trying to get at any chocolate in the house. And chocolate, they've been told, is toxic for dogs. Fern tells Nora, "What I'm saying now is, well, toxic-schmoxic."

When her mother doesn't say anything on the other end, Fern knows she's crying.

At the vet's, there's a Christmas tree decorated with dog biscuits and all the helper girls at the front counter — only irritating and incompetent on regular days — are this afternoon also dressed as Santa's elves with red velvet caps and jingle-bell belts. One of them, jingling all the way, brings Fern and her mother and Lucky (who walks unsteadily, but on his own, about two inches an hour) into an examination room.

Dr. Sanders comes in through the door on the other side of the room.

"Sorry about the festivities," she says.

They've gone to Dr. Sanders since she was just out of vet school and worked out at the Bone Animal Hospital with a portrait in the lobby of its improbably named founder, Dr. Bone. Now she has two kids and is onto her second marriage. She has been Lucky's vet practically his whole life. She stitched him up after the terrible fight with the two Dobermans, pulled his broken tooth, gave him all his boosters.

"Here's the part they don't tell you at the puppy shop or the animal shelter," she tells Fern and Nora. "They don't warn you that taking on a pet is a contract with sorrow." (Dr. Sanders herself has made several of these contracts. She has four dogs — all rescued from dumpsters or fires or grim situations. Dogs with suspicious natures or half their fur missing.)

Fern sits cross-legged on the floor and settles Lucky across her lap.

"If I can just give him this first," she says, tearing the wrapper off the Hershey bar. She breaks it into a few pieces and holds one under his nose to get him going. Piece by piece, while they all wait, Lucky eats the whole bar, then licks Fern's hand and looks around at everyone as if to say, "Okay, what's next?"

Dr. Sanders squats and, with a syringe, gives him a pinprick in his haunch.

"This is just a sedative. To relax him. He should be pretty out of it soon."

And within moments, he gives Fern a goofy look, then his tongue slips out of his mouth and his eyes get sleepy. The elf spreads a towel on the steel examining table and they lay Lucky down on his side on top of it. Dr. Sanders shaves the hair off a patch of his hind leg, near his paw, and gets the IV in, then starts the euthanasia solution.

"Stay close to him so he can smell you," she tells Fern. "Talk to him if you like. It's hard to know how much he's perceiving through the sedative, but I think it comforts the animal to have his human close by."

Fern pets Lucky and rubs his ears and tells him how she used to take him shopping with her and leave him in the car. And when she came back, someone was almost always there laughing at him sitting in the driver's seat, pressing on the horn with his paw, honking for her.

"What happens now?" Nora says.

"We wait a little while. Then I listen to his heart," Dr. Sanders says. She puts her stethoscope to his chest, and says, "Very faint now." Then, a moment later, she listens for a longer time, and they all stay very still until she looks up at them.

"It's stopped."

Fern bends down and kisses him.

"Lucky was a great dog," Dr. Sanders says. If she says the same thing about every dog she puts down, Fern doesn't want to know.

"You can stay with him awhile, if you want. When you're ready, you can use the back door to the parking lot. So you won't have to go through the party." She nods her head sideways, in the direction of the lobby, where Brenda Lee is singing "Rockin' Around the Christmas Tree."

Nora rubs Lucky's head, then puts a hand on Fern's shoulder and tells her, "I'll wait outside."

Left alone with her dog, Fern remembers how big and rambunctious Lucky seemed to her when she was a child, how insubstantial he appears now. A million pictures of him flip through her inner field of vision. She unfastens the collar with his nametag on it and puts it in the pocket of her pea coat. She puts her hand into the thick fur on his neck. He's warm. Warm, but so terribly still. This, then, is the essential element of death. The theft of animation.

She bends over and kisses his ear, then puts her mouth against it.

"You wait for me," she tells him.

In the parking lot, Fern and Nora stand facing each other and a future minus Lucky.

"I've been standing out here thinking about the dumbest stuff," Nora says. "Like no more surprise bones under our pillows."

Fern nods. "I know. And we'll have an unhairy sofa." Neither of them says anything for a little while, then Fern says, "The best thing about him, for me, was his there-ness. No matter who else has come and gone, he's always been there, filling in the blank, completing the scene." She stops for a second to gather up her emotions. "There were times, you know, when you needed things to change. But I was a kid; I needed them more to stay the same. That was Lucky — always the same. He liked his walks and his dinner at the same time every day and he'd turn exactly three times on his bed before he'd drop down and go to sleep. And he wasn't going anywhere on me. He was always going to be there, lying on his blue bed in the corner."

They are only a foot apart, which, in ordinary circumstances, would be the same as a mile. But right now, it's an easy fall into each other's arms, where they cry for much longer than Fern could have expected. After a while, it begins to seem to her that they are crying for more than Lucky, that they have both caught a glimpse of some broader palette of sorrow and have incorporated into this moment the sadness they have already encountered and that which still lies ahead. Even when it seems they should be done, they're not and just keep crying. Only when they finally break apart and start hunting down Kleenexes in coat pockets does Fern think what a long time it has been since she has been held by her mother.

And when they get into the car, Nora says "Come home with me. So you don't have to be alone tonight."

"Okay."

"Jeanne and I were just going to do something low-key anyway," Nora says. "We can make it even lower-key. I'll make cheesy eggs. We can have a non–Christmas Eve."

"Oh, Mom," Fern says, meaning too many things to go into.

At dinner, Vaughn is calm and happy, making a big mess on his highchair tray, breaking down his portion of eggs into lumps, then determining which lumps are eating lumps, which are throw-on-the-floor lumps. He is the only happy human at the table.

Nora and Jeanne try to help Fern by paying tribute to Lucky, to his great addlepated sensibility, his cockeyed journey through life. Fern can't quite chime in, isn't up to packaging Lucky in anecdote yet, but she is appreciative, for their stories, and for their company tonight, for the comfort of other living beings in the room with her.

Through a wash of pain, Fern sort of notices that her mother is doting on Jeanne in a peculiar way, slightly formal, as though Jeanne is a rare visitor from afar rather than the person Nora lives with. Fern is sorry for all of them. For herself, for losing Lucky. For Jeanne, who will soon, one way or the other, find out she is being betrayed. For her mother, who has been made vulnerable to disaster by one small shoddy aspect of her character, which is ridiculous, almost hilarious if you look at it from a certain angle. Fern can't quite get to that perspective tonight, though. Tonight, her mother just looks stupid and tragic, sitting on a kitchen chair, possibly about to blow up something good and essential for something that is almost surely beside the point.

After they've eaten, Nora insists on cleaning up. Jeanne puts Vaughn to bed in his crib in Fern's room. The cold weather makes him a sleepy baby, early to bed.

James calls looking for Fern, but she doesn't yet feel up to reassuring him that it was okay he wasn't here today.

"Tell him I'm already asleep," she says to her mother, then crawls into her bed, next to Vaughn's crib, then gets up and goes through her closet and drags out her old cowgirl blanket from the deepest recesses of her childhood and puts it on top of the pile of everything else she usually sleeps under.

Outside, where there had been a lot of snow blowing around, everything has now turned still and bitter. Fern can see the moon high and pale yellow, a coin going into a slot of black sky. She thinks of Lucky, out there somewhere in the universe, heading into the unseeable. And then she slides into a dreamless sleep, which lasts a few hours, until the night blows wide open with a crash. Fern, still half-asleep, runs through the darkened rooms and wipes frost off a front window to see what has happened.

antarctica

THE RENTAL CAR they've given Nora is an SUV. It's all they had left on the lot. It's a huge sucker, a total embarrassment. She roams around looking for parking spaces big enough, sinks low in the seat and hopes no one sees her. Her replacement car is due next week. They towed in her old one to see if there was a chance of putting it to rights, but it was totaled. The frame, the guy at the collision shop told her, was basically a parallelogram now, as opposed to a rectangle. He drew two diagrams with a pencil, to help her grasp the concept.

Neither the cops nor the insurance people inquired about any possible connection between her and whoever did this.

"Holiday drunks," one of the cops said, shaking his head as he filled out a report. Standing there with his paunch and his snap-holstered gun and a screeching walkie-talkie clipped to his shirt, he had such an air of authority on the matter that Nora almost started believing him along with everyone else.

After that, there was the hour or so of bad acting she had to do for Jeanne's benefit. Fern, astonishingly, just picked up the script and improvised on it.

"Oh, Mom, you loved that car. I can't believe people that drunk let themselves get behind the wheel. Of course, they probably don't even know they're driving."

And when Jeanne brought up the curious fact of Nora's being the only car hit, Fern reminded everyone of the damage (minuscule, but Fern didn't mention this) done to the bumper of the car in front of Nora's. She was trying to show Nora she had an ally. This alliance was completely unexpected. Nora didn't know what to make of it. She wanted to grab Fern and kiss her all over her face, was so grateful for something good in the midst of all the bad that was coming down.

Vaughn, in spite of having awakened all of them on numerous occasions, did not appreciate his own sleep being interrupted. He squalled for another half-hour before they could all get back into bed and Nora could feign exhaustion, turn away from Jeanne, and pretend to sleep.

She was still awake two hours later, in the long winter lag time before dawn, when the phone rang. Unfortunately, the phone was not on Nora's side of the bed. Rather, it rested on a stack of books of French feminist critical theory on Jeanne's side, an easy reach for her, even half-asleep. And so Jeanne was the one to receive the call, the one to make the acquaintance of Melanie, Pam's other lover.

Nora parks by Harold's apartment building. She has been sleeping on his sofa for the past week. He has been generous to her in so many ways that she has wound up crying at some point in nearly every day. She hopes he is home now because she needs to talk again. Basically, she needs to talk about every ten minutes. She needs sympathetic ears, shoulders to cry on, and has found a small population of these. Stevie, who is always there for her, even when she doesn't understand what Nora is doing. Geri in Admissions, although Nora suspects she would talk sympathetically with anyone who will stand outside the Administration Building and smoke with her. And Harold. He's her mainstay.

When she comes in, he's fresh out of bed, although it is early afternoon. This is his regular schedule, what with his work life being entirely on the swing shift. Nora finds him in the kitchen, fixing eggs over easy with roast duck. Duck is a staple in his diet. Apparently they always have leftovers at the restaurant.

He is wearing a short, navy terry cloth robe, his Arnold Palmer shave coat. This is part of a new, ironic drag that Harold finds amusing — fatuous manly accessories from the recent past. Soap on a rope, deodorants with virile brand names. In this apartment, he can be anyone he pleases. Himself, Dolores (Nora has finally met her), or the guy who uses all this stuff, whom she believes is Chad.

"Did you blow off work today?" he says. "Would you like some breakfast?"

"Thanks, no. I just had lunch. There's nothing happening at work. Mrs. Rathko is about the only person down there. She says she's using the holiday lull to redo her files on some color-coded system she read about. She subscribes to magazines like *Modern Administration*. I think she's really lurking around to see how bad I look when I come in. I'm sure this is so delicious to her, my life collapsing around me."

"Oh, I think it's already collapsed. Now's the part where you start to build it back up."

"Do you think so? How come it seems to me like I'm just paralyzed and sleeping on your sofa and reading all your Hollywood bios?"

"Cautionary tales for you. Required reading, really. Before you make any next moves."

"I wake up in the night," she tells him. "A little free fall. I start thinking, What if this is only the beginning of Melanie's mayhem? One night I'll be going to my car at school. Late, after a meeting. I'll feel her behind me, then the gun at the small of my back or the piano wire around my throat. Or I'll be at home, reading in bed, and hear the crackle of starter flames on the front porch."

"Stop."

"What I'm saying is maybe I should be calling the police."

Harold sits down at the table across from her with his plate. "What could you pin on her? She probably ditched the car she used. She wouldn't have used her own. Plus it would mean dragging the whole lesbo love triangle mess to the cops, who would probably like it a little too much. Besides, I think she has probably made her big statement. And you're staying away from her girlfriend, which is all she wants."

Nora doesn't say anything. Harold looks up suddenly from his eggs.

"You *are* staying away?"

"Oh yes. Not that I'm proud of it. She's been leaving messages."

The messages, she tells Harold, are of various stripes. "She's so, so sorry, she takes all the blame for what happened, she never thought Melanie would go this far. She wants to pay any damages. Then a few days ago, she left a new number. She's staying with a friend, up in Rogers Park. I'm not supposed to give the number to Melanie if she calls. Then yesterday, there was this kind of wail from the middle of the desert: Why have I abandoned her?"

"Do you know?" Harold says.

"Oh, there would just be so many steps, and I can't even imagine the first few. Calling her, okay. I can imagine that. Maybe meeting her at the apartment of her friend. Apparently she has eleven cats. That's about as far as I can get. What comes after that? I sleep with her on the sofa bed with the cats crawling around our heads. What then?"

"You could just call. Or answer the next time she calls. You could just step up to the plate."

Nora shakes her head. "I'm having some terrible failure of nerve. It's not really worrying about her nutball girlfriend, about her coming after me with a hacksaw. Sawing me to death and putting the pieces in her refrigerator. It's *me* I'm really afraid of. All those years ago, Jeanne saved me from this thing inside me, this tropism toward moronic passion or whatever. Say I run off with Pam, what happens a few more years down the line when the next Pam comes along? So, of course, I'm tempted to call. Of course, I'm not over her. But I think the best thing I can do is try to take the high road, be on my way, and not look back. I just wish I didn't feel so shaky about everything, so unsure which impulses to trust. I know I seem like a basket case. Fern and James, when I come over, they fix me tea. Herbal tea. As if real tea would be too stimulating. Like I'm on the big lawn at the institution and they have to speak in soft voices around me. It's not exactly what I want from Fern, but in a weird way it's the nicest she's been to me in years."

"I think maybe this has cut you down to size for her, made you more approachable."

"You know the worst part? Maybe I will have a little duck." She goes to get a fork and plate. "The worst part is that this thing I do, this thing I thought I was through doing but apparently wasn't. It's like a little relativity equation. I take the matter that's me and find someone I can use to blow myself into pure energy, into this place where all I am is desire. But that's not the worst part. The worst part is that I really don't know if what I find when I get way out there is my worst self, or my most authentic."

A little later, Harold has to get ready to go to the restaurant. It's New Year's Eve, and there's a special eight-course dinner. Plus a live brass oompah band to back up the singing bartenders.

"A *long* night of Bavarian merriment," he says. "Can you see these grease spots on my cummerbund?"

"Do you want the truth?"

"I guess I don't have time for the truth. The jacket will cover the worst of it. So, what are you going to do?"

"If I could be anywhere now, I'd be back home. I'd be making Jeanne that ghastly instant cappuccino stuff. You'd think she'd look down her snooty European nose at it, but instead she loves it. So that would be it — drinking a bad instant coffeelike beverage. Sitting in the kitchen, talking about tomorrow, which would just be another regular day."

Harold doesn't say anything.

"But you can imagine how far away and hard to get to that seems. Antarctica."

"You could use the New Year's thing. As an entrance ramp."

"No, no. She'd never fall for it."

But at eleven, Nora is driving up from Sam's, where she bought a bottle of Pomerol. She also has flowers. Nothing was open, and so she has pulled six limp 7-Eleven roses from their plastic tubes and rubber-banded them into something like a bouquet. She will look like a fool to Jeanne, standing on her doorstep (formerly known as *their* doorstep) loaded down with corny romantic clichés. Like Elvis coming to court Priscilla on the army base. Frank Sinatra trying to make time with Ava Gardner in Hollywood. *If* Jeanne is even home, which she probably won't be.

But when she comes up the front steps, Nora hears a barrage of gunfire inside and knows Jeanne is watching a video. Nora rings the bell and the noise stops abruptly and Jeanne opens the door.

Nora expects her to look haggard, like Madame X in the cheap hotel in Mexico City, like she's been through something. But she doesn't. She looks calm, unruffled.

She says, "Come in," but Nora can't find any inflection that would give a clue to her mood, nothing in her expression to tip Nora off.

The house, inside, also looks unruffled. All traces of the long, terrible Christmas they spent together here, after Fern and the baby cleared out, have disappeared. The pillows are fluffed up and back in place on the futon couch. The kitchen wall where the milk carton hit has been cleaned up. Even the air has a calm to it, enhanced by some chunky candles Jeanne has going on the coffee table.

The wine goes unopened. The flowers got dropped on the front porch next to the door. Nora didn't have the nerve to bring them in.

The two of them sit in the living room.

"I know being sorry isn't enough," Nora says. "It's too meager."

"Yes, it is too little," Jeanne agrees. "I am too angry. My anger would be too much bigger than your apology. And even if I weren't so furious at you, there is so much I need. I need you to be sorry *and* not love anyone but me. And I know you can't do that right now. And I want you to be the sort of person who wouldn't have let this happen. That's the worst of it, that you aren't that person. I want to exact promises from you, but what value would they have?"

"All I can ask is that you let me show you."

"But how much showing would it take? How long before you could hold me without me sniffing to see if I could smell someone else on you? If I stay with you, I'll know you have the capacity for betrayal. No matter how much time went by, I would fear your treachery had only moved into the shadows. What is love but trust, and how can I have that now?"

Nora nods.

"I am not trying to put you through the hoops," Jeanne adds.

"No, I know. Everything you say is true. I've left us with only less-than-great options. We could end it over this. I'll understand if you want to do that. Or we could go on, but you're right that it will never be like before. Not so easygoing. Blithe — blithe wouldn't be available to us anymore. I know I've made that impossible."

Jeanne sits staring at the flames of the candles, picking bits of warm wax off the sides. She has made several little cubes of wax, now set next to one another on the coffee table, dice without numbers.

"On the other hand," Nora says. "You'd have me over a barrel. You could push me around for a *long* time. Make me go to Korean restaurants and eat all those little pickled things. You could play those spacey mood tapes that make me insane. You could make me visit your family."

"Oh, my family would never see you now."

Emotion is such a tricky element. Nora is completely surprised at how stung she is at this rejection by a small group of women she loathes. And on moral grounds. She is now someone who can be rejected on moral grounds.

"The water heater burst," Jeanne says. "Tuesday. There was water everywhere."

"I think it was pretty old," Nora says. "I think it was already here and old when we bought the place."

"Bernice came over. She brought her Shop-Vac. Then we got a guy to replace it yesterday."

Jeanne has been on this side of the Atlantic so many years and yet every time Nora hears her overarticulate something utterly American, like "Shop-Vac," she falls a little in love all over again.

Jeanne is not simultaneously falling a little in love all over again with Nora. Her expression doesn't change, but she has brought their daily life together into this conversation, which is huge. Nora exhales silently, sensing they have moved past the place where Jeanne would have asked her to leave.

Later, toward morning, they are back in their bed, but their truce is tentative. Nora is crying; she has been crying off and on, for some time. "I'm just so grateful."

"Yes," Jeanne says. "I know. You are grateful and you are here, and we will go on together, for a while at least. To see if we can. But there is a crack in the vase now."

"I know," Nora says, "but just come here." She pulls Jeanne on top of her. She needs to be weighted down, needs a counter to the helium of folly.

sandbox

NORA WAS FLUSH with the sense that everything was just beginning. Tuesday and Thursday mornings, she went into work late so she could bring Fern to a group that gathered in an informal way at a play lot in the park.

Fern was thrilled by these outings. She seemed equally happy being bossy with the toddlers and being bossed around by a pair of twin sisters, who were older and basically ran the show around the swings and slide.

Nora was less well socialized, did less well with the mothers than Fern did with the kids. She could see that seeds of friendship were being sown among these women, but not with her. She suspected they found her a little standoffish, which she supposed she was (although she was also, in sequence, attracted to two of them). She hung around the periphery and listened as they revealed themselves in small bursts of conversation snatched from chasing down this wandering child, scooping up that fallen one. She saw how they expressed their self-satisfaction ironically, through small complaints about husbands or kids, which were really mechanisms for revealing the importance of men, around whom so many arrangements had to be made, the importance of children who required so many activities to satisfy their curiosity or creativity. Both the husbands and the children were positioned conversationally as accessories, a way in which these women defined who they were without having to reveal themselves directly.

Nora was shy about offering anything of her own along these lines. Her marriage seemed sturdy enough, but modest in scope; her husband steady but not important enough to brag about. Her child, by contrast, seemed so important that she couldn't talk about her at all.

When she was pregnant, Nora had no idea who she was about to bring into the world, and so Fern astonished her from her first months, when she already seemed like such a fully developed human being. When she began to talk, she was already full of things to say, as though she'd been waiting quite a while. Most recently, she had been revealing a battery of firm, considered opinions on many subjects. Everything about her was fascinating to Nora, every day thrumming with the possibilities of who Fern would be tomorrow.

At the moment, Fern was showing a small boy, Aaron, how to make a basic castle by packing a plastic bucket with damp sand from the sandbox they were sitting on the edge of, then turning over the bucket, tamping it onto a flat patch, then lifting the bucket to reveal the formation beneath.

"Where are the turrets?" he asked.

"Turrets are the next lesson," Fern told him, patient and professorial, and totally bluffing. "Turrets are next week."

Among the hopes Nora was pinning on Fern was that she would be the first person in Nora's life to whom she could give herself over completely, whom she wouldn't need to resist in any way. And so things weren't beginning just for Fern, but also for herself.

astronaut

NORA IS IN THE PARKING LOT of the Whole Foods on Clybourn. Her assignment for Vaughn's birthday party is appetizers. She stands bent over the open trunk of her car, the replacement for her old Jetta, this one green instead of navy. She is going through the bags to make sure she has everything. A shrink-wrapped package of smoked Scottish salmon dusted with dill. A wedge of Brie flecked with mushrooms. Crackers for the cheese, a loaf of pumpernickel for the salmon. Some hummus and pita bread. Vegetable pâté. Roasted red peppers. Little Italian olives, Fern loves these. She probably has too much. She should have made a list so she wouldn't overbuy.

She tries to keep her life small and organized these days — lists ticked off, promises kept — a place of recuperation and containment. She is not unhappy in these reduced circumstances, but rather has found comfort in the tighter fit, the tucking in, her life pulled taut around her.

At first she doesn't hear the engine at her back. When she picks up on the sound and identifies it, the vibration is hot breath on her neck. She doesn't have to turn around to know who it is. She doesn't have to turn around, period, but she does. The window on the passenger side of the truck descends with a low electronic whir. Pam leans across and unlatches and pushes open the door.

"Just a few minutes," she says. Her hair is longer. The crewcut is gone. She is wearing a gabardine jacket Nora doesn't recognize. Little clicks of time passing, having passed.

Nora can so easily imagine herself shaking her head, can see herself so clearly — saying no, she's sorry, she can't, and then getting into her own car, turning the key in the ignition, driving straight to Fern and James's apartment without casting a glance in the rearview mirror.

Instead, she climbs into the cab of the truck, a sequence of movements that feels like rolling back a huge stone and entering an old cave. Sheryl Crow is singing quietly from the tape deck. A bitter Sheryl, telling someone: "If it makes you happy."

Familiar smells cover the inert interior air like moss. Coffee and fries, Pam's musky cologne and the other scent about her that's sex. Pam doesn't say anything, doesn't look at Nora, only drives. They don't go far; Pam pulls into a deserted parking lot behind an abandoned warehouse off Elston.

"No one will hear my screams," Nora says when Pam has put the engine in neutral and turned a little to face her, letting the weak joke evaporate.

"You totally iced me," Pam says.

"I had to do something. I had to make a decision."

"But it was a decision for both of us, and you made it alone."

Nora wants to be able to say yes, but it was the right decision, she hasn't had a moment's doubt about it. She wants to say that the two of them talking would have only dragged out an inevitable end. A beautiful, coherent speech lies somewhere, for someone to make in a moment like this, a collection of words to balm exit wounds. But she can't make the speech; she can't find it anywhere inside herself. The plain fact is she ran back into her relationship with Jeanne and pulled the door shut. She thinks she's done the right thing, but she still has days when some floodgate breaks and she is awash in longing for Pam, as though no time at all has elapsed. But the Pam she misses is by now partly a creation of loss and desire. As for the real Pam, the justifiably angry woman sitting inches away from her, she can't tell her any of this; it's both too much to let her know, and information that is worthless. What value is there in saying, I may still love you but I'm never coming back?

Also, saying even these worthless words would be a betrayal of Jeanne, whom she has promised never to betray again. So all she can do is sit and inhabit the silence formed by Pam waiting for a reply Nora can't make.

Eventually Pam starts lightly drumming her fingers on the steering wheel. She is done waiting, and what she does next is unexpected and startling, not on any of the pages of the script of phantom connection Nora has written for the two of them, an aftermath of understanding and forgiveness. Pam has been writing her own script. She turns and clutches the front of Nora's jacket and pulls slowly. And Nora's response — also not what she would have expected — is to close her eyes, feeling first lips against her mouth, then teeth, then the sharp, swift pain of her lower lip being bitten, not playfully, but in dead earnest. She backs away, but refuses to put her fingertips to the blood she can feel welling up to the surface, running in a rivulet down her chin, dropping onto the collar of her jacket, then the dusty blue linen shirt she has put on for the party.

Pam reaches across to push open the door, inadvertently brushing the back of her hand across Nora's nipples, which, absurdly, stiffen.

"Tell your girlfriend you got that at yoga," she says as Nora steps out and, for an instant, feels like the astronaut on an ill-fated space walk, outside the craft, her line suddenly cut, drifting into the thin ether that lies just beyond the ordered universe.

one

FERN HAS the two cake layers baked and out of their pans, one set on top of the other. They list slightly to one side, but this is not so noticeable now that she has the frosting (chocolate) on. She is scripting in "Vaughn" with a tube of white icing. The celebrant himself is sitting in his highchair, gnawing on a bagel, watching as though he knows the cake is about him. Fern has already put his party hat on him.

James comes into the kitchen and laughs as soon as he sees Vaughn. "Your hat, man!" he says, and opens Vaughn's hand so they can high-five. Vaughn has almost got the high-five down pat. Then James spots the cake. "It's a work of art," he says.

"I'm glad I don't have to do all my writing in frosting," Fern says, squeezing out the tail of the "g."

"No, it looks perfect," James says. He has been out shopping for the forgotten condiment, sour cream, to go with the chili that's bubbling on the stove. "I got these, too." He sets a pot of foil-wrapped paper whites on the table. "To say, you know — spring is here."

After a morning of cold rain and fog steaming up from the ground, the afternoon has offered some watery sunshine for Vaughn's first birthday. Fern has the window open, and the cool air coming in above the radiator shimmers in waves and brings with it the fragrance of damp earth, last fall's dead leaves, the shoots of tulips in progress.

"Lucky would have his nose on the windowsill today. It's a real symphony of smells out there." Fern still misses Lucky more than seems normal to other people. They don't say "he was just a *dog*," but she can tell that's what they're thinking. But it was Lucky's dying that has made Fern see the line between life and death as not all that hard and fast. In the midst of missing him, she is often interrupted by the certainty that he is still with her, around the house, on the floor by her bed, wheezing a little in his sleep. And right now — she doesn't even have to turn and look — with his nose on the sill.

Fern has told everyone to come about three, and soon after that they arrive in a short burst — the buzzer going off, muffled thumping up the old wooden steps, then stooping as they take off their jackets, put down their presents for Vaughn in the living room, and come under the eaves, into the kitchen with their offerings for the party.

Jeanne has brought a giant box of chocolate truffles and a bottle of white wine. She is wearing a dress with a pattern of tiny flowers, a pale green cardigan clasped at the neck with a bumblebee pin.

"You're a vision of springtime," Fern tells her, and lets Jeanne kiss her on both cheeks.

Harold shows up with a mix tape he has made. "Songs with 'one' in them," he says, tapping the plastic case.

James goes for the boom box.

Russell has come with Louise's cornbread but, mercifully, without Louise. He is not happy about Fern taking on Vaughn, or about James having shown no particular interest in any sort of career beyond messengering, or about Fern going part-time at school and taking on extra hours at the psychic hotline. He thinks she is abandoning all her good plans. She can see his point of view. Nothing about her situation is ideal. She has taken on the care of someone else's kid, about a decade before she expected to be doing any parenting. Her partner in this enterprise is an underemployed depressive. Help from those around her has its limits. Her father's purse strings are tied up by Louise. Nora lends a hand with caring for Vaughn, but she and Jeanne are not the buoyant babysitters they used to be. Now they have their own troubles. As a unit they seem fragile. They make you feel as if you should not make any sudden moves around them, or drop anything breakable. So Fern is more on her own than she would like, and not really in possession of a grand plan, or even a reliable map. She is making do with the small patch of ground she's standing on, and the next step out from there.

Still, she has a sharpening picture of who she is in the world, how she wants to participate in the enterprise of being human, the ways in which she wants to be there for those around her. Somehow this goes along with being an observer and student of humanity. She will become an anthropologist; getting there may just take a little longer. Vaughn may have to be bundled up and put in the dog sled to visit the Nenets with her.

Tracy and Dale show up with beer, a twenty-four-pack, which seems excessive for an afternoon family party, but up in Wisconsin among Dale's family, this might only be the starter pack. Dale is short and compact, missing the tips of two fingers. He is sullen, or maybe just made shy by all these people who know one another well and him hardly at all. Tracy is edgy. When she and Dale came back down from Wisconsin in the winter, they found an apartment and took the baby back. But it wasn't even a couple of weeks before she called Fern at three in the morning from a club, sounding pharmaceutically enhanced, asking if Fern could pick up Vaughn because the babysitter might have gone home. When Fern and James got there, Vaughn was asleep in his crib, no babysitter in evidence. Fern suspected there had never been one.

After that, there had been a short sequence of bad conversations in which Tracy swung between indignant and defended, and remorseful and apologetic. What it came down to, when she was finally able to admit the truth, was that she didn't want to lose Dale, and he apparently felt that if there was going to be a kid in his house, it should be his kid.

It was in the middle of one of these talks — one where she and Fern were going over some materials on adoption, looking into all that would have to be done at some point — that Fern suddenly understood that as her future was merging with Vaughn's, she and Tracy were parting. Where once Tracy had seemed wiser and more experienced, now Fern feels so much the older one. She could even imagine a final scene — she and Tracy in their thirties, running into each other someplace boring and obvious, a Gap, a record store — and by then the calls and visits will have long since diminished, Tracy will have missed Vaughn's last two birthdays. They will have reached the exact spot where everything between them will have been said and done.

But as of now this separation has only just begun. Tracy has relinquished her place as Vaughn's mother, but is still looking around for a position she can occupy in relation to him, something other than failed parent. When she visits and it's only her and Fern and Vaughn, it's almost not awkward anymore. This gathering will be rougher, though. Fern can already see Tracy smelling judgment in the air.

Tough. She'll have to deal with it. This group was not the easiest to assemble, but together, they add up to Vaughn's family. They're all he's got.

By three-thirty, Fern is getting impatient with her only as-yet-unarrived guest.

"She was supposed to bring the appetizers," she tells James. "I think if you're the appetizer person, you should probably come a little early, but at the very least, you need to be on time."

Jeanne overhears and says, "She was going to Whole Foods. She's probably busy buying too many things." But Fern hears a slight raggedness in Jeanne's voice, an undertone of disappointment on the verge of exasperation.

"She'll be here," James says. "I'll put out some crackers and peanut butter."

Fern thinks he's kidding, but he's heading for the cabinets. *Guys,* she thinks.

By quarter to four, everyone is in a groove, sitting on the sofa and the living room floor, working through the crackers and peanut butter and the beer and the wine, even the chocolates have been opened, and Harold's tape is up to "Book of Love," which contains the line "Chapter *One* says to love her, you love her with all your heart," and Fern is pissed. She has moved beyond caring about little boxes of sushi and little Italian olives or whatever her mother is bringing. She is beyond delayed appetizers, deep into replaying the whole historical pageant of her mother's failure to show up. Then this anger snags on a suspicion. Nora is being held up by something more than spaciness or indecision at the deli counter. Some event has intervened.

In the same passage that Fern sees this, she also sees that whatever has happened won't stop her mother, that something fundamental has shifted between them. Nora is not going to disappear on her. Returning holds more importance to her than going away. Other things may happen, but this one bad thing, at least, is behind them.

From here, the noises of the party drop way into the background as Fern concentrates on helping her mother get here, willing her footfalls on the stairs. And it works. Fern hears the downstairs door open and shut, then Nora, not hurrying exactly, but taking the steps with deliberation. Then there is a momentary stop, a pause of preparation — a straightening of posture, a replacement of expression — as she gets ready to break through from wherever she has been to here, where she needs to arrive. Fern feels the precise pressure of her mother's hand on the knob. And the door opens.

MY THANKS TO
Stacey D'Erasmo, Elizabeth Hailey,
Mary Kay Kammer, Jayne Yaffe Kemp, Laurie
Muchnick, Barbara Mulvanny, Jean Naggar, Janet
Silver, Bill Spees, Sharon Sheehe Stark,
and to the Ragdale Foundation.